an Upper west side story

a novel

Rachel Cullen

Copyright © 2023 Rachel Cullen

Published by Lime Street Press

ISBN: 979-8-9863830-1-9

All Rights Reserved.

No part of this book may be reproduced in any form or by any electronic or mechanical means, including information storage and retrieval systems, without written permission from the author, except for the use of brief quotations in a book review.

For my middle daughter
My favorite Samantha
Always and forever

This is a work of fiction. Names, characters, places, and incidents are of the author's imagination or, if real, are used fictitiously.

Chapter 1

Jessica

New York City - 2004

"68th and Lexington, please," I mumble to the cab driver as I slide onto the slippery vinyl back seat and slam the door. When I look back on this day, the only possible bright spot is that a cab pulled up the minute I ran out of Brian's apartment building.

It's such a ridiculous cliché. At the same time, it seems only fitting that when I finally think I'm in a healthy relationship, I walk in on my boyfriend getting a blow job from Natalie, the chatty waitress at our favorite restaurant. Although, I think it's fair to say it can no longer be considered *my* favorite.

As the taxi crawls up Third Avenue in rush hour traffic, I replay the scene over and over again in my head. I used *my* key to open the door to his apartment - the one Brian gave me three weeks ago when he suggested we think about moving in together! Unfortunately, the apartment door opens directly into the expansive living room, and I got an unobstructed view of Natalie's bare ass. She was kneeling in front of the black leather couch with her head between Brian's legs. Her curly blonde hair was bobbing up and down at such an alarming pace that I would have been worried for her safety if the circumstances were different. Brian's eyes were closed (no surprise there), and Natalie was obviously preoccupied, so I had to clear my throat before either of them noticed I was standing there.

My cheeks burn as I think back to the look Brian gave me because it only revealed a hint of guilt that he'd been caught. There was no remorse or shame when his eyes met mine. And God help me; he didn't even have the decency to try to push Natalie away or run after me to explain. Instead, as I closed the door, I made the mistake of glancing back, and I saw him put his hand on top of Natalie's head, in that *special* way men have, to encourage her to resume what she'd been doing previously. I'm simultaneously furious and mortified when I think back to my phone call with my parents only a few days ago. I told them I thought Brian was close to proposing – yet another thing my mom will judge me for.

The cab is stuck in the middle of the intersection at 42nd Street and hasn't progressed in three light changes. I can't sit here for another twenty minutes in bumper-to-bumper traffic while listening to my driver talk nonstop on his cell phone in a language I don't understand and can barely identify; it sounds a little bit like Russian, but I don't think it is. However, my options on this chilly April evening are pretty slim, and I know I'll be even more miserable walking twenty-six blocks in heels and an unlined trench coat.

My fingers are wrapped tightly around my cell phone; they've been that way since I got into the elevator in Brian's building. I knew I would lose service as soon as the doors closed, but Katie was in the middle of a rant about her boss, and there wasn't a chance for me to interject. I planned to call her back as soon as I got to Brian's place, but that was before I was distracted by a naked woman with my boyfriend's penis in her mouth. My phone continues to vibrate in my palm, and I feel bad for ignoring Katie's calls, but I'm sure she'll forgive me when she finds out what happened.

At the light at 53rd Street, it occurs to me that Katie may not be the only one trying to reach me. I flip open my phone and scroll through the list of recent calls. My heart sinks as I spot Katie's number nine times in a row. After what I just witnessed, it seems highly unlikely that Brian would be calling me, and I'm angry with myself for even hoping it would be him, but I can't help it. I want an explanation for what happened because it doesn't make sense! We sat on that same couch two nights ago and shared Chinese food while watching *American Idol.* Then we had sex in Brian's bed and fell asleep in full spoon position, with Brian's body glued so tightly to mine that I woke up in the middle of the night with my sweaty t-shirt stuck to my back. How could things change so much in forty-eight hours?!

* * *

"What happened to you?" Katie demands as soon as I open the door to our apartment. I still have one foot in the hallway and haven't even had the chance to wriggle my key out of the finicky lower lock, but Katie is looking for answers.

"Sorry," I reply quietly, finally wrenching the key free and shutting the door behind me.

"You look awful," Katie says, looking me up and down and shaking her head slowly from side to side before taking a hefty sip from the glass of red wine in her hand.

"Thanks," I reply, attempting a sarcastic tone, but I know she's right. I grabbed a quick look in the lobby mirror at Brian's apartment building before I got in the elevator, and it wasn't a pretty picture. My dirty blonde hair was limp and lifeless, all of my eye makeup had pooled underneath my eyes, and my cashmere shell had lost its shape and bunched over the waistband of my skirt, and this was *before* I encountered the porn scene in Brian's living room.

"Seriously, why are you home? What's going on?" Katie asks, her tone sounding sincere. "Weren't you walking *to* Brian's apartment from the subway when we got disconnected?" she questions.

"I was," I say, not bothering to correct the unnecessary detail that I was already in the elevator when the call dropped. "Let me get a drink before I tell you what happened," I say, grabbing the nine-dollar bottle of wine from the fridge that I opened last night. I contemplate drinking straight from the bottle because it feels like that kind of night, but I decide against it and open the cabinet to grab one of the Ikea wine glasses we bought on our shopping spree last year. I notice that we only have five glasses left, already having broken seven from our initial set. One of the many things I was looking forward to about moving in with Brian was trading our mismatched, budget rental for his sleek grown-up condo – including a fully stocked bar with ample, fancy glassware.

I throw my coat over the back of a kitchen chair and make my way over to the couch, where Katie's wineglass is almost empty. Her usually brilliant white teeth have a faint purplish tinge, which confirms that this is at least her third glass of wine, but no more than her fourth. After living together for four years, I know almost everything about Katie, including the corresponding shades of purple teeth for each glass of wine.

"So?" Katie asks, hugging her coltish legs to her chest.

I take a breath, drain half my glass of cheap white wine, and then tell her the entire story. Somehow it takes me fifteen minutes to tell her every detail, even though I was in and out of Brian's apartment in about sixty seconds. When I'm finished, Katie looks at me to make sure I have nothing else to add and then begins the obligatory tirade as the best friend of the aggrieved girlfriend. I nod along as she makes countless points about Brian's worthlessness, vulgarity, and incompetence, but my heart isn't in it. Of course, I'm still mad, but I'm no longer livid like I was when I walked out of his place. Now I'm just heartbroken and confused and wish I could go to sleep and wake up to find out that it was all a bad dream.

Chapter 2

Robin

I've lost count of how much wine I've had to drink because every time I take a sip, my overzealous date refills my glass. At first, I thought it was considerate that he was being so attentive and super convenient that the sommelier had left the wine chilling in an ice bucket right next to our table. But now I think my eHarmony date is turning out to be a creep who just wants to get me drunk and see if I'm the type of girl who has sex on the first date.

"Tell me more about what it's like to work at Victoria's Secret. Do you spend a lot of time with the models? Do you get to try out the lingerie?" Howard prods while plucking an insanely large shrimp off the rim of his iced glass and dunking it into a tiny bowl of cocktail sauce.

I desperately regret telling him anything about my job over our one pre-date phone call because it's clear he didn't listen to a word I said. "I don't work *at* Victoria's Secret," I say, willing my eyes not to roll upward as I speak. "I work at the parent company, L Brands, and I am an assistant brand manager for Victoria's Secret skincare."

"Oh," Howard says, clearly disappointed with this news. He leans back in his chair and gives me a puzzled look as he grabs his highball glass, swirls the ice and vodka, and contemplates his response. "Can you get promoted to work with the bras and panties?" he asks suggestively as if it just occurred to him that there's still hope for whatever gross fantasy he's envisioning to play out.

"I just realized that I told my roommate I'd help her with something. I didn't realize it was so late. Thanks for the wine," I say, pushing my chair back from the table and reaching down to grab my purse off the floor. I've thought about ditching bad dates before, but I've never actually done it. It must be the alcohol fueling my fire, or perhaps I've finally reached my limit of gross Manhattan men, and I'd rather sit home in sweatpants for the rest of my life than endure any more of this torture.

"You're leaving?" Howard asks, gobsmacked at the turn of events. "We haven't even ordered dinner," he declares.

"I know, sorry about that," I apologize, as I shrug on my coat. I hate that I apologize, but years of good manners make it impossible for me not to, even if I am walking out on him.

"What did you say about your roommate?" Howard asks. "Maybe we could all go back to your place together?" he suggests with a sleazy smile.

"Oh my God," I mutter as I turn to leave the table. I've forgotten any iota of regret that I had at ditching him.

* * *

"So, how was it?" Jenny asks as soon as I walk through the door. "It couldn't have been very good; I haven't even finished this episode of *Law & Order*," she jokes.

"It was awful," I moan, kicking off my pointy-toed boots and making a beeline for the fridge to see if there is anything worth eating. "Why are all guys so gross? And why do I keep going out on these ridiculous dates?" I complain.

"Because you're a hopeless romantic, and you believe that your perfect man is waiting somewhere out there for you," Jenny replies, moving down on the couch to make room for me and my cold sesame noodles.

"I'm done. This was my last date," I declare.

"You'll be back online tomorrow. But I'll pretend to believe you tonight if it makes you feel better," she says with a smile.

"What am I going to do without you?" I sigh. I've asked Jenny this question at least ten times a day since we found out she matched with Boston Medical Center for her residency and will be moving there next month.

"You'll be fine," Jenny assures me, but her tone is not convincing. "Any luck with the roommate search?" she asks.

"Not yet. I'd rather move into a three hundred square foot studio than live with any of the crazy people who will probably reply to my ad on Craigslist," I lament. I feel bad making Jenny feel guilty for moving since I know she has no choice, and she has to go to Boston to continue all of her fancy doctor training. But I still can't help feeling sorry for myself. Jenny's going to be living with one of her med school classmates, who is also moving to Boston, and my other best friend from Duke just got engaged and is moving in with her fiancé in a loft in

Brooklyn. Meanwhile, I'm working at a job I don't love (which is only a minor step up from the job at Citibank that I hated), I go on countless first dates with horny investment bankers, and I'm going to end up living with a stranger because I can't afford to pay my rent.

"You don't mean that!" Jenny exclaims, clearly horrified at my statement. "You can't give this place up!" she reminds me.

"I know, I know," I sigh. Our apartment is one of those unicorns in New York City that you hear about but don't believe really exist — it's a rent-controlled "classic six" in a stunning pre-war doorman building on the Upper West Side. For anyone unfamiliar with Manhattan real estate terminology, which was me until I moved here, that means our apartment has two bedrooms, two and a half bathrooms, a kitchen, a living room with a working fireplace, and a dining room.

With my student loans, I can't afford the reduced rent on my own, even though we are lucky enough to have Jenny's aunt's name on the apartment lease. The market rate for this place would be five times what we pay each month, and people in the building actually pay that! And some people have even bought their apartments outright, but I can't fathom that kind of money.

"I'm sure someone will turn up if you actually *post* the ad," she says, and I don't miss the accusation.

"Tomorrow's a new day," I reply, trying to sound optimistic. "I think I'm going to go to bed. It's been a long day," I say. The combination of chardonnay and sesame noodles makes me queasy, especially when I have to think about sharing this beautiful apartment with some crazy stranger.

Chapter 3

Tory

"I can't believe you're thinking about moving out," Anna says, draining her can of Pabst Blue Ribbon and tossing the empty back into the metal tub that holds four more identical cans floating in an ice bath, waiting to be drunk.

"I'm twenty-six years old; I can't live with my parents anymore," I tell her. "It's pathetic," I add firmly. I finish my own can of beer and pop open another with a satisfying crack that can only be achieved from this specific type of cut-rate aluminum. This watered-down bargain-basement beer would be disgusting anywhere else, but at my favorite dive bar on the Upper East Side, sitting in a faded leather booth with sawdust on the floor and smoke in the air, there's nothing better.

"Living with *your parents* is not the same as anyone else living with their parents," Anna tries to argue.

"You have your own apartment," I remind her.

"I have two roommates, and I'm in a fourth-floor walkup; it's hardly something to envy. I'd kill to have your place," Anna says.

"But then you'd have to live with my parents," I tell her.

"Your parents seem fine," Anna gushes.

"That's because you've never spent more than five minutes with them. They put on a good show whenever *company* comes over," I say, trying to make a joke out of it, but it's not feeling very funny.

"I'm pretty sure I would suck it up for my own floor in a brownstone, one block from Central Park," Anna says.

There's no good way to respond, so I take another sip of my drink, grab the stained paper menu from between the salt and pepper shakers, and pretend to agonize over the selections as if I don't get the same thing every time we end up here.

"How do I find a roommate?" I ask, hoping this isn't a stupid question.

The look she gives me with her raised eyebrows is worth a thousand words, but she doesn't make any of the comments I'm sure she's dying to make, and for that, I am grateful. "I don't think you want a roommate. If I could afford to live anywhere alone where I didn't think I was going to get murdered in my sleep, I would definitely choose to do that," she says.

"I thought you liked your roommates," I question Anna, replaying previous conversations in my head where she has mentioned the two girls whose names I can never remember. Anna and I both started at Hachette Book Group the same week about two years ago. Anna took a more linear path to her job as an assistant at the massive publishing company. She graduated summa cum laude from Columbia with an English major and was "lucky enough" to land a job getting coffee, submitting expense reports, and taping up boxes of books in the hopes of one day actually getting to edit or write something that uses her Ivy League education.

On the other hand, I barely graduated from Tulane and then spent two years traveling around Europe after graduation, trying to figure out what I wanted to do with my life. I was on a friend of a friend's yacht in Greece on September 11th, 2001, when the towers were hit in New York, and then three weeks later, when I could finally get a flight home, I was back in Manhattan because that felt like the right thing to do. Even with the glaring gap on my resume, I landed this job without any trouble – one of the perks of my parents' connections. I told them that I might want to be a writer, and this is what my dad found for me. Although, I might as well be folding clothes at The Gap because there is just as much of a chance of me writing something there as there is in my current job.

I don't like to put a damper on Anna's dreams, and I'm no closer to figuring out my own, so I try to pretend that we are in this together, working our way up the publishing ladder, but it's hard to muster enthusiasm for administrative support.

"They're fine," she says unconvincingly, "But I would much rather live alone."

"I think I should have at least one roommate," I say, thinking out loud.

"You're crazy," Anna laughs, but I can tell she isn't upset

even if she doesn't understand why I want to move out or live with a stranger.

"There are websites where I can find someone, right?" I ask, ignoring Anna's smirk at my ignorance. "I heard someone talking about it the other day at work."

"Are you looking to move into someone's apartment? Or are you looking for someone to move in with you?" Anna asks.

"How could someone move in with me? I don't have anywhere to live?" I protest.

Anna sighs and shakes her head like she can't believe what she's hearing. "I don't understand why you can't just move out and get your own place?" Anna asks as she finishes off another beer.

"We make the same amount of money. If you can't afford to live without roommates, then neither can I," I state. Once the words are out of my mouth, I realize how snotty it sounds and wish I could take it back. I also wish the waiter would come by so we could order the extra hot buffalo wings – I haven't eaten much today, and the watery beer is going straight to my head.

Anna purses her lips, and I know that she's pissed. I'm sure I deserve a snide remark or worse, but I'm not in the mood. I want to eat something and go home and fall into bed. Anna must take pity on me, or she can't be bothered because her reply is quite pleasant. "I feel like *you* could afford your own place, but if you want a roommate, you should try Craigslist," she offers.

"Thanks so much. I'll look that up tomorrow," I reply.

"It's late. I think I'm going to get going," Anna says, sliding her petite frame down the bench and grabbing her maroon velvet blazer off the hook at the end of our booth. I'm about to beg her to stay for "one more drink" when exhaustion takes over, and I realize I don't want to stay either. My stomach has given up on me, and I can only hope my liquid diet won't result in too much of a hangover tomorrow morning.

"Want to share a cab?" I ask, scrambling to get my Louis Vuitton clutch from the end of the bench and get to my feet on the sticky floor.

"I'm going to take the subway," Anna says as she weaves around the tables on her way to the front of the bar.

"But it's after midnight," I argue. I rarely take the subway during daylight hours, but I've never taken it at this hour.

"You do know that it's open twenty-four hours a day?" Anna teases. She flashes me a smile that reveals dazzling white teeth that could have been perfected with orthodonture in her teenage years but instead has given her an adorable, quirky grin with one slightly crooked front tooth. I know I'll lose the argument, so I decide not to bother.

Third Avenue is far from deserted when we exit the bar. It may be one in the morning on a Tuesday, but it's still Manhattan, and it's called "the city that never sleeps" for a reason. Anna heads south and west toward the Union Square subway station, and I raise my arm to flag a cab going uptown. It feels like it's dropped about thirty degrees since earlier today, which is not uncommon for late April, but it makes it almost impossible to figure out what to wear. I should have worn something warmer, but I can't resist wearing new clothes right after I get them. I glance down at my super low-rise Diesel jeans and the cropped halter top that leaves at least six inches of my stomach exposed, and I'm secretly thrilled at how toned my abs look, even after a night of drinking, despite being covered in goosebumps.

Thankfully a taxi pulls up while I still have feeling in my fingers and toes, and I greedily swing open the back door and dash into the backseat, praying that the heater is turned on and that the driver doesn't have pervasive body odor. "80th and Madison, please," I say, collapsing against the cracked vinyl seat.

"You got it," the driver replies, in a thick New York accent that catches me by surprise. I expect him to follow up with a question or comment because he seems like the chatty type, but we ride up Madison Avenue without another word. I can hardly hear the music at first, but then I realize that the radio is playing classical music at a barely perceptible volume. It takes a minute, but I recognize the piece as Brahms' Violin Sonata Number Three. I'm so surprised by this unexpected turn of events that as we pull up to the corner of my street, I almost tell the driver that when I was twelve, I performed this piece at Carnegie Hall. Then I think better of it, tip him five dollars, and make the same prayer I always do when I come home – that neither of my parents is still awake.

Chapter 4

Jessica

It's been four days since I walked in on Brian getting head from the waitress. He called me the next night, and when I didn't pick up, he left a lame message on my answering machine asking me to call him. I haven't returned his call, and he hasn't attempted to reach me again. I'm not sure what I expected, but it certainly wasn't this. Okay, that's a huge lie; I know exactly what I expected. I thought Brian would come to my apartment that night begging for my forgiveness, and if not that night, then certainly the next morning. I envisioned bouquets of flowers and possibly even jewelry and, most of all, an explanation for why he cheated on me!

Instead, I'm left wondering what happened and questioning every moment of our relationship: Did I do something wrong? Was Brian cheating on me the whole time? Did he ever have feelings for me?

A loud cracking noise disturbs my inner monologue, and I

realize that Max is angrily snapping his fingers at me, trying to get my attention. "Hey, earth to Jessica. Are you done with those slides yet?" he asks, glaring at me over the top of his massive computer monitor.

"I'm almost done," I reply sheepishly. I stare back at my computer screen and sigh. It's not surprising that Max is pissed off that I haven't finished these slides yet; these are quite basic and should have taken me forty-five minutes, not two hours. "I'm finishing up the pie charts on the last page," I say, but when I look up, I see that he's no longer sitting at his desk. So I get busy double-checking the data on the last slide and adding the appropriate images and logos before emailing it to Max – better late than never.

It's a few minutes after ten-thirty in the morning, and I hear laughing from the office kitchen down the hall. Although there is no official morning coffee break, this seems to be the time when many people on our floor gravitate toward the new Keurig coffee maker for their second, third, or sometimes fourth cup of the day. Thankfully, I'm not here early (or late) enough to even need a second cup of coffee at this hour. In this office, I'm one of the lucky ones, or at least that's how I look at it. I come in at eight-thirty, and I leave at five-thirty. Considering that I work at a consulting firm, only a few of us can say that. I don't make the same type of money as my "peers" – the twenty-six-year-old consultants who work eighty- or ninety-hour weeks and have racked up hundreds of thousands of frequent flyer miles but never seem to have time to use them. But they look miserable and downtrodden; every day is another client crisis. On the flip side, they probably aren't still living with a roommate and eating Ramen noodles for dinner.

When I started at the Rhode Island School of Design, I had big dreams of what I would do with my art degree. By the time graduation rolled around, I was a little more realistic and had taken several graphic design courses as a hedge, even though I majored in photography. In all my visions, I never imagined I would work at a management consulting firm, but somehow, I've been here over three years, and because the pay is halfway decent and the benefits are pretty good, I have no real reason to look for another job. I'm one of four graphic designers that create countless PowerPoint presentations. Actually, I don't even really *create* the presentations, I take the sloppy slides that some young analyst has thrown together, along with copious handwritten or emailed notes from the team's manager or partner, and I turn them into a beautiful presentation. Then some power-hungry Harvard MBA comes in at the last minute, tweaks one of the charts, and takes credit for ninety pages of my work. Then I come back the next day and do it all over again.

I press send on my email and wait to hear Max's computer's obnoxiously loud inbox notification alert him that my slides have arrived. "About time," Max grumbles as he opens the attachment. I know better than to expect gratitude, but does he have to be so snarky about everything? I open my mouth to say something to that effect but think better of it and take a sip of my lukewarm coffee instead. While Max's maturity level may hide it, he is technically my boss and bears the title "Head of Graphic Design," not only for the New York office but for all the offices in North America and

Europe. There's a woman named Marie who is his counterpart and manages design for Asia and Australia. I've only worked with her once on a massive project that required round-the-clock graphics support. I pulled an all-nighter to help the team in Beijing. It took me days to recover, but Marie was so much better than Max; it would almost be worth it to work nights if I could trade bosses.

"I'm running out. I'll be back in a few minutes," I tell Max. I grab my purse from the bottom drawer of the filing cabinet and head out of our shared office before Max can reply. It's a beautiful spring morning, and the expansive tulip-laden sidewalks of Park Avenue are filled with men in shirtsleeves and women in light dresses; it's like all of Midtown got the memo to come outside for a mid-morning fashion show of this year's spring collection. I try to absorb the optimism and enthusiasm from the air, but it's useless. I have no reason to be wandering around out here, especially with a pile of work waiting for me back in the office, but I thought the fresh air would help clear my head. Since that's proved unsuccessful, I call Katie to see if that lifts my spirits. My other option is a muffin and latte from Starbucks, and I can't afford that luxury.

Katie picks up on the second ring, and I feel slightly better at the sound of her voice. "Hey, is everything okay?" she asks, sounding worried.

"Yeah, it's fine. I'm having a slow morning and wanted to say hi," I lie.

"Oh, good. I thought maybe you had heard from Brian," she says.

"Nope, still haven't heard," I say miserably, turning left

on East 53rd Street to minimize the number of bystanders who could witness my possible meltdown.

"Sorry, Jess! That's not what I meant," Katie apologizes. "He's such a schmuck," she adds, tossing out one of her favorite insults. Katie didn't hear a lot of Yiddish growing up in Western Ohio, but she's picked up some key phrases since moving to New York.

"Do you think I should call him?" I ask Katie as if we haven't spent countless hours discussing this over the past four days.

"I think you should do whatever you think is right," she says. This is the same answer she gave me last night; it isn't any more satisfying this morning.

"I'll think about it," I sigh.

"Can we talk more later tonight?" Katie asks. "I have to get ready for that audition."

"Oh my God, I'm so sorry!" I say. "Yes, go get ready! I'm sorry to keep you. Let's talk tonight."

"Don't worry about it. I still have a couple of hours, but I want to do some more vocal warm-ups, and you know I like to get there early," she says.

Even after being roommates for four years, I barely understand her "professional" life. Katie dreams of being on Broadway one day. She goes to an alarming number of auditions and spends much of her day reading lines and rehearsing songs, but her income comes from waitressing and bartending at an upscale strip club. "Good luck! I mean, break a leg!" I shout at her through the phone, hoping that this will finally be her breakthrough.

"Thanks! Let's meet for drinks at Rio Grande tonight – at

six? I think tequila may be the answer to your problems," she jokes.

"Okay, that sounds good." Suddenly, I can taste the salt on the rim of the glass mixing with the tart frozen liquid, and I have the push I need to get me through the day.

"There's also something I want to tell you tonight," Katie says, and quickly follows with, "But it's not a really big deal or anything – okay, gotta go!" And with that, she's gone.

My excitement over the margaritas disappears and is replaced with dread. I don't know what Katie wants to talk about, but it won't be good with how my luck's been going.

Chapter 5

Robin

I'm not usually one for procrastination, but I've put off posting this roommate ad until the last possible minute. Jenny moves to Boston in less than a month. At first, I hoped that if I ignored the situation, it wouldn't be real, and I'd never have to live with someone else. But my unwillingness to face reality is going to leave me scrambling – I'm going to end up living with someone horrible, creepy, and desperate. Visions of the movie *Single White Female* dance through my head, and I try to get the image of an early 1990s Jennifer Jason Leigh out of my head while reminding myself that it's fictional.

The messages in my Microsoft Outlook inbox continue to pile up, and I know I must get back to work, but I promised myself I would post this stupid ad today. As if they aren't under my control, my fingers know I need to stall, and they click on my internet browser and open my eHarmony account. I swore that I was abandoning all online dating sites, and at a minimum, I was taking the week off, and here I am glued to the screen twenty-four hours later - my lack of willpower is a disgrace.

Then, a calendar reminder pops up to remind me that my weekly team meeting is in conference room B in five minutes. The meeting is usually a waste of time as my boss's boss spends the whole time talking just to hear herself speak. However, now I have the deadline I desperately need. So I pull up the ad I hastily wrote last night and read over the words one more time to see if there is any way to improve the listing or, by some miracle, to guarantee that only normal, friendly, non-stalkers apply.

Seeking female roommate to move into a classic-six apartment in a doorman building on the Upper West Side. Seeking a young, single professional who likes watching romantic comedies after a long day at work, gossiping late into the night, and drinking too much wine on the weekend. Must split rent and utilities evenly. Rent portion is $1200 a month.

I read it again, and it seems okay. I've never written a roommate ad or read one before, but it captures all the basics. I enter the required contact information and hurriedly press submit just as Christy walks by my cubicle to pick me up for the meeting. Christy is the junior financial manager of the skincare brand, and although we have very little in common outside of the office, we are inseparable inside these walls.

"I hope this doesn't take too long," Christy moans. "I barely ate breakfast, and my stomach is growling. Oooh, let's get Shake Shack for lunch!" she suggests excitedly.

I laugh because I can't help myself. Christy is *always* hungry and constantly snacking on something or talking about what she just ate or what she plans to eat, which is rarely healthy. But the perplexing and only *slightly* annoying part of the equation is that Christy is super thin and claims to barely work out. I tell myself that it's just part of the unfortunate inequities in life, but it doesn't stop me from coveting her insane metabolism. "I think I'm going to have to pass on Shake Shack today and get yet another salad. It's also only ten-thirty – if I eat now, I'll be dying later. You know I like to wait to eat as late as possible so the afternoon doesn't feel so long," I remind her.

"Suit yourself. I'm thinking chocolate shake and a bacon cheeseburger," Christy says, ever so slightly licking her lips, like she can already taste the greasy fare.

We are last to arrive in conference room B and quickly slip into the two remaining seats at the large oval table. We both attempt to match the professional demeanor of the other men and women in the room, although it is always clear that we are the youngest ones here, no matter how we conduct ourselves.

Janet taps her dry-erase marker on the whiteboard and clears her throat to let us know that she is ready to begin. Janet is the Director of Marketing for beauty, which includes fragrance, skincare, cosmetics, and accessories. I know that I should respect her as a fellow woman in the workplace. I'm pretty sure that's what I am supposed to do. I recognize that she has a lot of responsibility, runs a large team, and reports directly to some guy who is so senior that I've only seen his picture. But at the same time, I despise her. Janet is one of those women who doesn't like other women. I can't tell if it's because of the whole glass ceiling thing where she thinks that there's only room for one woman at the top, so everyone else is her competition, or if she's the type who *never* got along with other girls, even in elementary school. But whatever it is, it sucks.

"We are ready," Frederic says, drawing out the words in his charming French accent. Frederic is my direct boss and the senior brand manager on skincare, and everyone adores him, especially Janet.

"Then let's get started," Janet says, looking around the room and shaking her head as if she's already disappointed in the results of the weekly skincare update before it's even begun. Frederic runs through our sales numbers and revised forecast and even manages to put a positive spin on the slight hiccup we had with research and development on our new bath scrub formula. Per usual, Janet is mesmerized by Frederic's upscale Parisian accent combined with his jet-black hair, olive skin, and delicate bone structure, which leaves most people wondering why he chose a career in brand management instead of modeling.

"We are good?" Frederic asks after he finishes his presentation and looks up from his Moleskin notebook.

"Yes, yes, merci Frederic," Janet gushes, smiling only at him. "Let's get the finance and production update, and then I have some news to share," she announces ominously.

I shoot Christy a look, but her eyes are glued to her laptop while her boss presents the detailed financial update, and I can't catch her eye. My mind races as I try to focus on the remaining updates, but I'm too worried about Janet's announcement to concentrate. The last time Janet made an unscheduled announcement, several managers were reassigned to different brands, and a couple of people ended up without a job. Although now that I think about it, that did happen in an email, and it probably *was* planned, but still, I'm terrified. She's now seated at the head of the table, and I sneak a glance at her as if, somehow, I can read her mind. Janet taps her left hand's long, pink acrylic nails on the table and scrolls through her Blackberry with the other hand. It looks like she isn't paying any attention, but I know from experience that she's absorbing every word of the manufacturing report while reading her emails. She may be a bitch, but she's an excellent multi-tasker.

When all the reports have been read, Janet stands up again and walks to the whiteboard at the front of the room. She picks up the blue marker and starts to write a series of words on the board: "Old, Dated, Tired, Stagnant, Boring."

Frederic glances at me and shrugs as Janet is writing to indicate that he also has no idea what's going on.

"Does anyone know what these words describe?" Janet asks the room. All five members of the skincare brand team look around the table at each other, but not a single one of us offers a response.

"Anyone?" Janet asks again, but the silence continues, and if at all possible, it gets even quieter in the room as if the first one to make an audible noise will be called upon and singled out to answer the question.

Janet sighs with exasperation and then goes on to answer her own question as if she knew she couldn't count on us. "These words describe our current product," she announces with a flourish.

A gasp of surprise escapes my lips, and my hand flies to

cover my mouth, but not quickly enough to prevent the entire team from staring directly at me. I feel my cheeks grow hot, and I know they are a bright shade of crimson, but there is nothing I can do to hide this additional level of embarrassment. Janet exhales loudly through her nose, not unlike a bull in the center of the ring, and Frederic shoots me a sympathetic smile.

"It doesn't bode well that you are so shocked by these consumer descriptions of your brand," Janet says, glaring at me. There's no good way to respond, so I give her a small head nod that hopefully conveys subservience and pray for her to move her attention elsewhere.

"Our skincare line no longer fits the Victoria's Secret brand image," Janet continues. I tune out while she drones on for ten minutes about the brand's personality and how the packaging shape doesn't speak to our target consumer. I know that this is a key component of my work, and this part of it is by far the most interesting piece of my job – it certainly isn't reconciling discontinued product barcodes with their replacements. However, Janet even manages to make the best part of the job tiresome with her endless monologue. Her long-winded speeches rarely contain pertinent information, so I'm caught off guard when she says, "Robin will be spearheading the skincare brand refresh to see if she's ready for the promotion to brand manager. Under the guidance of Frederic, of course."

I'm simultaneously stunned, elated, and terrified. Janet is looking at me expectantly. It seems like she's making a declaration rather than asking a question, but I hate awkward silence, so I reply, "Challenge accepted," before I can think of anything else. There is faint laughter around the room, and my cheeks are on fire for the second time in less than thirty minutes. Christy mouths the words, "It's okay," but I know she's lying to make me feel better.

Janet picks up her BlackBerry and Smythson crocodile notebook and pushes her chair back from the table – her signal that the meeting is over. As she walks out the door, she calls back, "Robin, get something on my calendar for next week so you can give me an update on the refresh," and without any further instruction, she disappears.

Chapter 6

Tory

It's taken me a couple of days to get around to it, but at Anna's suggestion, now I have decided to scroll through Craigslist to search for a place to live. There seem to be thousands of posts for people seeking roommates. Some are vague, and I can barely tell what they're offering, while some are so specific that they spell out the number of shelves offered to keep personal items in the bathroom and refrigerator. What they all have in common is that they are all incredibly bleak and make it almost impossible for me to imagine myself renting a bedroom in some stranger's apartment.

I scan over what must be the two hundredth ad today and catch the phrases "No personal items allowed in common rooms!" and "Basement bedroom with shared bathroom and no kitchen access on weekends!" and with a heavy sigh, I know that I'm never going to make this happen. And then I hear my dad's raised voice. It's muffled at first, so I can't make out the words. I almost put my head under my pillow, like I used to do when I was younger, but instead, I get up from my desk and walk toward the door so I can hear what he's saying.

"I don't owe you any explanation!" My dad yells as he stomps up the stairs. The sound of the soft leather soles of his wingtips is muted on the oriental rug, but I've always been able to gauge his mood by his footsteps. My mom's heels go clickety-clack on the marble hallway floor outside my door, and I listen closely to discern whether she's following him up to their bedroom or if she's retreating back downstairs.

"You're a pig – I hate you!" my mom screams, and her voice cracks on the word 'pig' as if she's holding back tears.

I stand motionless by the door as I wait to hear if he'll shout something back at her or, worse if he'll come running back down the stairs. But after two moments of complete silence, my mom's stilettos retreat down the hall, and I hear the ding of the elevator and know that she must be going at least a few floors down, or she would have taken the stairs.

It wasn't until late in elementary school that I realized it was unusual that we had our own elevator. It was probably because half of the kids in my snobby private school also lived in nine-story brownstones with elevators, and the other half lived in penthouse apartments. This is likely one of the many reasons that Anna thinks I won't be able to make it on my own or doesn't understand why I would want to. Just then, I hear my dad thundering down the stairs as he yells, "Pamela, don't think this is over! You asked for it!" and then he continues to spout more drunken nonsense as he makes his way down the stairs.

Fueled by the idea of living far away from my parents' dysfunctional relationship, I quickly respond to three of the least offensive ads and ask to come in for an interview. I press send on the Craigslist messages before I can change my mind.

As expected, my parents are sitting at the dining room table on Sunday morning, drinking coffee and sharing sections of the *New York Times* as if nothing happened the night before. When I see them together like this, it always makes me doubt myself. Maybe *I'm* the one who misunderstood? Maybe I didn't hear him correctly when my dad called my mom an "unlovable whore?" Is it possible to misunderstand when my mom cries that she wishes she had never met my dad? It's not as if this feeling is new, but every time it happens, it fills me with self-doubt and insecurity. I vow to either record them the next time it happens or move out – hopefully, I'm on my way to option number two with my apartment visit today.

"Where are you off to?" my mom asks. She places her china cup in its saucer and carefully gives me a once-over with a pinched look on her cosmetically enhanced face.

"I'm going out," I reply sharply.

"We can see that," my father adds. He carefully folds the business section of the *Times* and places it on the linen tablecloth next to his plate.

"I'm meeting a friend," I offer, hoping this appeases their curiosity.

"Isn't it a bit early for you on a Sunday morning?" my dad chides.

I want to counter with a snotty reply, but unfortunately, he is correct. It is rare that I am out of bed before eleven on a weekend, and even then, I'm usually still in pajamas until the early afternoon. I admit this is probably something I should be ashamed of at my age, but the new independent me will be different.

"I'll be back this afternoon," I say. It takes all my self-restraint not to elaborate on my response, but I manage. It takes even more restraint not to grab a pastry from the basket of fresh-baked warm muffins, croissants, and danishes sitting untouched in the middle of the table, but I don't feel that it bodes well if I can't make it out the door without relying on my parents' personal chef.

They have both returned to their newspapers, and neither acknowledges my comment or seems to notice as I disappear down the stairs and out the door to meet my new life.

* * *

I ring the buzzer to apartment 3B as instructed in the email and pray that this is better than the other two hellholes I've visited this morning. I wanted to jump in a cab and go straight home after the last place, but I felt like too much of a failure, so I instructed the cab driver to go to the corner of Avenue A and East 3rd Street as planned. There's no response, and I can't help the immense feeling of relief that comes with the silence. Just as I'm about to walk away, knowing that I tried and did my best, a crackly voice erupts over the call box. "Who is it?" she demands angrily.

"It's Tory. I'm here to see the apartment? We exchanged emails? The Craigslist posting?" Everything I say ends with the lilted tone of a question, further evidence of my uncertainty and discomfort.

"Third floor," she replies gruffly, and then the door buzzes loudly as it unlocks. I immediately grab for the scuffed, tarnished door handle because she doesn't seem like the type that would be forgiving if I missed it and needed her to buzz me in again.

The lobby is small and dimly lit, with rows of mailboxes on the wall to the left. I can't imagine what I would do with packages, deliveries, or dry cleaning, but I decide not to worry about that yet. The carpeting on the stairs is an indescribably ugly color, somewhere between brown and gray, almost worn down to the concrete foundation in the center of each step where the traffic is heaviest.

I hesitate outside the door of apartment 3B and then knock softly on the door, reminding myself that *I'm* the one who wants to move out and that this is all under *my* own control.

"Who is it?" the same voice calls out, sounding annoyed.

"It's Tory. You just buzzed me up," I say, unable to hide my own irritation.

There are footsteps on the inside of the apartment, and then the door opens to reveal a woman in a light-yellow Juicy Couture sweatsuit with two dark brown Pippi Longstocking-style braids and hot pink lipstick glaring at me.

"Hi," I say, mustering a smile.

"Hey," she utters through tight lips.

"I'm Tory. You must be Carla?" I ask, offering her my hand.

She stares at my outstretched arm like a foreign object,

then turns and walks back toward the corduroy futon in the middle of the room, sits down, picks up the remote control, and turns on the television. I feel like I'm in an episode of *The Twilight Zone*. I exchanged multiple emails last night with Carla. We discussed the apartment and living together and planned to meet this morning. And yet now she's looking at me like I'm some crazy trespasser.

"Am I missing something?" I blurt out.

"Huh?" She says, looking up at me.

"When we emailed last night, you said you were looking for a roommate, and then we decided that I would come over here this morning to meet you and see the place," I say to her. "And you also said that you had a large, modern two-bedroom apartment?" I question, using my arms to gesture to what is now very clearly a small, grungy studio.

"Oh, yeah. I was really drunk last night," she says, and her lips curl up into something that could be interpreted as a smile.

"So, you were lying to me? You were trying to trick me?" I ask, attempting to grasp the situation.

"My friend dared me to do it," she says. "But you have to admit - it is kind of funny," she adds.

"How is this funny?" I yell at her. "Who does this?" I say, incredulous at her level of disrespect and insolence.

She's snickering as I march out the door, and I feel hot tears form in the corners of my eyes as the humiliation starts to sink in. I stomp down three flights of stairs, and by the time I reach the bottom, I've already accepted my fate – I will live with my miserable parents forever.

Chapter 7

Zach

The waiting room doesn't look anything like I expected it would. I'm not sure exactly how I pictured a psychologist's waiting room, but this looks more like an interior designer's office than a doctor's office. There are recent issues of *The New Yorker, New York Magazine,* and *The Economist* on the black glossy coffee table in the center of the sparse room, but I'm too anxious to read anything. I glance at my watch *again,* and it's only two minutes later than the last time I looked. My appointment is supposed to start at two o'clock. I wonder if she runs on time or if she's like most other doctors, and the appointment time is just a guideline but has no actual bearing on when I'll see her.

At exactly two o'clock, the door opens, and a petite redhead dressed head-to-toe in black calls my name. Instinctively, I glance around to make sure she's talking to me, even though I know I'm the only one in the room.

"Are you ready?" she asks, motioning with her left hand

toward her office; in her other hand, she's holding a yellow legal pad.

It is such a loaded question that I almost laugh out loud; however, I immediately worry that my laugh will be the first note she writes about me on that legal pad, and I swallow it into my throat. My high school guidance counselor was the first person to suggest that I "see someone." That was fifteen years ago. In the rural town in New Hampshire where I grew up, no one went to therapy – or a "shrink," as they called it. My parents wouldn't even meet with the counselor when he asked them to come in and talk about it. If I remember correctly, their exact response was, "Zach is simply smarter than everyone else in the school, including *you*; that doesn't mean he's crazy."

Then my advisor at MIT mentioned that his psychologist had helped *him* gain confidence in social situations, and I'm pretty sure I was supposed to take that as a hint, but I didn't. It wasn't until a couple of months ago when I reluctantly ended up going out for drinks after work with some new hires, that I finally got the push I needed.

"Zach, are you coming?" Dr. Green calls out, and I realize that I've gotten lost in my thoughts again, and I'm unsure how long I've been sitting here making her wait for me. Now at least, I know what she'll write first about me in her notes.

"Yes, sorry, I'm ready," I say as I stand up from the cream-colored sofa and walk toward her.

Dr. Green's office looks more like I imagined a psychologist's office would look, with a small desk, floor-to-ceiling bookcases filled with expensive-looking books, diplomas covering the walls, a long leather couch on one side of the room, and a club chair directly across from it. I assume the couch is for me and quickly take my seat - I opt to stay seated and hope she won't ask me to lie down.

Dr. Green gets settled in the club chair, crosses her short legs at the ankles, places the legal pad in her lap, and looks at me expectantly. The silence hangs in the air, and I wait for her to ask, "What brings you here today?" or "What can I do for you?" but she just stares at me and smiles. I'm not uncomfortable with silence. In fact, I'm usually annoyed when people feel the need to speak solely for the sake of breaking the silence. However, after a solid minute of staring at each other, Dr. Green must be declared the winner of the contest because I'm the first to crack.

"This is my first time talking to a psychologist," I blurt out.

Dr. Green nods but unfortunately doesn't say anything, so I feel like it's still my turn. "I'm not sure what to say. Do you ask me questions? Should I tell you about myself?" I ask.

I worry that she isn't going to respond again, but she shuffles slightly in her chair and then finally starts to speak. "We can talk about whatever *you* want to talk about. It can be helpful if you tell me specifically what you want to talk about, but we can also just talk, and some of the issues you want to address may surface naturally – whichever you prefer," she says.

I'm not thrilled with her answer. I work well with strict guidelines and clear goals – this loose methodology does not mesh well with my personality. "I suppose I'll tell you about myself and why I'm here – that seems like the most efficient way to do things," I say to Dr. Green.

"Whatever you prefer, Zach – the time is yours."

I remind myself that she is a professional and that I've chosen to be here today, but it's hard not to be annoyed with her laissez-faire attitude.

"I'm an only child. I grew up in a small town in New Hampshire. Both of my parents still live there. My dad is an accountant, and my mom is a librarian. I'm twenty-nine. I went to MIT for undergrad. I double majored in computer science and mathematics. After graduation, I worked at Microsoft for three years and then transitioned to a job at Expedia, which is where I work now. I live on the Upper West Side," I say, trying to think of what else to tell her.

"That's an impressive resume," she says. "Can you tell me a little bit more about *you*?" Dr. Green asks, pointing at her own chest when she says it, which is somewhat confusing.

"I like to swim. I'm not a big drinker, but I enjoy the occasional glass of wine or scotch. I'm single," I offer, wondering if this is the type of information she is looking for.

Dr. Green jots several items on her notepad. I wonder what I said that she finds particularly noteworthy and if she'll share it with me. Unfortunately, she simply nods and gives me a blank expression. I get the impression that I'm disappointing her. This feels like I'm failing a test, and I *never* fail tests.

I'm determined to give it one last attempt and see if I can get a more positive response from Dr. Green. "I've always done well academically, and this success has carried over into my professional life, but it's not quite the same in my personal life. I have friends and acquaintances, but..." I say, and then I trail off before I finish my sentence.

Finally, Dr. Green looks pleased with what I've said. She is leaning forward in her seat as if she is hanging on my every word. "But what?" she asks.

"I'm twenty-nine years old, and I've never had a *real* girlfriend," I say to her. Of course, this isn't entirely true, but it's close enough for now, and I'm not about to reveal more details to a stranger. I said the exact same thing about not having a girlfriend a few months ago to those new hires, and I wait for her to give me the same shocked look followed by a pitiful smile. To her credit, she doesn't even flinch.

"Do you want to talk more about that?" she asks with an air of indifference like it doesn't matter to her one way or the other. That's certainly not the reaction I got from the inebriated twenty-somethings who grilled me all night like I was some kind of freak show.

"I guess so," I reply as if this isn't the sole reason I'm here. Dr. Green adjusts her position again in the chair, and I have to stop myself from asking her why she hasn't chosen a more comfortable chair if this is where she sits all day long.

"Tell me a little bit more about what you mean when you say *real* girlfriend. Does that mean you haven't had a meaningful relationship? Do you mean that you haven't had a long-term relationship? Have you ever been intimate with a woman?" Dr. Green asks.

Considering how few words she's said up until this point, this is a lot to take in all at once, especially given that they are all yes or no questions. I have different answers for each one, and if I'm going to talk about it, it seems like a lot more than a yes or no is required.

I have the sudden urge to lie down so I can stare up at the

plain white ceiling instead of making eye contact while I share my humiliating dating history. Lying down on a psychologist's couch seems to be something people only do in movies or on television, but I can see the real-life appeal. Regrettably, it seems too late to lie down at this point in the appointment, so I recross my legs and begin to share. "I've been on many first dates and second dates. But I don't often make it past the third date," I say. This is not exactly the truth, but, it feels close enough.

"Hmmm," she says. "Why do you think that is?"

Although I came here of my own free will, I'm suddenly not in the mood to share much with Dr. Green. I could share my fear that women will despise me once they get to know me. Or I could tell her that I'm scared I'll fall in love with them, and they'll break my heart into a million pieces, then turn around and laugh in my face. But instead, I shrug and say, "I don't know."

"Are you intimate with these women?" she asks nonchalantly.

This is the question I was dreading, but of course, I knew it would come up. "Yes," I say with tremendous hesitation, "And also no."

"Would you care to say more about that?" she asks.

I sigh again and check my watch to see that the fifty-minute session is finally nearing the end. I guess all the long pauses and awkward silences took up more time than I thought. I think it's unlikely that I'll return to Dr. Green's couch, so I decide to tell her the truth. "I *do* have sex since I think that's what you're getting at," I reply.

"It sounds like there's more to that response. Do you want

to say more?" Dr. Green asks. I'm unsure if she's asking this question out of personal or professional interest, but it's clear that she's interested in my response.

The short answer is that I do *not* want to say any more about it, but then what's the point of coming here to talk about things? I try to work out an answer that will be satisfactory while not leading directly to Cassie.

"To use your words, I'm *intimate* with some of my dates, but it rarely leads to sex."

"And why is that?" she asks bluntly.

I was hoping she would leave it at that, but it seems nothing is off the table in our first session. "I almost always change my mind right before it happens. I can't go through with it," I say.

"Is it a physical issue?" she asks cautiously.

"No. There's no problem physically," I reply. I was prepared for her to ask this question. "I just can't do it. I think I'm going to be able to, but then I stop right before it happens and end up leaving. Which is why I don't have a lot of third or fourth dates."

"So, you just leave the woman right as you are about to begin intercourse?" she inquires.

"Usually, yes," I reply.

"Oh," she exclaims as her eyes widen, and then her face snaps back to its neutral expression.

Chapter 8

Jessica

Katie has already secured a table and is waiting patiently for me when I arrive at Rio Grande. She is easy to spot in any room, and I'm not the only one staring at her as I make my way toward her table. Half of the men here can't keep their eyes off her, although if they ever got up the nerve to approach her, they would quickly find out that none of them stand a chance since Katie only has eyes for women. Katie is blessed with a body, face, and hair that usually only exists with significant airbrushing. I'm ashamed to admit that I hated her the first time I met her. My aversion only lasted about half an hour, and at that point, I realized that she was smart, funny, and just the right amount of sarcastic, but my initial instinct was to assume that no one who looked like Katie would be a good girlfriend, let alone a good roommate.

I'm only fifteen minutes late, which isn't bad for me. Even with the best intentions, I can never seem to make it anywhere on time, except for work – somehow, I arrive at my desk at precisely eight twenty-nine each morning.

"I'm so sorry I'm late," I say, trying to catch my breath as I slide into the seat across from her and hoist my laptop bag onto the empty chair next to me.

"It's totally fine," Katie says. She's obviously used to my tardiness, but I still feel guilty every time. "I ordered drinks," she says, gesturing to the two frosty margaritas on the table, "But I've only had a few sips of mine. I didn't want to be wasted by the time you got here," she laughs.

"They're called *crack margaritas* for a reason," I reply, using the moniker my friends and I have adopted for the extra-strong drinks here. I hold my glass up to toast her before taking a long sip of my drink – I can smell the tequila when the glass is still several inches away from my face, and that's definitely the kind of drink I need right now.

"How was your audition?" I remember to ask. I've been so preoccupied with my own problems this week that I haven't been much of a friend. I promised myself that I wouldn't dwell on Brian tonight, and shifting the conversation to Katie is a great way to do that.

"I'm not sure," Katie replies. "At first, I felt good about it, but then I talked to someone afterward and found out that they asked her to sing three songs, and they only had me sing one," she sighs and covers her face with both hands.

"I'm sure that's because they only needed to hear you sing one to know how good you are! They were probably giving that other girl several chances to sound good, but they couldn't find any song that worked for her," I say encouragingly.

Katie removes her hands from her face and gives me the big, brilliant smile that I know I will someday see on a stage or screen. "Is that because Broadway casting directors are well known for giving people several chances?" she smirks and takes a hefty sip of her drink, but I can tell she feels a bit better. "They said we should hear about callbacks in the next few days, although I'm not going to hold my breath."

"Fingers crossed," I say, and I hold up my right hand to emphasize my point and show her that my fingers are, in fact, crossed. I'm not sure what it is, but something about that movement jostles my memory, and I recall that Katie wanted to talk to me about something tonight – that was the reason we were meeting for drinks. "Was there something special you wanted to talk about tonight?" I ask her.

Katie hesitates before she replies, and with that subtle movement, I already know that whatever she has to say is going to be bad news. "I was going to tell you the other night," she begins. She doesn't have to clarify for me to know which night she is referring to – it's the night I saw Brian's penis in another woman's mouth. "But *obviously*, that wasn't the night to talk about anything other than what an asshole Brian is," Katie continues.

"Uh-huh," I say, unable to say anything else as I wait for the inevitable bad news.

Katie fidgets with her straw before she says anything else, and I wonder just how bad this is going to be. "If I had known how things were going to go with you and Brian, I never would have done it. I feel awful about what I've done," Katie begins.

"What are you talking about?" I ask her. I'm not sure if

it's the crack margaritas or if Katie simply isn't making sense, but either way, I have no idea what she's talking about, and I think she may be trying to tell me that she's sleeping with Brian now, but that doesn't make sense for numerous reasons!

"I signed a lease to move in with two girls from work. I'm so sorry!" she cries, and I can see tears starting to roll down her cheeks. She keeps going before I have a chance to say anything. "You were planning to move in with Brian, and we didn't renew our lease, and they found this great apartment on East 67th Street, and I had to give them an answer immediately, or they were going to ask somebody else, so I said yes. Now you obviously *aren't* going to be living with Brian, and they won't let me out of the lease, so I have to move out," Katie says, finally stopping to take a breath after her rambling speech.

"Oh wow," I reply. "It's okay, sweetie." I wasn't expecting this, but I probably *should have,* considering that the plan was for me and Brian to move in together, and then Katie would have needed somewhere else to live. I'm so relieved to hear that there isn't more heartbreaking news about Brian that it takes me a minute to realize the direct implications for me.

"It's not your fault," I say to Katie, reaching across the table to pat her arm. She's still sniffling, but even with black lines of mascara running down her cheeks, she's still the most beautiful woman in the bar.

"I'd rather live with *you,*" she implores, "But there's nothing I can do about it now."

"It's okay," I say again. "I was *supposed* to move out. You had no way to know that Brian was a cheating scumbag," I say, and then feel a wave of sadness wash over me as I picture

Brian and the slutty waitress hooking up on his couch right now. I'm sure by this point they've progressed to his bedroom, or maybe it was just a one-night stand, and he's done with her and moved on to someone else, but in my head, it will always be the two of them on that couch. "When do you have to move out?" I ask quietly.

"The end of the month," Katie says gently. "Our lease isn't up for another three months, but I checked with the landlord, and he said we could move out earlier if we want," Katie says sheepishly. "Or you can stay until the lease is up," she adds.

"I don't think I can afford to stay there on my own," I sigh. "I mean, I guess I could technically afford it, but I'd have to use some of my savings, and that doesn't seem very smart," I say to Katie. I shake my head as I try to grasp the impending logistics through a tequila haze. "I guess I'm going to need to find a new apartment and a new roommate," I say pitifully and then signal for the waiter to order another margarita. I want to put off thinking about my shitty situation for at least the rest of the night.

Chapter 9

Robin

Yesterday afternoon was miserable. By the time I got back to my desk after the meeting, I was panicking. I hadn't heard everything Janet asked me to do, but there was no way I could admit that to her or even to Frederic. He may be an understanding boss, but accepting that I zoned out and have no idea what I'm supposed to do is above and beyond. Christy was able to give me a few details, but she admitted that if it doesn't concern her directly, she doesn't pay any attention. I spent hours staring at a Word document, trying to put together a to-do list for a brand refresh, but the page was still blank two hours later. After complaining bitterly about not having enough responsibility, I might not know how to *do* anything once I've finally been given a chance!

The hours of fruitless work meant that I didn't get any of my actual work done, so I was at the office until eight forty-five finishing my weekly sales report. By the time I got home, I was too tired to make anything other than cereal for dinner, although Jenny was quick to tell me that pouring Special-K and milk in a bowl was not *making* anything. I had been so busy all afternoon that I hadn't even thought about the roommate ad I'd posted that morning.

* * *

"I posted an ad for a roommate yesterday," I tell Jenny. She's lying at the opposite end of the couch, paging through a *People* magazine, and her head pops up as soon as she hears me.

"Did you get any responses?" she asks excitedly.

"I don't know. I haven't checked yet," I say. "I can't imagine anyone would have responded yet – I just posted it yesterday."

"Let's check!" she says, bouncing off the couch and practically running over to the desk we have set up in the corner of the living room with my computer. My mom's school gave all the teachers massive discounts on Apple computers last year, and Jenny and I were lucky recipients of this Power Mac G5. It was a godsend since it replaced the Dell monstrosity I got in 1994, my freshman year at Duke.

"I'm sure there's nothing there," I tell her again, but I peel myself off the couch and follow her to the computer anyway. I login to the special Hotmail email I created to use with my Craigslist account, and I can't make sense of what I see on the screen.

"Holy shit!" Jenny exclaims. "Are those all responses to your ad?" she asks.

"They can't possibly be," I say to her, but since this email account is brand new and I've only used it for this ad, there's no other explanation. "I *just* posted the ad – how could I have one hundred and seventy-four replies?!" I practically shout.

"That means you'll have a lot of options," Jenny says – always the optimist. "Let's start reading!" And she pulls over a chair from the dining room so that we can each sit at the desk and scroll through the replies.

An hour later, I moan, "This is hopeless!" as I finish my third glass of wine – even though I swore I wasn't going to have a second.

"They're not *all* bad," Jenny says unconvincingly, but even she's having trouble finding a bright side to this disaster. "What about the one who works at the library? She'd probably be quiet," Jenny says hopefully.

I shoot her a disgusted look. "She also has three pet ferrets."

"Right – I forgot that part," Jenny says, and I can tell she is trying hard to conceal a smile. "Wait, here's one." Finally, after over a hundred terrible emails, I can no longer bear to look, and Jenny has taken full control of the computer. "This one says that she's twenty-seven. She's single. She's a paralegal. Her favorite movie is *Sweet Home Alabama*," Jenny says, wrinkling her nose.

"Hey, that was a cute movie," I reply, defending my love of cheesy rom-coms. "She sounds good. Maybe I should write back to her and have her come by for an interview?"

"Oh. Oh no," Jenny says, staring intently at the screen.

"What? What is it?" I ask.

"I don't think she's going to be a good fit after all," she sighs.

"Why not?" I inquire. I was already mentally crafting my email and debating whether I should ask if she liked other Reese Witherspoon movies or if I should wait to ask that in person.

"She wouldn't be moving in here alone," Jenny says.

"I thought you said she's single?" I question.

"She is. But apparently, she has a two-year-old son," Jenny tells me. "The email says that he's pretty quiet, but she would be hoping her new roommate would be interested in splitting childcare responsibilities...." Jenny says, trailing off.

"Oh, my God! What is wrong with people?! I'm never going to find a roommate," I wail.

"Well, there was that one girl who looked pretty good – as long as you are okay with letting her use the apartment on Tuesday and Thursday nights for her coven to meet," Jenny laughs.

I throw a pillow at her and collapse back on the couch in despair.

Chapter 10

Tory

I've essentially given up on the idea of ever being able to move out of this townhouse. I'll never be able to make enough money to afford a decent place to live on my own, and I'm not willing to live in any of the horrible places that I *can* afford.

I snapped at Anna yesterday when she suggested that I ask my parents for a loan. I know I should apologize to Anna because it's easy to see how my behavior could be confusing. I've made up arbitrary rules about what I consider to be acceptable and what constitutes crossing the line into spoiled brat territory, and for some reason, I've determined that I'm still on the right side of that line. However, if they give me money for an apartment, then that would be one step too far. I'm sure they wouldn't even be willing to give me money to rent an apartment, but it's a moot point since I won't ask.

Suddenly, the dinner bell chimes and I remember that I promised my parents I would join them for dinner tonight in the dining room. I roll off my bed and feel more like an angsty teenager than a twenty-six-year-old woman. I begrudgingly slink down the stairs and pray that dinner is quick and my parents aren't fighting.

The beginning of the meal is surprisingly calm, and my mother tells us about some charity luncheon she attended at The Pierre that day and my father informs us that he'll be in Zurich and Brussels the following week for meetings. We all make inane comments about how delicious the dinner is; although none of us had anything to do with the meal preparation, and it's the same salmon, asparagus, and lemon rice we have every Tuesday because my mother insists on it.

I'm about to excuse myself from the table and call the meal a success when my father barks my name. "Tory, tell me about work."

I push my chair back in and sigh; I was so close to a clean getaway. "What do you want to know about it?" I ask him.

"Are you still just the secretary or working in the mailroom, or whatever you do there?" he says, dismissively waving his hand.

"I'm not a secretary, and I don't work in the mailroom," I say through clenched teeth. "I'm a publishing assistant."

"It's all the same thing. It's not a real job, you don't need any skills to do it, and you barely make any money," he says calmly and swirls the overpriced red wine in his crystal glass before smelling it again and taking a sip, looking like the villain in a bad movie.

I want to scream at him, but I've learned from experience that there is nothing to gain from that, and honestly, that's what he wants me to do – I tell myself that I won't give him the satisfaction. "I'm putting in my time as an assistant so I can work as an editor or a writer one day,"

"But is that ever going to happen?" he asks. "You've been doing the same thing for two years, and as far as I can tell, you still have the same menial job," he says flippantly.

I look to my mother to see if she will defend me or at least tell him to stop being such an asshole, but she looks down at her empty plate and refuses to meet my eye.

"Isn't it time you give all of this up and focus your efforts on finding a husband to support you? You're still very pretty, but you aren't getting any younger. Men aren't going to be interested in you for much longer," he says as if I'm nearing my expiration date.

"I appreciate your concern," I say snidely, pushing my chair back from the table.

"I'm just telling it like it is, Tory. Just look at your mother," he says, waving his hand in her direction. "She was even more beautiful than you when she was your age, although she certainly had other issues. I think it's fair to say that you have a better body than she ever did – at least from what I can tell."

I look at my father in abject horror and then at my mother (there is no way she can continue to ignore his behavior). However, she is still staring into her lap, and I am dismayed to realize that she isn't going to say anything to him. Her desire not to get in a fight tonight is so strong that she won't even come to my rescue.

My father ignores my reaction and plows on, intent on finishing his diatribe. "If your mother had waited a few more years, I would probably have picked someone else, but she got me before she got too old – that's what you need to do too. How else do you plan to support yourself?" he laughs.

I storm out of the room and up the stairs before I *accidentally* throw something at him or stab him with my fish knife – he is lucky we had salmon instead of steak tonight! I'm so enraged that I'm shaking when I slam my bedroom door – I'm not sure if I'm angrier at his crass comments about my body, his degrading comments about my work, his total lack of respect for my mother, or that my mother remained silent through it all.

Although I swore it was pointless to look at Craigslist again, within moments of being back in my room, I'm scouring the site to see if there are any new postings or any amazing posts that I simply missed the last fifty times I looked at the site.

On the bottom of the second page, an ad catches my eye with the words "classic six" in the listing. I scan the ad, and it seems too good to be true, but after dinner tonight, I'm determined to give it another go. I type out a quick reply to the wine-drinking rom-com lover and hope for the best as I press send.

Chapter 11

Jessica

"You're never going to believe what I found!" Katie says cheerfully when I open my bedroom door at seven forty-five in the morning.

"Why are you up so early?" I croak. "And why are you so ridiculously chipper?" I pad into our tiny kitchen and forgive Katie's annoying joviality when I see that she has already made a pot of coffee.

"I have an audition later this morning, and I want time to rehearse," she says.

I try to remember if she mentioned it last night, but most of it is a blur – sadly, the past three nights are all a blur. Some might say that I'm not dealing with being cheated on or losing my roommate in a healthy way, but I call it "coping."

"I found a really good apartment listing for you," Katie says. The look on my face must convey my lack of excitement bordering on dismay because she stumbles over her words as she tells me about it. "I just feel terrible about how this is all happening. I want to help you find somewhere great to live. I've been looking at listings all morning, and there's a lot of super weird ones out there, but this actually looks pretty great," she rambles.

I take a long sip of my coffee and sigh before I respond. "It's not your fault, Katie. You don't need to feel bad about it. It's Brian that needs to...."

"But I do!" Katie cries, cutting me off mid-sentence. "Just take a look at this ad. I think you should go check out the apartment – you could go there after work tonight?" she suggests, and her voice gets suspiciously high at the end of her sentence.

I've known Katie for several years, and we don't have the kind of friendship where I always know what she's thinking (although honestly, I think people who say that are full of shit), but I do know her well enough to know when she's keeping something from me.

"What aren't you telling me?" I ask her, attempting to keep my tone light even though the coffee isn't doing much to help my hangover yet, and I have a bad feeling about all of this.

"Don't be mad," Katie begins as she holds up both of her hands like miniature stop signs. I believe those three words are a sure sign that I'm *going* to be mad because why else would she preface her statement with them?! "I sent a response to the woman who listed the apartment, pretending that I was you, and made an appointment for you to go see it tonight at six o'clock," she blurts out. Then, she ducks and holds her hands over her head as if bracing for an attack.

"Are you serious?!" I ask her, stunned that she would overstep like this.

"I'm only trying to help. I emailed you all the information. Please don't be upset with me," she pleads.

"I've got to get ready for work," I say stoically, grabbing my mug as I turn to walk down the hall to the bathroom and then slamming the door shut for full effect.

The day goes by surprisingly quickly. There is a huge client presentation tomorrow, and everyone in the office is frantically making changes to the final decks - which means that I'm swamped. We are so busy that Max orders lunch for the three of us and charges it to the client. I know that the consultants eat dinner at their desks three to four nights a week, and it all goes on some giant bill, but it's very rare that the graphics department gets a free meal.

I only have time to think about my fight with Katie a handful of times during the day, and most of them are the few moments my eyes are off the screen while I'm in the bathroom. I'm not sure why I'm so annoyed with her. I know she is only trying to help. It's probably because she feels guilty for moving out or, more likely because she genuinely wants to make sure I end up with a good living situation. Either way, I *should* be happy to have her assistance, but for some reason, it really pisses me off.

I don't have time to think about Katie again until seven fifteen, when the final presentation is complete and has been sent out for printing and binding. I'm rarely here at this hour, and although most people in Manhattan wouldn't consider this to be a "late day," it's late for me, and unlike the consultants, I certainly don't get paid to work more than forty hours a week.

As I'm about to shut down my computer, I pull open my AOL account and scan the listing and email exchange that Katie sent me this morning. The apartment *does* look pretty great, and I've done a cursory look at listings over the past few days, and everything I found looked terrible. I think my anger this morning was an overreaction and likely just a reflection of how pissed off I am with Brian and the situation – not that Katie sent a few emails in my name to help me out.

I print out everything, so I'll have all the information and throw it into my messenger bag with a quick wave to Max on my way out the door. I know that Katie said I was going to be at the apartment at six tonight, but seeing as it's well over an hour past that now and I'm still in Midtown, that obviously isn't going to happen. The apartment is on West 78th Street near Columbus, which isn't too far from an F train stop, and I'm only about a ten-minute walk to the train, so I decide that this is the best way to go. I'm hoping if I have good train luck that, I can get there by seven forty-five, and although that is much later than six, it still feels like a reasonable time to arrive. It doesn't even occur to me to take a taxi to get there a few minutes earlier.

* * *

When I arrive at almost eight, I double-check the address against the paper I'm holding in my hand to ensure I'm in the correct place. The building is far nicer than I imagined it would be. I've walked past this building dozens of times while strolling through the Upper West Side, and it's one that always caught my attention due to its ornate stonework and wrought iron balconies. I remember learning that several of these beautiful buildings were originally constructed and operated as hotels, but I'm not sure if this is one of those. This 78th Street gem is a pre-war doorman building that's in immaculate condition, and it's actually closer to Central Park West than Columbus Avenue, which means it's mere steps from the 79th Street entrance to the park.

I'm still gaping at the building's façade when a uniformed doorman with closely cropped gray hair underneath his perfectly fitted hat opens the door and asks if he can assist me. He leads me to the desk while I fumble with my papers and try to find my potential roommate's name and apartment number. "I'm supposed to meet Robin Cromwell – Apartment 9C," I tell him when I finally manage to locate the information.

"And whom should I say is here to see her?" he asks in a polished voice with a slight accent that I can't pinpoint.

"Jessica Barlowe?" I reply although I phrase it as a question as if I'm unsure of my own name.

The doorman gives me a silent nod and picks up the receiver, presumably to call up to Robin's apartment. While I wait, I look around the well-appointed lobby and remind myself to buy a bottle of wine or flowers or something for Katie on the way home to apologize for how I acted this morning *and* to thank her for finding this place!

"You can go on up," the doorman says to me as he

replaces the receiver in its cradle. "The elevator is just over there," he says, pointing toward a row of three shiny gold elevators in the back of the lobby. I thank him and make my way over while I wonder how it's possible that there's a girl my age who lives here and is looking to rent half of her apartment for $1200 a month! As the elevator glides up to the ninth floor, I determine that it must all be a mistake. The price listed is wrong, or this is all some sort of trap, and there's going to be a serial killer waiting for me when I get to 9C.

I'm practically hyperventilating when I get off the elevator, and if the doors hadn't already closed, I'd probably be heading back down to the lobby right now. But I've come this far, so I follow the expensive-looking carpeting down the hallway until I see the door marked 9C and hold my breath while I ring the doorbell.

A girl who looks about my age opens the door. I know that I should mentally think of her, and of myself, as a *woman*, but I still refer to and think of all my friends as *girls*. She is about my height, or maybe a little shorter, and has wavy blonde hair that falls past her shoulder. She has a pretty heart-shaped face with brown eyes and a beautiful complexion, or else she is great at doing natural make-up that makes it look like she has great skin. She's wearing a wrap dress that I could never pull off. It shows off her curvy hips and shapely waist and suggests abundant cleavage, although it's tasteful, and I'm guessing it's what she wore to work that day. In my three-second appraisal, I surmise that she doesn't look like a psychopath and could be a normal roommate, so either the monthly rent was a typo, or I have just lucked into the most amazing living situation possible.

"Are you Robin Cromwell?" I question.

"I am," she replies warmly, but that's all she says.

"I'm Jessica Barlowe. I was supposed to be here earlier, but I got stuck at work," I say, hoping this serves as both an apology and an explanation.

"Oh gosh," Robin replies, looking down at the floor.

"I'm really sorry I'm late. I usually only work until five, sometimes five-thirty, but today I was stuck working on a client presentation, and I didn't get out of the office until after seven," I ramble. "I could come back another time if this isn't good for you?" I offer.

"Do you want to come in for a second?" she asks.

I'm unsure why I'm only coming in for a second, but maybe she's on her way out, and she wants to rush through some questions or compare calendars to find another time to meet, and it would be awkward to do that while standing in the hallway.

"Of course," I reply. I walk into the front hall and try not to gawk at my surroundings. I can't believe that there is an actual front hall with an entry table and two closets! This area alone is almost as big as my current bedroom. I can glimpse the kitchen off to the right and the edge of the living room in front of me, and I'm trying to imagine if I would bring any of my Ikea furniture or just toss it all and wait until I could afford something nicer that would match the apartment.

Robin leads me to the living room, but she doesn't sit down on the brown leather couch (which isn't quite as fancy as I thought it would be) or offer me a seat.

"I feel terrible about this," Robin exclaims.

"About what?" I ask her.

"I felt like we had a connection from our emails, and I was looking forward to meeting you," she says.

I smile and nod but don't say anything. I feel a pang of guilt that Katie was the one writing the emails; however, I read through them, and Katie did a great job of impersonating me, so I feel like they were relatively authentic.

"Then, when you didn't show up, I got so worried. And I've gotten so few normal responses to my ad, and time is running out, and I panicked ..." Robin says, trailing off.

"Again, I'm so sorry about getting here late! I'm usually quite punctual. Okay, if we're being honest, I run about ten or fifteen minutes late to everything," I say, trying to make a joke, but I notice that she doesn't smile.

"The other person got here right at seven-thirty for her interview, and I just assumed that you weren't coming," Robin says.

It takes me a minute to figure out what she's saying, but it hits me like a blow to the stomach when I finally get it. "You found another roommate?" I ask although I know the answer.

"Sorry," Robin says.

"It's okay," I tell her. "I shouldn't have gotten here so late. I guess I'll keep looking," I sigh, although I know I will never find the unicorn that is this apartment.

We just met and didn't owe each other anything, yet I can tell that we both feel we've let the other down.

Chapter 12

Zach

My weekday routine rarely varies. After work, I go to the Equinox gym near my office, and unless the weather is terrible, I walk forty blocks to my neighborhood and stop somewhere on the way to pick up something for dinner. I take a quick shower as soon as I get home, sit on the couch with a legal drama or CNN on low volume, and eat dinner while I work on my laptop until it's time to go to bed.

The aroma of Kung Pao chicken fills the elevator, and I'm debating if tonight will be *CSI* or *Larry King* when the doors open on the 9th floor, and I veer right toward my apartment and the promise of a hot shower and a pair of sweatpants. I stop in my tracks when I see a woman leaning against my door, with her face buried in the crook of her elbow, quietly sobbing.

It is such a cliché to be unnerved by a crying woman, but

I simply can't help it. My mom is not an emotional person, and I can count the number of times I've seen her cry on one hand. I didn't spend a lot of time around other women growing up, so on the rare occasions that I am around crying women or honestly people displaying strong emotions of any kind, I never know the right thing to do. For a moment, I contemplate turning around, getting back on the elevator, eating my dinner in the lobby, and hoping that the crying woman has vanished when I return. But this seems cowardly, and at the end of my session with Dr. Green, we discussed doing things that push my boundaries and taking risks, so with that in mind, I head down the hall.

She must hear me approach her because she looks up when I'm a few feet away and starts rubbing her eyes with the cuffs of her jacket. Her eyes are red and puffy from crying, her nose is running, her dark blonde hair is plastered to the side of her face; and I almost do a double take as I absorb how beautiful she is and how familiar she looks.

She looks at me and then looks at the door she's been leaning on as if putting the pieces together. I shrug and attempt to give her a casual look, but I'm sure I appear creepy and ridiculous instead.

"I'm so sorry. Is this your apartment?" she asks.

"It is," I say, and I have the urge to apologize to her for my door.

"Let me get out of your way," she says with a sniffle as she grabs a black messenger bag off the ground and slings it over her shoulder.

"Is everything okay? Is there anything I can do to help?" I

ask quickly. Although this is well outside my typical comfort zone, the thought of losing this sad, beautiful woman makes me even more uncomfortable, so it rolls off my tongue somewhat easily.

"Not unless you're looking for a roommate," she says.

She must regret what she says because she instantly holds up both of her hands and says, "I'm kidding, I'm kidding. I'm sorry, I've just had the worst week of my life, and then I thought things might be turning around, and it looks like I just missed out on a once-in-a-lifetime apartment because I was too stubborn to take a taxi. Or maybe I simply have terrible luck," she sighs. "Anyway, I apologize for causing a scene outside your door – this isn't like me. Although it seems pretty fitting for how my life is going right now."

The words she's saying make it seem like she's going to leave, but her feet are still glued to my welcome mat, and I am wracking my brain to try and think of what I can say or do to prolong this conversation.

"I'm sorry you've had such a bad week. Were you looking at an apartment on this floor? I didn't know that there were any currently available," I wonder aloud.

"One of your neighbors was looking for a roommate. I guess her roommate is moving to Boston to start her residency, and she wants someone for the other bedroom," she says. By this point, her face has returned to its normal color, and her green eyes are almost sparkling in the dim hall light.

"Of course, Robin and Jenny," I say as if we are old friends. I *have* met both of them on several occasions during my tenure in the building (waiting for the elevator, in the laundry room, and at the mailboxes), and they even invited me to a party one time, but I didn't attend.

"Right," she says and gives me a small smile. My knowledge of their names seems to give me a hint of credibility and potentially makes me less of a stranger. "I was supposed to move in with my boyfriend in a couple of months when my lease was up, but that's not happening. I don't know why I'm telling you this. You're trying to get into your place and eat your dinner, and I'm this crazy person crying in your hallway," she says, gesturing at my paper bag of Chinese takeaway.

"Don't worry about it. Sometimes it feels good to get it off your chest," I say to her. I'm desperate to hear more about her living situation with this boyfriend. I also think that Dr. Green would be pretty proud if she could see me right now.

She exhales loudly, and I'm sure she's going to leave, but then she shifts her bag to the other shoulder and keeps talking. "I walked in on my boyfriend cheating on me last week, and then my roommate and best friend told me that she signed a lease for another apartment because I was *supposed* to be moving out," she takes a breath but quickly continues before I can offer my sympathies or express any horror that someone would dare to cheat on her. "I haven't been able to think about finding a roommate or another apartment, but my best friend is so kind that she did all of this searching for me and found this amazing opportunity at Robin's apartment, and then when I showed up tonight, I was over two hours late, and Robin had already found someone else," she laments, and it looks like she might start crying again.

"That's awful," I tell her. I wish I was more eloquent and could find better words to express my feelings.

"Well, thanks for listening," she says. "I should get going. I've got hundreds of hours of Craigslist postings to search, even though I'll never find anything as good as this again," she laughs half-heartedly.

"I *am* actually looking for a roommate," I blurt out.

She laughs and gives me a funny smile, but it's clear that she thinks I'm joking because, of course, this is a preposterous idea.

"I'm sure this sounds ludicrous, but I *am* looking for a roommate; I just haven't gotten around to posting an ad yet," I lie.

"That's very nice of you..." she says awkwardly, but she's already starting to back up – putting distance between herself and the crazy man in the hall who just suggested she live with him.

"Never mind. Please forget I said that. I didn't mean to scare you off," I say, regretting everything I've said for the past ten minutes.

"Don't worry about it. I was the one who unloaded my whole life story on you," she jokes. "I should get going anyway."

"I'm Zach," I say, clumsily sticking out my hand for her to shake.

"Oh. I'm Jessica," she replies, taking my hand even though it's clear she finds it to be unnecessary.

My next steps continue to feel out of character, or maybe more like an out-of-body experience, but what do I have to lose? Although I've just met Jessica, there is a powerful attraction that is not merely physical – I try to put her familiar face out of my mind. I am almost ill at the idea of her getting into the elevator and never seeing or talking to her again.

"Let me give you my email address so you have it in case nothing better comes along," I tell her. Meanwhile, I put my takeaway bag on the floor and root around in my backpack for a notebook and pen to give her my information. She doesn't attempt to flee while I'm doing this, so I keep going and eventually hand over a sheet of paper with my name, personal email address, and home phone number. I'm about to suggest that she could look around at the apartment while she's here, but thankfully I realize how that may sound and keep my mouth shut.

"It's the same size and style apartment as Robin and Jenny have," I offer, and it's something to fill the silence.

"I definitely appreciate it, and I'm sure your apartment is really nice," she says wistfully, "But I'm just not sure that it would work."

"Yeah, you're totally right. It was a crazy idea," I say again.

Before I realize what she's doing, Jessica grabs the pen from my hand, writes something on the bottom of the page I'd given her, then tears it in half and hands it to me. "This is my email and phone number," she shrugs. "I'm not sure what's happening tonight, but this has been such a terrible stretch, and you are the first nice thing that's happened all week. I can't imagine moving in with some random guy, but maybe there's a reason we met tonight, right? Nice meeting you, Zach," she says, and with that, Jessica disappears down the hall toward the elevator.

Clutching her contact information in one hand and my Chinese food in the other, I practically float into my apartment on the heels of one of the most unusual and inexplicable interactions I've ever had. I have no idea what steps to take next, but I don't even take my laptop out of my backpack, as I'm certain that I won't be able to focus on any work tonight.

Chapter 13

Tory

I have two Louis Vuitton hard-sided suitcases and one Gucci weekender duffle open on my floor, and I have no idea where to begin. I've always considered myself to be a "good packer," but that's for vacations or even extended trips – I have no idea what is required to *move out* on my own. I assume that my room will sit here untouched, with the exception of a bi-weekly cleaning, so I'm not under any pressure to pack everything up.

An hour into my packing endeavor, it's clear that I will need more than three overpriced pieces of luggage. I think back to packing for college, and I know that I had cardboard boxes and duffel bags, but I have no idea where they came from or where they went after I came home from Tulane. I know I told Anna I wanted to do this alone. Still, when I dial the number for a local moving company, I assure myself that it's normal to use movers in my situation. When they ask if I also want them to handle the packing and unpacking, I *do* hesitate before accepting the additional services.

Robin said that her roommate would be happy to leave her bedroom furniture if I wanted to use it, or she would put it in the storage unit in the basement – it's up to me. I only glanced in the bedroom when I was there for my interview, and now, I can't recall what the bedroom set looked like. I have no idea what new stuff will cost, but I'm pretty sure that even the cheap stuff is expensive. The only furniture I currently own is what is in my bedroom in the townhouse, and now that I think about it, *I* don't actually own that; my parents do. I send a quick email to Robin telling her that I would love to accept her generous offer of keeping the items in the bedroom and confirm that this Friday still works for me to move in. As I look around the room at my custom-made Italian furniture, I feel a hint of relief that my room will be here intact, waiting for me – just in case. Now all I need to do is tell my parents that I'm leaving.

It's ten at night, and my parents are sitting in opposite corners of the living room. My dad is sitting on the couch reading the paper with a glass of scotch (probably his third or fourth of the evening), and my mom is at the antique writing desk working on her note cards with a glass of white wine perched precariously next to her well of ink. I'm almost certain that my mother is one of the last people in 2004 to write with a fountain pen and to find the occasion to send ten to fifteen handwritten cards a week – thank you notes, requests for donations to her charities, invitations to lunches, the list never seems to end.

It's convenient for my announcement that both of my parents are in the same room, but puzzling, nonetheless. With nine floors and countless rooms in our house, I can't figure out why my parents both gravitate toward the living room in the evening when they clearly want nothing to do with each other. Thankfully they rarely scream at each other – although, like toddlers who cover their eyes and think no one can see them, my parents seem to believe that I don't know about their loathing for each other. But even when they aren't fighting, they rarely speak – unless it's to criticize me, but still, they spend most of their time within thirty feet of each other. Perhaps it's purely habitual, and at one point, they did enjoy the other's company, or maybe neither one is willing to concede the territory, and they are both too stubborn to move. Either way, it works in my favor tonight.

I clear my throat in an attempt to get their attention, and my dad looks up from his paper, but my mom continues to gaze at her notecards.

"Do you guys have a minute?" I ask cautiously, hating that I feel more like a teenager than the grown-up I am.

"Make it quick," my dad barks. "I'm heading up to bed soon. I've got an early start tomorrow."

I wonder if my dad's critical early start involves a squash game, a massage, or breakfast with a bloody mary at Pershing Square. I know that he never goes into the office before ten, and even then, it's not like there is a *required* start time.

When your entire job is to assist the team that manages your family's fortune, the hours aren't too strenuous.

"I'm listening, but I can't turn around," my mom calls out. "I'm in the middle of an important letter, and I'll muddle the ink if I stop now. Just go ahead, Tory, and say what you need to say."

My father has one eye on the paper, and I've only got the attention of the back of my mom's head; unlike some of my friends' moms, she is not one of those overly observant parents who claim to have "eyes in the back of their heads." I think this might be the best I can expect from my parents, and perhaps it will make it easier if they aren't focusing on me. I take a deep breath and let it out. "I'm moving out."

"Who is he?" my dad says without missing a beat.

"No, it's not like that. There's no guy," I reply.

"You know that we changed the terms of your trust after you blew all of that money traipsing around Europe for two years like some sort of Paris Hilton wannabe," my dad sneers. "Your monthly allowance stays the same as it is now, and you can access the rest of it in four years when you turn thirty. Unless you fuck up again," he adds.

I wince at the reminder of my irresponsible behavior and the sad dig about my allowance. It takes all my willpower not to tell him to take his monthly handout and shove it – I already need to dip into the extra funds due to my paltry assistant salary, and now with monthly rent and food costs, they will be an absolute necessity.

"Where are you going?" my mother asks without turning around.

"I'm moving to the Upper West Side," I reply.

"Ugh," my father scoffs. I'm not sure the last time he was on the west side of the park, and I'm certain he views everything that isn't in our neighborhood, or Wall Street, or right near Lincoln Center as a dump.

"How will you afford it?" my mom asks.

"I'll have a roommate," I tell her. I wish this conversation would end and I could run back to my room, but now that I've started it, I'm going to stay here and answer their questions, even though I'm not sure they care about my responses.

"A roommate?" my dad laughs maliciously. "You didn't even have a roommate in college. We paid for that fancy dorm where everyone had a suite and room service."

I bite my tongue because there is no point in correcting him. While he is off-base on the room service, it is true that I was in the rich kid dorm and that I've never had a roommate.

"Who is she?" my mom asks at the same time my dad asks, "Who let you sign a lease with *your* income?"

Although my mom *still* hasn't turned around, her questions are far less obnoxious, so I reply to her first. "You don't know her." And then to my dad. "I didn't have to sign the lease; I'm moving into her apartment."

My dad looks like he's going to follow up with another obnoxious comment, but instead, he closes his mouth and directs his full attention to the *Wall Street Journal*, de facto dismissing me from the conversation. "Do you know her from Spence?" my mom asks hopefully, referring to the elite all-girls private school that I attended (as did she and her mother).

Even my father looks back up for a moment as if my answering "yes" to this question would make everything a bit more palatable. I almost give them the answer they want in order to placate them *and* make my life easier in the short term, but in the end, I opt for a different, more manageable lie. "I know her from work." Because I'm having trouble even admitting to myself that I'm about to move in with a complete stranger.

Chapter 14

Jessica

"Any luck?" Katie asks. Her silky hair tickles my arm as she peers over my shoulder to glance at the computer screen.

I rub my sore eyes, which are a result of staring at the monitor for the past four straight hours, and give her a look that conveys exactly the type of luck I've been having.

"I take that as a *no?*" she asks, though the question is clearly rhetorical.

"There are no affordable apartments and no normal roommates! I'm going to have to move back to Sonoma and pick grapes," I moan.

"Stop being so dramatic," Katie says, draining her glass of wine as if to emphasize her point. "Besides, it wouldn't be that bad; you'd get all the free wine you want, *right?*" she laughs.

Katie is one of the few people who can joke about this, and even *she* is coming close to crossing the line right now, considering my dire situation. When people ask where I'm from and I tell them I'm from California, most people on the East Coast assume I'm from L.A. since they know shockingly little about the most populous state in the country. Although recently, with that new ridiculous show *The O.C.*, people have expanded their geographical knowledge to ask if I'm from "The O.C." Then, they get oddly excited when I tell them I'm from Sonoma, and we establish that it's just north of Napa Valley. However, it's nothing compared to what happens when I tell them that my family owns two vineyards in Sonoma. At this point in the conversation, most people have already developed a mental picture of me strolling through picturesque vineyards with a glass of wine in my hand, counting my family's fortune.

I learned long ago that attempting to correct this distorted image is pointless. Most people have never been to a vineyard. If they have, they went for an afternoon of drunken winetasting, and simply hearing the word *vineyard* conjures up romantic images of beautiful valleys and endless glasses of Pinot Noir. Only those of us who have experienced a working family vineyard know that it's tireless backbreaking work and complete and total dependence on mother nature. Somedays, I can't believe I actually "got out," but I have too many problems to think about that victory right now.

"Are you even going to consider moving in with Zach?" Katie asks me.

"I should never have told you about that," I laugh. "You're like a dog with a bone."

"I just think it's worth considering," Katie says. "It's 2004; you can have a random guy for a roommate, the same way you would have a random girl. Joey had a girl for a roommate," she offers. Someone else might think she is referring to our mutual friend, but of course, I know she is referring to Joey Tribbiani from her favorite TV show, *Friends*.

"And then they started dating, and it got weird, and she had to move out!" I exclaim.

"Okay, fine, maybe that was a bad example. What about *Three's Company*?" Katie says and laughs.

"How about an example of actual people who have done it and made it work, and not sitcom characters?" I ask.

"I'm sure there are tons of people. I just don't happen to know any of them. That doesn't mean it won't work for you. And you need to find *something*. I'm moving out next week," she says quietly – now all the playfulness is gone from her voice.

"I'm aware of the date," I say bitterly and then follow it with, "I'm sorry, I'm just really stressed."

"Can we talk about the Zach option for a minute, and then I'll drop it?" Katie asks.

"Promise?" I demand.

"Promise."

"Fine," I relent. "Let's talk about it."

"It's a great location and a great building," she says.

"Yes."

"The pictures of the apartment he emailed you look beautiful – they actually look a lot nicer than Robin's apartment – and the rent is just as affordable," Katie reminds me as if I haven't looked at that email a dozen times since Zach sent it to me. The day after I met him, he sent over some pictures with a brief description of the apartment. He told me that he was planning to post his ad soon, but he'd give me the right of first refusal since he told me about it first. I haven't had the heart to look and see if his posting went live yet since it's been four days, and I haven't gotten back to him, but it hasn't shown up in any of my searches.

"I know. It's basically too good to be true," I reply.

"And you said he seemed like a nice guy," Katie says.

"But he's totally random! What if he's a serial killer? Or a terrorist?" I ask her.

"Any of the people you are going to find on Craigslist or the rest of these sites are going to be random, and maybe Robin is a terrorist – I don't think you're being a very good feminist if you're only assuming that guys can be totally psycho," she adds with a bewitching smile that I'm sure is an asset to her on stage and off.

"What if it doesn't work out?" I question.

"What if it does?" Katie retorts.

"What if it's awkward because of sex stuff?" I ask, and I know how stupid it sounds as soon as I say it.

"What are you, twelve?" Katie laughs. "What do you mean by sex stuff? Are you planning on having sex with him?"

"No! I may never be ready to have sex with anyone again," I moan. "But what if he brings a girl home? Or what about showering?" I ask.

"I'm pretty sure you shower by yourself no matter who your roommate is. And you have your own bathroom," she reminds me. "You are creating excuses to make this impossible. It could work if you want it to," she tells me, and I detect a hint of annoyance in her voice that wasn't there earlier.

* * *

The following morning at work, I'm behind schedule before I even sit down at my desk. There are two eighty-page Power-Point decks that need graphics revisions by three o'clock this afternoon. As I shrug off my coat and start to thumb through the pages while my computer warms up, I notice that there are changes on almost every slide, and most of the changes appear to be significant. I open the files and begin to turn the chicken-scratch pictures into striking data-driven visuals. I try not to let my younger self see this older, lame version – the one that is proud of waterfall charts and Harvey balls. But occasionally, she slips in and wants to know where all my edgy black-and-white photos have gone.

I barely have time to go to the bathroom for the next six and a half hours. I don't take my eyes off my screen while I eat the ham sandwich that Max unceremoniously tossed on my desk, and I certainly don't have time to think about Zach's apartment. I only have time to think about these two presentations – one for a bank in Ohio and one for an insurance company in Missouri. But then it's three fifteen, and everything stops. It's like someone rang the dismissal bell at school, and I'm the only one who didn't grab my backpack and run out the door. Of course, there are still people in the office going about everyday business, but the two big project teams have taken their presentations and run off in their suits to catch flights to the Midwest, and Max abruptly announced he was leaving for a doctor's appointment. Now I'm all alone, and the phrase, "Hear a pin drop," keeps coming to mind. There's always something that needs to get done, and I'm sure if I checked my project list, I'd find lower-priority decks that need my attention, but I'm exhausted and decide to treat myself to a coffee and cookie from the break room and at least thirty minutes of internet surfing for clothes I can't afford.

Halfway through my fantasy browsing spree, I think about Zach. It takes me a minute to figure out why. The Dolce and Gabbana model looks a little bit like him. I lied a bit when Katie asked me if Zach was cute. My answer was somewhere in between "I didn't notice" and "Not particularly." Brian has killed whatever part of me would otherwise ever want to date or trust a man again, so it didn't seem relevant, and I didn't want Katie to bug me about it, but he would also have to have gouged out both of my eyes for me not to notice that Zach is attractive. He doesn't actually look like the D&B model, but they both have wavy dark brown hair, light brown eyes, and chiseled facial features. Zach was almost even cuter than this model because of his slightly dorky messenger bag, unassuming khakis, and navy crewneck sweater that made him look more like the captain of the forensics team than a supermodel.

Before I can overthink it or come to my senses, I log into my AOL account and pull up Zach's email. I skim what he wrote before hitting reply, and they *don't* seem like the musings of an axe murderer (although I'm not sure I'd know what those look like). My email is short and to the point and probably way too formal.

Dear Zach,

Thank you so much for following up about the roommate opportunity. If it is still available, I think I may be interested. Would you be free to meet for coffee today or tomorrow so we could talk about it more? I can be flexible about time and location.

Thanks again,

Jessica

I hit send and then pull it up again to reread what I wrote, and I cringe at every word. I probably just lost *this* apartment as well by being a total loser!

Chapter 15

Zach

It's my third time in Dr. Green's waiting room. It would be a stretch to say that I feel comfortable here, but it is starting to feel like a *routine*, and I do like routines. Although, my focus at the moment is exclusively on the email I received from Jessica right before I left the office.

"Zach, are you ready?" Dr. Green asks. I was lost in my thoughts and didn't even notice that she'd opened her office door and stepped into the waiting room. She's wearing a different version of the same outfit she's worn the previous two weeks – dark wool slacks and a pastel sweater set. I briefly wonder how many of these sweater sets she owns, if she wears them on a rotation, and if I'll be here long enough to see all of them.

"Yes," I reply quickly, following her into her office.

"How has your week been?" she asks once we are seated in our respective spots. I contemplated lying down on the couch this week, but now that I've done two sessions sitting up, it seems weird to start now. I feel like she would ask why I chose to lie down today, and I don't want to explain my rationale, so the ship might have sailed on this one.

For a second, I debate whether I should even tell her about Jessica. It would be so easy to simply talk about my week at work (even though Dr. Green has no clue what my job entails), and then we could rehash my lame date from the other night, and before I know it, the session would be over. But that feels like a waste of time when this development with Jessica is all I can think about.

"The week has been good. I may have a roommate moving in with me," I say casually.

"I didn't know you were looking for a roommate. Tell me more about that," Dr. Green says.

"It all happened kind of quickly, but this woman, Jessica, might move in with me. We're having coffee tonight – right after this – to discuss the details," I tell her.

She pauses and writes something in her notebook, and I have to fight the somewhat irrational frustration that she is taking notes about me. "When did your previous roommate move out? How did you meet Jessica? I imagine it's tricky to find the right person to live with, but it must be a necessity for most people with such astronomical rents in this city," she adds more to herself than to me.

I decide on a half-truth, although I don't need a doctor to tell me there's an issue when I'm keeping things from my doctor. "I hadn't *officially* started my search yet when I happened to meet Jessica in the hall outside of my apartment." This part is true. I don't say that the last time I had a roommate was over three years ago, in my old building, before

I bought this apartment. And that I had no need for or intention of having another roommate until I met Jessica.

"I'm sure this makes me sound ancient, but are you concerned about any potentially awkward situations with a female roommate?" Dr. Green asks.

"I don't think it's that unusual," I reply. "We have separate bedrooms and bathrooms."

"And I assume there's no romantic attraction?" she says as if it's a foregone conclusion. "You obviously wouldn't want to enter into a living arrangement where there could be those kinds of complications."

I contemplate contradicting her, but it seems like she's already moved on. And besides, even though I already think Jessica is beautiful, smart, funny, and I want to be around her, I can't imagine dating her – I couldn't take a risk like that again.

Jessica is sitting at a table in the corner when I arrive. It's hard not to notice the similarities when I look at her, but I blink a few times as if that's all I need to do to erase any images from my mind. Jessica's hands are wrapped tightly around a white and green Starbucks paper cup, making it look like the beverage was ordered more for hand-warming than drinking on this chilly early May evening. I peek at my watch and am relieved to see that I'm right on time – she must have arrived early. I catch her eye and motion to the short line, hopefully a clear indication that I will get a drink before I join her. She waves in return, so I assume she understands.

It's just my luck that it appears to be the barista's first day on the job. It takes him two tries and over five minutes to froth the milk, and I'm about to cancel my order when he finally gets it to work and then hands me a venti chai latte (even though I ordered a tall) and gives me a sheepish grin.

I'm ready to apologize when I reach the table, but Jessica beats me to it. "I can't believe you had the patience to wait for him," she jokes. "I ordered a latte, but I couldn't take it. I gave up."

My shoulders instantly relax at the sound of her laugh. I hadn't realized how tight they were until I felt them drop as I slipped off my jacket and slid into my chair. "What did you get?" I ask her.

"English breakfast tea," she says, turning her cup around to display the string that is hanging limply down the side. "It seemed like he couldn't mess that one up," Jessica says, smiling again.

"I should have thought of that," I reply.

"What about you?" she asks, pointing to my drink. "Hope it's good; there's certainly a lot of it," she comments playfully.

"It's a chai latte. At least, it's supposed to be. But I only ordered a tall. I could never drink this much milk," I tell her, quickly wondering if I've revealed something too personal.

"Ooh, I love chai. I always forget to order it, and then I hear them call someone else's order and wish I had gotten one," she says wistfully.

I'm about to tell her that she's welcome to some of mine, but I've already taken a few sips, and it seems way too personal to offer to share a drink. But once the moment passes, I wonder if I messed it all up by not offering, and now, she's going to think I'm rude.

"Do you want to talk about the apartment?" I ask her. I'm looking to change the topic and also get to the point if that's what we are supposed to be meeting about. I don't want her to think I'm wasting her time.

"Yes, of course," Jessica replies.

I wait for her to say something else or ask a question, but she just takes a sip of tea and looks at me expectantly. "As I think you saw from the pictures, it's a two-bedroom and two-and-a-half-bathroom apartment, so you would have your own bedroom and bathroom. I leave for work around seven-thirty in the morning, come home at about eight-thirty at night, and do a little more work. I don't have a lot of guests over, but of course, you're welcome to. Hmm, let's see. The apartment is already wired for cable, and there's a cable box and TV in your room if you want to use that, or I could move it if you don't," I tell her, and from the look on her face, it's clear that I'm rambling.

"That all sounds great. Your apartment is the nicest rental I've seen. And I've looked at a lot of places," Jessica adds. "I'll admit that I was a little worried about living with a guy and about the random way we met in the hall. But after thinking about it, I don't think it's any weirder than finding a room-mate online, right?" she asks, clearly seeking confirmation.

"Right," I reply. I try not to get distracted by her shiny dark blonde hair and beautiful green eyes. I tell my brain to ignore the pull that makes me feel drawn to her – it's only because she's nice and easy to talk to.

"Can you tell me about your previous roommate? I've

been living with my best friend Katie for the past four years, but she's moving in with some of her other dancer and actor friends," Jessica explains.

I don't know why I didn't anticipate this question, but of course, she would want to know what happened to my previous roommate. Without time to think through it, I panic and tell her about Ely, my roommate from my old apartment. I tell her that he moved to Chicago because he got a new job. Although that is technically true, I think it counts as a lie of omission. It's only after I tell her about Ely that I come up with several other responses that are much closer to the truth, but it's too late for that now.

When we hug goodbye and make plans for her to move her stuff in over the weekend, I am filled with a mix of excitement and fear, and it is unclear which emotion is stronger.

Chapter 16

Robin

"Tell me all about her?" Jenny demands. Her voice is familiar and comforting, but having to talk to her on the phone means she might as well be in China and not just two hundred miles away in Boston. Though I suppose the time difference is a bit easier this way.

I'm curled up on my bed with my favorite blanket and the cordless phone tucked under my chin. Even though Tory is out with her friends, and my door is closed, I still feel like I should keep my voice down in case she comes home unexpectedly. "She's okay," I sigh. "She has really nice clothes."

"That's already an upgrade. You can shop in her closet. All I had were scrubs, jeans that were too low-rise for your taste, and my leather jacket," Jenny giggles.

"You *have* to get rid of that!" I yell gleefully into the phone, and then tears spring to my eyes, and I stifle a sob.

"Are you okay?" Jenny asks.

"I'm fine. It's pathetic. I just miss you. It's not the same without you," I say, grabbing a tissue from my nightstand to wipe my face.

"I miss you too!" Jenny says. "You know I didn't want to leave," she says, replaying the conversation we've had a zillion times over the past few months.

"I know. And I'm sorry for being sad. I really *am* excited for you, and I don't want you to feel bad about moving or feel bad for me. I'm totally fine," I say, trying to force a smile to make my voice sound brighter. "It's just been a tough few days."

"Because of Tory?" Jenny asks.

"No. No, she's fine. I'm not sure we're going to be great friends or anything, but she's fine. I'm also not sure she's ever used the stove before, but that's a different issue," I joke.

"So, what's going on?' she inquires.

"Just work stuff. It's this project I'm supposed to be doing for Janet," I say.

"Ugghh," Jenny says, and I love her for it. I just have to say her name, and Jenny understands why it's so terrible – she has all the background and can be instantly supportive with one groan. "What happened at your meeting?" she asks, referring to the update meeting I was supposed to have with Janet this past week on my brand refresh ideas.

"I got lucky again. I put together a bullshit list of ideas and some fancy brand marketing terms, and for the third week in a row, Janet's assistant postponed my meeting at the last minute due to *emergencies* in her schedule," I say.

"That's great,' Jenny says.

"Yes and no. It's great that she didn't yell or me or fire me, but I still have no idea what I'm doing! And now, when I finally meet with her, she's going to want to know what I've been working on for the past month, or however long it will be by the time I meet with her."

"Can't you ask Frederic for help?" Jenny suggests.

"I tried...but he said that he knew I could do it on my own," I lament.

"I even looked on the internet today for ideas," I tell Jenny.

"Isn't that the kind of research you are supposed to be doing?" she asks.

"I don't think I'm supposed to be researching "the best ways to refresh a brand" on Google," I say, and I can hear Jenny cackling in the background.

"I apologize in advance if I'm overstepping, and I know nothing about your job, but isn't this the kind of thing you've been doing for the past few years? I feel like you aren't giving yourself enough credit," she says.

"I don't know. It's been like a factory the whole time I've worked here. I run the same reports weekly, analyze the same sales and forecasting data, and manage the inventory," I say.

"I hate to say this, but that's not how I pictured your job," Jenny admits.

"It's honestly nothing like I thought the job would be when I first got here," I say to Jenny. I distinctly remember how excited I was to get the job offer. I'd been told that they only hired MBA graduates. I finished Duke at the top of my class and was lucky to get hired at Citibank right after graduation. But after two years in a rotational program, I knew I didn't want to work in any form of banking, and I couldn't afford to go back to school and take out any more loans.

When I heard about the position in brand management at Victoria's Secret, I applied on a whim and was thrilled and surprised when I got the job.

I continue for Jenny. "I thought it would be much more creative and all about advertising, packaging, and customer research. Up until now, it's been all Excel and PowerPoint – I might as well have stayed at Citibank," I joke. "But now they expect me to do all of those fun, creative things in order to get a promotion – which is great, but I don't think I know how to do any of them!"

"I feel so bad," Jenny says.

"What are you talking about?" I ask, totally thrown off by her statement.

"We've lived together for the past four years, and I really had no idea what you did," she confesses, but I can tell she's smiling.

"It's okay. That's only because it wasn't remotely interesting until now. I think this is the most I've ever talked to you about work. Other than complaining about Janet," I laugh.

"And we spend most of our time talking about your dates," she reminds me.

"Speaking of dates. This roommate search and all my work issues have left me no time to search on Match.com," I protest.

"Hundred-hour work weeks in the ER have the same effect," Jenny says.

"Alright, I suppose I shouldn't complain," I say.

"Speaking of, I need to get some sleep. I've got to be back at the hospital in six hours. I should be asleep right now," Jenny says.

"Thanks for sharing some of your sleeping time with me," I tell her.

"Of course," she replies. "And hang in there. You're going to be fine."

"I know," I reply, even though I'm not entirely sure.

Chapter 17

Tory

This new living situation may result in the best unintentional diet I've ever been on. When dinnertime rolled around on my first night in the apartment, it became shockingly clear that I was ill-prepared. Robin kindly pointed out that she'd cleared two shelves in the fridge for me to use and had done the same in the pantry. She explained that things like spices, oils, and condiments were communal and indicated that we could probably share items like milk and eggs in the future.

The first night was easy - I ordered a Greek salad from Seamless Web, and Robin made something with chicken and rice. I stopped at Zabar's after work the second night to get groceries, but when I got home, it didn't seem like I had gotten any food that could actually be used to make a meal — not that I really know *how* to make a meal. I had an apple and smoked salmon for dinner that night, and I'm pretty sure Robin thinks I have an eating disorder.

Last night I went out with Anna after work, and although we were at a wine bar with a limited menu, I made sure to order almost every appetizer they offered, so I wouldn't have to face the kitchen when I got home. Now I'm leaving work, and I could stop and pick up dinner or get delivery once I'm home, but I don't want restaurant food. My breakfast is a protein bar, my lunch is either soup or salad from the deli next to my office, and I want to eat a real dinner that doesn't come in a plastic container.

It's pathetic that I'm twenty-six years old and just realized that I've never cooked or grocery shopped for myself. I *thought* I had cooked for myself, but I'd actually only opened a well-stocked fridge or pantry and re-heated a meal or selected a few gourmet items to put on a plate (which were usually already sliced, peeled, chopped, etc.) I resented our family meals, but even when I missed dinner, there was always a meal saved for me in case I wanted to eat later, and when I was younger, our cook would often prepare special meals just for me if I didn't like what my parents were eating.

Of course, Robin isn't going to have any sympathy for my current plight – who would?! But as I grab a large pot, crack some eggs into it, and then try and figure out how to get the heat to work on the stove, I wonder if she would stop staring at me like I'm a total crazy person if she knew how I grew up.

Robin is sitting on the couch with a plate of pasta on the coffee table in front of her. It smells delicious, and I try not to covet her meal while looking into my bowl of watery egg soup.

"What are you watching?" I ask tentatively from my position in the doorway between the living room and the dining room.

"*The West Wing*," Robin replies. She pauses the show with her TiVo remote and then asks, "Have you seen it? Oh wait, that's a stupid question; you wouldn't have asked what it was if you'd seen it."

"I haven't watched it, but of course, I've heard of it," I reply lamely.

"Do you want to watch it? You'll catch on. I mean, you're five seasons behind, but it's okay," she laughs nervously. "Or we can watch something else if you want. This is on TiVo, so I can watch it later," she explains.

I slowly make my way into the living room and sit down on the couch across from Robin. I make the mistake of putting my bowl down on the coffee table, and Robin glances at it and exclaims, "What *is* that?!"

"It's supposed to be scrambled eggs. But I'm not much of a chef," I reply, trying to make a joke.

Robin does not have a poker face, and I swear she's dying to ask me at least a dozen questions about my deficiencies, but she must have been brought up well because all she says is, "I made way too much of this pasta. There's plenty left if you want to heat some of it up."

If my parents were here, I would have graciously turned down her offer and eaten every bite of my undercooked eggs just to prove to them how well I'm doing on my own. However, my parents are eating a gourmet meal in their brownstone, and likely trading insults across the table like normal couples would pass the salt. "I would love some pasta," I reply, eagerly hustling to the kitchen to exchange my eggs for something edible!

* * *

Over the next few days, Robin and I develop a bit of a rhythm. It's still a far cry from a solid friendship, but it feels a lot less awkward than right at the beginning when I felt like I was trespassing. Robin leaves for work in the morning before I do, but when I get up to shower, she makes oatmeal and drinks her coffee in the kitchen. We don't talk much in the morning, but we tell each other to "Have a good day," and that's more positive communication than I got while living with my parents, so I consider this to be a win.

The evenings still have a "first date" feel to them. We are both overly polite while taking turns in the kitchen, and I can tell that Robin thinks my eating habits are weird, but she keeps her thoughts to herself. Last night I offered to order sushi for both of us, and Robin was hesitant at first. I thought it might be because she didn't like sushi, so I told her she could pick something else. It turned out that her initial reluctance was because she had chicken sausage that was one day away from its expiration date, and she didn't want it to go bad. Once she convinced herself to put the sausage in the freezer and eat it another night, she was completely on board for sushi. I couldn't even pretend to relate to her dilemma and felt guilty for food I'd thrown out over the years or that had been thrown out on my account when I changed my mind or my plans at the last minute.

Over sushi, we watched *The West Wing* for the third

night in a row. Robin played a selection of episodes from previous seasons in an attempt to get me up to speed. She provided play-by-play commentary through most of the episodes to add the background and share her opinions on the characters and storyline. When she initially suggested this activity, I thought it was going to be terribly annoying, and I wasn't sure how to get out of it. But after the first episode, I was hooked on the show and found Robin's comments funny and her voice soothing.

Now I'm walking the last block to the apartment, struggling to balance two overflowing Zabar's bags. I still have no idea what type of groceries to buy, and at the rate I'm spending, I'm going to need to dip into my savings account just to buy produce. My dinner tonight is a collection of things from the hot pre-prepared section, and I was astounded when the clerk weighed my dinner and put a sticker for $23 on the package. I thought I was making an economical choice, but I might as well have ordered in again! I'm also pretty sure that they mismarked most of the fruit prices. I know the grapes said $2.99, but the big bag I got rang up for over $10. I'm sure that I should have complained about it, but I haven't shed all my privileged upbringing, and I can't quite fathom haggling over prices – it's enough of a culture shock that I'm even noticing them.

I'm already looking forward to another evening on the couch, drooling over Rob Lowe, when I open the apartment door and find all the lights are off, and it's eerily quiet. I don't have many data points to work with, but Robin has gotten home before me every night so far, and like clockwork, she's been preparing her dinner to the sound of Alicia Keys when I've walked in the door.

I call out, "Hello," and feel instantly stupid - it's clear that no one else is here. I've yet to be alone here in the evening, and it's irrational, but I feel a little bit scared. I rush around and turn on all the lights in the common rooms and then switch on the television for background noise, and I feel slightly better.

Even though my groceries cost well over a hundred dollars, it only takes two minutes to put them away because there really isn't that much food. I'd never given any thought to the fully stocked Subzero refrigerator in our brownstone or the cabinets bursting with every type of food I could imagine. I realize that I don't know if Roberta oversees grocery shopping or if that's part of Lorraine's duties. And I never bothered to think if she shopped every day, or a few times a week, or had groceries delivered – it was like everything else in the house, it just magically appeared.

After putting away my pathetic array of goods, I change into my favorite Juicy Couture sweatpants and a faded Tulane t-shirt I got my first week of freshman year. Considering the menial work I do all day, which often includes manual labor, these clothes are far more suitable to wear to work than what I'm required to wear. This is what runs through my mind as I hang up my gray pencil skirt and toss my wrinkled Thomas Pink blouse into the dry-cleaning pile.

I contemplate transferring the twenty-three dollars' worth of hot buffet items onto a plate but quickly conclude that they will look even less appetizing that way, and I'll likely just make a mess. With my dinner in one hand and a hefty pour from a ten-dollar bottle of chardonnay in the other, I make my way to the couch for my first night alone in my new apartment.

I was looking forward to a few more episodes of *The West Wing*, but it feels weird to watch them without Robin. I know she's seen them already, so it won't be like she's missing out or anything; it's just that it feels like *our thing*. I'm done with dinner and still haven't found anything I want to watch. There are a ton of shows I've never seen before and a few that I have, but nothing piques my interest. Instead of watching something just for the sake of background noise, I grab the manuscript out of my bag that I took from the slush pile at work. My boss claims that the slush pile is a wonderful opportunity for underlings like me to get experience editing and for unknown authors to get their day in the sun, but I know she's full of shit. She just dangles the carrot, and when an actual junior editor slot opens, she hires someone from the outside or brings in her nephew the way she did a few months ago.

Still, I pick up the manuscript and my blue Tiffany pen and decide to give this one a chance. Even if the book is terrible, I'm still awestruck that someone had the courage and stamina to write an entire book and submit it for consideration.

When I hear the key in the lock, I have no idea what time it is, but I'm on page forty-seven, and I've jotted down meaningful notes on almost every page.

"Hi," I say to Robin as she comes in and automatically hangs her coat up in the front hall closet.

"Hey," she replies. It's only a single word, but she sounds either incredibly tired or like she's been crying.

"Is everything okay?" I venture.

"Yeah, well, no. I mean, it's fine," she says, contradicting herself.

I put my pen inside the manuscript to save my place and put it down on the coffee table. "Do you want to talk about it?" I ask her.

She pauses for a moment as if she's considering it and then shakes her head. "No. It just wasn't the best day at work, that's all. I'm going to go to bed," she tells me.

"Okay," I reply, but she's already halfway down the hall, and I don't think she heard me. Seconds later, I hear Robin's muffled voice, and from the cadence, it's clear that she's on the phone. I guess she did want to talk about it; she just didn't want to talk to *me* about it.

I pick up the manuscript and try to get back in the right mindset. I aim to put all thoughts of Robin and roommate bonding aside. I have somewhere to live that isn't under my parents' roof, and it's a decent apartment in a nice neighborhood – I should be thrilled and stop trying to make it more than it is.

Chapter 18

Jessica

"**A**re you sure that isn't too heavy?" I yell to Zach.

"It's fine," he replies, but his voice is strained, and it looks like he might collapse under the weight of the enormous box of books he's carrying. I know that books are supposed to be packed in smaller boxes so they don't get too heavy, but I ran out of those and only had giant ones left. I decided to fill those up with books instead of bedding, which is what the writing on the boxes advised.

Katie and I packed up all of our stuff over the past two days and then rented a U-Haul to take everything to our new apartments. Katie got several of her friends to help us carry everything from our apartment into the truck, but they all had to get to work and rehearsals, so on this end, they were only able to unload as far as the lobby. It's clear that Zach's doorman isn't too happy to have my belongings strewn all over the lobby. Apparently, I was supposed to make a reservation to use the freight elevator, but now that I'm here with all my worldly possessions, there isn't much he can do about it - except give me dirty looks and basically ensure that all my future packages will be mysteriously misplaced. Thankfully, Zach is here and has been great about helping me get everything upstairs.

"How much is left?" Zach asks as we ride up the elevator to the ninth floor. He's resting the gigantic box on the floor, and I'm sure he is regretting the day he met me.

"Only six or seven more boxes," I say. "And the bed," I add with a wince.

I can't even imagine how Katie is managing on her end. Even if all three of her roommates are helping her move in, she's in a walk-up! She also brought a lot more furniture with her than I did. Since Zach's apartment was completely furnished, I told Katie she could take the living room furniture. My bedroom at Zach's place (it's hard to think of it as anything else yet) already had a desk and a dresser in it. They were much nicer than my old stuff, so the only real furniture I've brought with me is my full-size mattress, box spring, headboard, and a nightstand.

"You couldn't find movers?" Zach asks. I genuinely can't tell if he's joking or annoyed – the latter would certainly be justified.

"Katie got a quote from a moving company – I think they were called Moishe's Movers? And she said it wasn't worth it. She said we didn't have that much stuff and we could save a lot of money if we did it on our own. I think she was wrong on this one," I sigh.

"We're almost done," Zach says, offering a kind smile that

I surely don't deserve after making him spend his entire Saturday afternoon hauling my boxes.

Two hours later, I am lying on my fully assembled bed in my new room. I still need to unpack, but I'm surrounded by all my boxes, and all my stuff is *here*. I called Katie to check in while we were taking a quick break, and she said that they hadn't even gotten half of her stuff upstairs, and most of her helpers were about to leave. I felt bad for her and simultaneously relieved that I didn't have to deal with that, and then guilty that I felt relieved to be here.

My door is three-quarters of the way open, but still, Zach wraps his knuckles lightly on the door to make me aware of his presence. "How are you doing?" he asks.

"Great. I think I may wait to unpack until tomorrow," I tell him.

"I can understand. Today was a long day. I'm going to order a pizza for dinner. Would you like some? What kind do you like?" Zach asks.

"I would love pizza," I reply. At that exact moment, my stomach audibly growls as if Zach needed additional proof of my hunger. I realize that I've had nothing to eat all day since a Luna Bar early this morning. I've been too busy to be hungry, but now I'm ravenous, and it's unclear if I'll be able to wait thirty minutes (or longer!) for our pizza to arrive.

"I'll eat anything," I tell him. "Wait, let me get it," I say, reaching down to the floor to find my purse and hopefully my wallet. "It's the least I can do."

"I couldn't let you pay for dinner on your first night," Zach says, and when he smiles, there's a tiny dimple on his left cheek that I hadn't noticed before.

"Thank you so much," I reply, too tired to argue. "I'll get the next one," I say, but Zach is already out of the room and dialing the pizza place, so it's unclear if he heard me.

Thinking back over the past twelve hours, I can't believe that I ever imagined Zach being a serial killer or psychopath or even remotely sketchy. He is such a nice guy, and I would never have been able to move in here without his help. Brian may have ruined my ability to trust a future boyfriend, but Zach might be able to help restore my faith in men in general – even if I've sworn off dating for the rest of my life.

Chapter 19

Robin

I open my eyes a split second before my alarm goes off, and I'm painfully aware that it's a Monday. There's nothing noticeably different in my room or in the small amount of sunlight that is peeking through the cracks in my drapes, but my whole body feels the weight of the beginning of a long week. Right now, I wish I were the type of person that could call in sick just because they don't feel like going to work, but my conscience wouldn't let me do that. I feel like Tory might be someone who plays it fast and loose with her sick days and then instantly feel guilty for my baseless assumption.

As if on cue, I hear the ancient apartment door open and shut. Tory mentioned last night that she was going to go to a sunrise yoga class in the morning and asked if I wanted to go with her. The idea of getting up any earlier than I have to on a Monday seemed crazy, especially to stuff myself into spandex and attempt poses that are nearly impossible alongside skinny, flexible girls like Tory. Although maybe there's something to morning yoga since Tory sounds energized and upbeat as I hear her moving around the apartment, and I can barely pull myself out of bed.

The shower's steam helps a bit, although it still feels like a Monday. As I rinse the conditioner from my hair, I review my day's schedule. First, we have our weekly budget meeting at ten. I'm almost ready for that; I still need to double-check a few things when I get to the office. Next is a monthly "lunch and learn" from noon to two, though I can't remember today's lackluster topic. It will be the same platter of wraps and slightly wilted salads that they always serve. At which point, I will have to decide if I dare eat two of the small wraps so I'm not hungry all day and risk the judgment of the rest of the room. Somehow, everyone else only requires a few leaves of lettuce or the corner of a wrap to be "so full" except for Christy – she'll probably eat four wraps and claim she's still hungry, and everyone will think it's adorable because she's a size zero. The VP of sales is presenting to our whole department at three, and his meetings always take forever, so that will probably run until five. This means I'm basically in meetings the whole day, and I still need to find time to get my regular work done *and* make some progress on the brand relaunch presentation for Janet. The mental run-through of my day is already overwhelming - by the time I finish blow-drying my hair, I'm ready to crawl back into bed.

I planned out my outfit last night to save time this morning. I opted for a navy J. Crew sheath dress and my favorite red Nine West slingbacks that have been mistaken a couple of times for Manolo Blahniks. Admittedly, the people who made this mistake knew nothing about shoes and simply knew the brand from watching *Sex and the City*, but I still think it counts. I sigh when I look at myself in the mirror and try to focus on the things I like rather than those that I don't. I have no idea where I read or heard this, but at some point in college, I came upon the advice to "find three things you like when you look at yourself, and the things you don't will simply fade away." That's not entirely true, but it can be helpful. I focus on my flawless complexion (thanks to good genetics), my bewilderingly perky D-cup boobs (also good genetics), and my muscular legs (which look even better in heels). These three attributes keep me from fixating on my wide hips and somewhat doughy stomach.

My attention is drawn upwards, and I toy with the idea of adding beachy waves to my long, straight blonde hair, but there's no way I have enough time for that. I rarely wear any makeup, which seems both ironic and a point of contention for my colleagues in the cosmetics group, so I make some extra effort today for all my meetings and give myself a smokey eye and pale, glossy lips.

All it takes is one step into the kitchen and a look at Tory's face to confirm that I look different than I usually do. Unfortunately, I can't read her initial expression to know if the difference is positive or negative.

"Wow, you look great!" Tory exclaims. I guess this gives me my answer, but of course, I instantly wonder if that means I usually look like crap when I leave for work – one of my superpowers is turning a compliment into an insult.

"Thanks," I reply without much enthusiasm. I debate whether I should tell her that she also looks great or if it would sound insincere. I decide not to say anything because in the week since Tory has been here, she has looked fantastic every day, and I haven't said anything yet, so it would seem weird to start now when she doesn't look any different.

"Do you have something special?" Tory asks.

"Just some meetings. Is it too much?" I ask her, suddenly nervous that I look like I've overdone it for a day of boring presentations.

"No, not at all. I didn't mean that you didn't look good the other days. I was just reacting to the dress, shoes, and make-up," she apologizes and immediately winces.

"I get it, and thank you," I say more sincerely this time. "When I first started at this job, I dressed up almost daily. But I've gotten a lot more casual as time has passed – I don't think I realized just *how* casual," I laugh.

"I wish I could be more casual. Unfortunately, my boss insists that everyone dresses like this," Tory says, indicating her immaculately tailored pants, silk blouse, and what I think may be actual Manolo Blahniks. "Even though nothing about my job requires me to be seen or heard," she says. I offer a small laugh, but it feels mildly uncomfortable like I'm laughing at her job.

"Oh my gosh, I've got to go!" I exclaim, catching a look at the time on the digital clock on the oven.

Tory swivels her neck to look at the clock as if she needs to confirm for herself. "You do!" She agrees. "You're usually gone by now."

She hasn't lived here very long, but she's picked up on my

schedule and is correct that I should be long gone by now. I hate being late, especially on a Monday when I have so much to do!

"I've got to go, bye!" I say to her as I grab my purse off the counter and run out the door.

Miraculously, the elevator door is open, and I begin running down the hall and yell, "Please hold the elevator!" as I try not to trip in my slingbacks. I'm not one to scream in the halls, but the elevators in our pre-war building are high on charm and low on speed, and if I miss this one, it could be five minutes until it comes back.

I practically jump into the elevator as if it were a moving subway car and cry, "Thank you!" And then bend down to adjust the straps on my shoes without even glancing at my companion (and commute savior). When I stand up, I look at the woman next to me, and she seems familiar, but I can't place her. I've heard from friends that it's typical in Manhattan not to know any of the people in your building, even your next-door neighbors. Jenny and I must be the exception because we know everyone on our floor and a lot of people in the building. Maybe it's an exaggeration to say that we *know* them, but I recognize almost everyone from the building, and I know the names of everyone on our floor. I swear I recognize this woman, but I don't think she lives in the building.

She must notice me staring because she looks straight back at me, but I'm not expecting what comes next. "I'm Jessica," she begins. "I came to interview to be your roommate, but I showed up really late, and you had already found someone," she adds helpfully.

"Oh my gosh, that's right!" I say as if she needs me to confirm this for her. "What are you doing here?" I blurt out before I can stop myself. Although it seems like a perfectly reasonable question – what *is* she doing here?!

"I moved in down the hall with Zach this weekend," she tells me.

"Oh!" I reply, unsure what else to say.

"It was random, or maybe fate, if you believe in that," she laughs. "I met him in the hall as I was leaving your place, and he said he was about to post an ad for a roommate, and then one thing led to another," she says, looking somewhat sheepish.

"I didn't even know he was looking for a roommate," I say. "Although I don't know him very well," I add.

"He's a really nice guy. I think it's going to work out well," Jessica says.

Just then, the elevator dings, and the door opens into the lobby where a woman from the fourth floor is waiting impatiently with her giant double stroller, and an older man from the eleventh floor is enjoying a cup of coffee from the corner deli and waiting patiently, as if he has all day.

"We could all hang out sometime?" Jessica suggests as we walk toward the exit, although it sounds like more of a question the way her voice goes up at the end.

"Yeah, sure," I say. "My new roommate is Tory – we could all get together," I offer.

"That would be great," Jessica replies as she turns to walk down Columbus Avenue, and I break off to head west toward the subway. "It's a date!"

I smile at her comment, as this is hardly what I would

consider to be a date, but considering the type of dates I've been going on, maybe I should.

Chapter 20

Zach

"**A**re you heading out?" Tom asks.

"I was going to go. Do you need me to stay?" I ask him.

"It's fine. We can walk out together. I wanted to pick your brain about the new site updates that are due to come out next month," Tom says.

"Of course," I reply. I put my laptop and a few folders in my messenger bag, sling it over my shoulder, and meet Tom at my office door. Tom is more involved in the company than I imagined a CEO would be, but he's the first CEO that I've met, so I don't have a basis for comparison.

Tom has a few questions for me as we walk through the mostly empty eighteenth floor to the elevator bank, and thankfully, I can easily answer all of them. With business out of the way, we wait in mildly uncomfortable silence for the elevator to arrive. Tom must be at least twenty years older than I am, and from what I've gathered, he has a wife and three children – the oldest one just started college. Although I've worked with Tom since I joined Expedia three years ago, we don't have much of a relationship outside of the office, and I'm perfectly happy with that. However, at a time like this, it would be nice to have something to talk to him about – especially if we are alone in the elevator for the next eighteen floors. As the youngest member of the team, I never feel excluded when I hear that others have socialized outside the office. I have no interest in golfing at their country clubs or sailing on the Hudson, but I'm sure Bob, George, Sally, and the rest of our team wouldn't struggle to make conversation if they were in my position.

Tom breaks the silence. "How was your weekend, Zach? I remember being your age and living in the city – there's nothing like it!"

Suddenly I feel younger than I normally do around him and my other colleagues and wish we could return to the uncomfortable silence. "It was nice," I reply and cringe at how lame it sounds. My weekend was fantastic. I helped Jessica move in on Saturday, which was exhausting and nerve-wracking. Then it rained all day Sunday, and we were both so tired from moving that we stayed in, and she unpacked while I got some work done, and we ordered dinner and watched a movie. I know I can't relay this to Tom for multiple reasons. First of all, he'll be disappointed that I didn't do something more interesting, and second, he'll have no idea why I suddenly have a roommate. "I hung out with friends," I add. "How about you?" I ask in an attempt to shift the focus of the conversation.

"You know, the usual weekend. Maggie had a track meet

on Saturday, and Paul had a race in Connecticut on Sunday. But I still snuck in eighteen holes both days," he says with a wink.

I know I should remember this because he talks about his kids all the time. Maggie must be his daughter, and Paul is his son who is in high school – I wonder what kind of race it was – I probably shouldn't ask. It takes me a second, but then it comes back to me. His son is some sort of all-state or nationally-ranked rower, so it must have been a crew race or boat race or whatever the right terminology is for that sport. I rack my brain for a follow-up question that won't make me sound stupid and come up with something vague enough that will hopefully work. "How did he do?" I venture.

It must have been okay because Tom's face lights up as he begins to respond. "His boat finished second, but it was an extremely tight race. The eight that beat them are all seniors and all committed to D1 schools for next year. Paul's still a sophomore – although Princeton and Penn have both indicated that they want him," Tom says proudly. With that comment, the elevator dings, signaling our arrival in the lobby and the end of our conversation.

I would ordinarily stop at the gym on my way back from work, but tonight I'm anxious to get home and see if Jessica is home yet – maybe she wants to order dinner again or watch a movie? She said that she typically leaves work at five-thirty, but that doesn't mean she goes straight home. I have no idea what her plans are tonight or any night. I try to pause and get some perspective. I need to maintain as much of my routine as possible. Jessica only needed a new place to *live*. She already has friends, a job, and a life in Manhattan. I can't assume that she is going to change anything other than where she's sleeping and showering now that she is my roommate. As I remind myself, all she's signed up to be is my roommate – I can't forget that.

* * *

When I arrive home from the gym a little over an hour later, with a lonely bean burrito stuffed in a paper bag, Jessica is sitting on the couch in flannel pajama pants and a tank top flipping through the television channels.

"Hi!" she says cheerfully. "How was your day?"

I'm more excited than is probably appropriate to find Jessica here and making herself at home. I try to keep my tone neutral when I respond. "Hey. It was good. How was yours?"

"It was pretty slow, which was kind of boring. I don't like it when I have so much to do that I feel like I'm always behind, but it's also annoying when there's not enough work. I like it when there's just enough work to keep me busy until five-thirty. You know what I mean?" she asks.

"Kind of like Goldilocks," I reply, instantly wishing I could take the words out of the air and shove them back into my mouth. She's going to think I'm such an idiot – I can't believe I said that! I'm about to apologize for my lame remark and make an excuse, but her face breaks into a grin, and she rewards me with her laugh. "Exactly," she chuckles. "Did you eat dinner yet? I made this chicken, rice, and spinach thing that my aunt makes, and there's a lot left over. It doesn't look that great, but it tastes good," she promises.

"That sounds amazing. Are you sure there's enough?" I ask.

"There's a ton! I called my aunt for the recipe, and I didn't think to change any of the quantities, so I made the same amount as she does when she's feeding the family," she says.

"I'm going to go rinse off quickly, and then I'll warm it up if that's okay," I say to Jessica, although her focus seems to have shifted back to the television.

I throw my burrito in the fridge and silently promise that I'll bring it to work tomorrow for lunch. I can't remember ever seeing anyone other than the assistants on my floor bring their lunches to work, but it seems wasteful to throw it out, and I'm definitely not going to turn down Jessica's offer to share her home-cooked meal with me.

After a quick shower, I change into sweats, join Jessica back in the living room with my dinner, and sit in the over-stuffed club chair perpendicular to Jessica's couch. This may be the first time I've ever actually sat in this chair, as I always opt for the couch. It seems way too intrusive to sit down right next to her, especially when this monstrosity of a chair is right here. The interior decorator, who the realtor convinced me to use, picked out and ordered all the furniture in the apartment. I like most of what she chose, but I've always thought that this chair looked way too big and not particularly comfortable, and as I awkwardly sink into it with my plate on my lap, my suspicions are confirmed.

"Have you seen this?" Jessica asks, nodding her head to indicate the movie playing on my ostentatious forty-eight-inch television set. That may be the only item I pushed back on with the decorator in the apartment. She said it would look ridiculous, and she might be right, but I really wanted the big flat-screen TV.

"*Ocean's Eleven?*" I ask her. "I've seen it a few times," I reply. "Have you?"

"I saw the beginning, but I didn't see the end," she admits sheepishly.

"Are you serious?!" I ask her.

"I know. I heard it was great and I really wanted to see it. I rented the movie with my ex, and he didn't like it, so we stopped it in the middle," she says.

"Seriously?" I question. I now have another reason to hate her ex-boyfriend, not that I needed one.

"We have to watch it," I exclaim. "I have it on DVD if you want to start at the beginning." I can't tell what channel this version is on, but I assume it's on Showtime or HBO, and it appears to be about one-third of the way through.

"Oh, that's okay. This is fine. I know I've seen this part already," Jessica says. "Are you fine to watch it?" she inquires. "I know you've seen it already," she adds.

"Of course. It's a great movie. I'm happy to watch it," I tell her.

We both relax back in our respective seats, which is easier for Jessica than for me and settle in to watch the movie. Against the glow of the screen, I take a few glances in her direction during the film while I know she's not looking and marvel at how it's possible for two people to look so much alike. If I didn't know better, I'd swear Cassie is right over there on the couch.

Chapter 21

Tory

I have fifteen minutes until I need to be back at my desk to answer the phones. So I need to hurry to get outside and soak up a few minutes of this perfect spring day. It's lunchtime on the first Friday in May, and Park Avenue is packed. Men and women are standing in the middle of the sidewalks with bare arms and rolled-up shirtsleeves, tilting their faces up toward the sky to feel the warmth of the sun. Faces that have been wrapped up in scarves and bulky sweaters since November are finally free, and there's a collective smile across midtown that only happens a few times a year.

I peer into the window at Hale & Hearty to gauge the line and check if there's any chance I'll be able to grab lunch and make it back in time. I'm pleasantly surprised to see only a handful of people in the shop – lunch plans must be delayed today due to sidewalk sunbathing, and I'm not going to complain. I order the same things in my salad that I always get when I come here – grilled chicken, broccoli, cucumber, artichoke hearts, hard-boiled egg (whites only), tomatoes, and fat-free Italian dressing. As I wait for the man in the black t-shirt and hairnet to make my salad, I listen to the woman next to me place her order. She asks for fried chicken, avocado, cheddar cheese, walnuts, bacon, croutons, and regular ranch dressing. The first thought that sneaks into my head is in my mother's exact voice: "That's not healthy; why is she even bothering with the pretense of eating a salad?" I tell my mother to shut up so I can hear my next thought: that her salad looks much better than mine. My next thought is that it looks like something Robin would order. In the short time we've been living together, I've noticed that she likes to cook (and seems very capable of doing so) and she likes to eat things that taste good and doesn't seem to feel bad about it. As the guy hands me my salad and gives me change for my twenty, I ponder ordering something like that the next time I come here for lunch, although I wonder if I will be able to do it without hearing my mother say, "A moment on the lips, a lifetime on the hips...."

The afternoon passes surprisingly quickly. One of the big authors we publish has a book coming out in a few weeks, and I get to help with the logistics for several launch events and book tour stops. A couple of years ago, I wouldn't have wanted anything to do with second-rate party planning; however, I now have perspective and know that this is actually about as exciting as it gets here for an assistant.

Anna stops by my desk at four fifty-five with her Canal Street knockoff Dior saddlebag over her shoulder. "Are you ready to go?" she asks.

"It's not even five," I reply without looking up from the manuscript in front of me.

"Since when are you not ready to leave before five? Especially on a Friday?" she adds.

Anna is one hundred percent correct. I am always ready to leave and usually the first one out the door. So it's not surprising that she's confused by my behavior.

"I know. I'm sorry. I want to finish this," I say to her, still without looking up from the bound pages in front of me that are now covered with my notes.

"What are you working on?" Anna asks. She picks up a binder and stacks it on top of a tower of identical three-ring binders to make room for her butt to perch on the corner of my desk.

"It's nothing. I mean, it's probably stupid, but I just want to finish it now that I've gotten this far," I reply, which doesn't remotely answer her question.

"Finish what?" Anna asks.

I take a breath before I answer, knowing that once I say it out loud, I can't take it back. It's not that it's a big deal to read unsolicited manuscripts. And it's not unusual for assistants to try to get noticed or make a name for themselves. And it's common for assistants to care about their jobs and work hard. It's just that it's abnormal for *me* to do any of these things, and everyone knows it – especially Anna.

"I grabbed a manuscript from the slush pile a little while

ago, and I think it might be pretty good. I've been making some edits, and I may show it to Paula," I tell her.

Anna leans over and shuffles through the pages with her thumb and forefinger. "Are you trying to rewrite it? That's a lot of notes," Anna says and then manages a laugh, but there's something off about her tone.

"You're right. It's probably too much. I don't even know if I'll ask Paula about it – she probably won't make time to read it if I do," I say and laugh to show that I know this is a dumb idea.

"Yeah, probably," Anna agrees. "We're going to PJ Clarkes for drinks. One of the guys I went to school with is bartending there tonight, so we're going to start there. Come meet us if you want," she offers.

"Okay, thanks for the offer. Maybe I will," I say to Anna as she walks toward the elevator, but I already know I won't. I can't put my finger on it, but something shifted just now between us that doesn't make me feel great. I might be imagining it, although I don't think I am. It's like there's always been this dynamic where we both knew she was the smart one who was good at her job and would be the one to succeed, and I was just the rich girl here biding my time. But now that I'm interested in something and there's a tiny, although unlikely, chance that it could mean something, it's like I've thrown off the balance, and Anna doesn't like it.

I shake my head back and forth as if I can physically dislodge the negative thought from my head before I dive back into the last five chapters of the manuscript. It's then that I notice the red light on my desk phone – I must have missed a call earlier when I was in the bathroom or in Paula's office. I navigate through the menu, and it appears that I have three missed calls and new voicemails – how did I miss three calls? Hopefully, there's nothing urgent from Paula on here. The first is from earlier this afternoon – it's my mother asking me to call her back when I have a moment. That one can definitely wait until this weekend or whenever she calls again. The second is from my father reminding me that I need to be at brunch on Sunday morning or I won't get my check. My cheeks burn as I listen to his condescending tone, and I stab at the keypad to erase his message. The third message is from Robin, and her tone is light and breezy. She says she is meeting up with two people from our building tonight at six o'clock at a bar down the street and wants me to come. In a completely opposite reaction to my father's message, my face lifts, and my whole mood brightens with this invitation.

I hurriedly pack the manuscript in my bag and assure myself that I'll finish editing it this weekend, and it wasn't like Paula was going to look at it tonight. With a spring in my step and thoughts of Anna and my parents shoved to the back of my head, I hustle out of the building and into a cab to get back to the Upper West Side to change and meet my roommate and potential new friends for drinks.

Chapter 22

Jessica

Zach said the bar was on the corner of West 70th Street and Columbus. I didn't bother to ask him which corner because I figured it would be obvious – I was wrong. I've walked around all four corners of the intersection like a complete moron, and I still don't see anything that says Shalel Lounge. I'm almost ready to give up and walk back to the apartment when I notice stairs leading below ground across the street on the Northeast corner of the intersection. It hadn't occurred to me that the bar wouldn't be at street level. I narrowly avoid a bike messenger as I run across the street to look for a sign, and now that I know where to look, I easily spot the name Shalel Lounge above the metal railing.

There is a slight chill in the air due to the stone floor and subterranean location. The bar is crowded and dark, even though the sun is still high in the sky on this early May evening, and I glance around nervously in the dim light to see if Zach has already arrived. I'm about to grab the empty seat at the end of the bar when I feel a hand on my shoulder. I spin around to see Zach's smiling face, and I let out an audible sigh of relief that is hopefully muffled by the noise around us.

"We have a table in the corner," Zach says, motioning to the back of the bar. I see Robin at the table, and she raises her glass in acknowledgment.

"Do I order here? Or is there a waitress?" I ask Zach.

"There's a waitress for the tables, but it's pretty busy, so it might take a while. You should probably get something here if you don't want to wait," he suggests.

"Can I do that? Won't the waitress get mad?" I ask him, sounding ridiculous even to my own ears. I don't know why I'm so nervous and asking so many questions – it's like I've never been to a bar before!

"I think it's fine. We'll just leave a big tip," Zach says casually.

My awkwardness is replaced by an unwelcome feeling of anxiety, and I miss the feeling from a few seconds ago when I was only worried about my weird behavior. It hadn't occurred to me that we'd be going to a "fancy bar" – I hadn't allocated that kind of money to alcohol this week. I take another glance around, and now that my eyes have adjusted, I notice that it's not a basement dive bar but more of a cocktail lounge that's too cool to be on street level. I remind myself that even if the drinks are fifteen dollars apiece, I can just have one and call it a night – I don't have to spend my carefully budgeted weekend funds on this Friday happy hour just because I'm here.

While I was lost in my thoughts, I didn't notice Zach sneak between the barstools and get the bartender's attention. "Jessica, what do you want?" he asks.

I'd love a martini, but I'm not willing to risk the price tag. My next choice would be a vodka soda. I know the cheapest option is always beer, even though I'm not really in the mood. "I'll have a beer," I reply. "A wheat beer if they have one," I add.

I'm still fishing in my tiny purse for the loose bills I rolled up and shoved in the bottom when Zach hands me a cold glass of straw-colored beer with a lemon wedge perched on the rim.

"How much?" I ask him.

"Don't be silly. I've got this," Zach says as he motions for me to walk in front of him to our table.

"Thanks," I reply over my shoulder. Maybe I *should* have ordered the martini, but I quickly admonish myself for being greedy.

By the time we reach the table, it looks like the fourth member of our group has arrived. A striking woman with long chestnut-colored hair stands beside Robin, shrugging off a fitted blazer to reveal a cropped tight white tank top, low-rise jeans, and about six inches of seriously toned abs in between. Living with a waitress at a gentleman's club means that I've spent my fair share of time around beautiful women, but I still have a terrible habit of staring when I meet someone who is objectively attractive. I try not to be too obvious as I scan her visible six-pack, and then I catch sight of her nipples poking almost indecently through her shirt and assure myself that I'm not the only one staring.

I glance over at Zach, and I'm shocked and impressed that he's not ogling Robin's new roommate. Instead, he's shaking her hand and appears to be doing a much better job than I am of making eye contact. Finally, it seems to be my turn, so I place my beer on the table and offer my hand. "Hi, I'm Jessica. I'm Zach's new roommate."

"Nice to meet you. I'm Tory," she says.

We all take our seats, and I quickly look down to try and figure out what kind of first impression I'm making on Tory – I need to look down because, at that moment, I can't even remember what I'm wearing. I have on an emerald, green silky camisole top. Although I don't even need a bra to go for a run, I've got on a bandeau strapless one to prevent the exact nipple issue that Tory doesn't seem so concerned about – although if my boobs looked like that in a white tank top, I'd wear one every day. I'm also wearing a pair of black, slightly low-rise bootcut jeans, but those also aren't very exciting. I remember turning thirteen, and I asked my mom when I would stop looking like a skinny boy, and she assured me that my time would come – she said I would fill out and get my curves, just like her. It's fourteen years later, and I'm still waiting.

I tune back into my surroundings just in time to hear a question directed at me. I smile and tell myself that I must focus on the conversation. "I'm a graphic designer at a consulting firm," I say to Tory. I'm almost positive that she asked about my job, and the look on her face says I got it right.

"What about you?" I ask and then kick myself as I'm sure this topic was already covered while I was zoned out and wishing I had her body.

"I'm an assistant at a publishing company. It's a terrible job," she adds.

"Why is it so terrible?" Zach asks.

"It's really boring, and most people do it because they want a career in publishing, but..." she trails off.

"That's not what you want to do?" Zach asks, trying to be helpful.

"I don't know," Tory replies.

The logical next question would be to ask her what she *wants* to do, but asking someone what they really want to do, if they haven't volunteered it, feels much more personal.

Robin changes directions and puts the question to Zach. "Where do you work?" I thought she might already know the answer, but since we are all getting to know each other, it feels perfectly acceptable and a good icebreaker, if nothing else.

"I work at Expedia," Zach replies. "What about you, Robin?"

"I work at Limited Brands? Do you know what that is?" Robin says.

Zach says that he does, while Tory and I say "no" simultaneously.

"It's the parent company for Victoria's Secret and several other retailers. I work in brand management for Victoria's Secret skincare," Robin says.

Just then, our waitress arrives, looking slightly frazzled, and asks if we are ready to order. My beer is almost gone, and I'm already feeling full from the heavy beverage, but I don't want to switch drinks now.

"I'll have a Cosmo," Tory says loudly. "And we'll have a

round of tequila shots. Make them doubles," she calls to the waitress, who is already backing away. Then, Tory laughs and says, "Nothing like a few shots to get the conversation going, am I right?"

The waitress brings our shots in record time; it's as if she had the bottle of tequila in her apron and sets them down in the center of the table with a small plate of salt and a bowl of limes. They are at least triple shots, if not larger, but Tory doesn't miss a beat; she picks up her tumbler of tequila and motions for us to do the same. "To new roommates!" she says.

Robin looks at Zach and me and then back at Tory, and we all shrug before forgetting the salt and downing the fiery liquid. I frantically search for a lime wedge to balance the burn and feel only slightly embarrassed that no one else takes one. My life has certainly taken an unexpected turn in the past month. I thought I would be living with Brian in a pretentious condo on the Upper East Side and anticipating an inevitable Williams-Sonoma registry. I'm not sure what the future holds now or who these people will turn out to be to me, but I have a feeling it could be a lot of fun.

Chapter 23

Robin

I hear the phone ringing as I'm fumbling with my key in the lock, and my frustration grows at the likelihood of missing what I'm sure is a call from Jenny. Finally, the lock clicks open on the fourth ring, and I run to the phone and grab the handset, breathlessly saying, "Hello!"

"Finally!" Jenny says, and I slump onto the couch with relief that our game of phone tag is over.

"I know! I can't believe it's taken so many days to make this work," I laugh.

"We wouldn't have this problem if you ever turned your cell phone on," Jenny chides. "You're like my parents. You know that it isn't just for emergencies or when you want to make a call, right? That little phone can be kept on to receive calls, too," she says, poking fun at my cell phone habits.

"I know. I promise I'm working on it! Every time I leave it on, it rings at the most inopportune times, and then I turn it off and forget to turn it on again," I say.

"You'll get there," Jenny laughs.

"Alright, enough about that. How are you? How is life as a doctor? How many lives have you saved? Tell me everything that's happened since we last spoke!" I demand.

"I think you've watched too many episodes of *ER*," Jenny jokes. "My first rotation is in the coronary care unit, but it's a lot more charting and prescription writing than crash carts and code blues – although that's probably for the best," Jenny says.

"I still can't believe you're a *real* doctor," I say, quickly trying to amend my statement. "That's not what I meant. But, of course, you're a real doctor, and I know you're great at it! It's just that I'm here trying to make decisions about body lotion, and you're really *doing* something."

Jenny tries to reply, and I cut her off. It's not on purpose; I'm just not done with my soul-searching soliloquy yet. "How did this happen? It feels like yesterday that we were registering for our freshman year classes, and now, poof – here we are! And not for nothing, but I got a higher grade in Intro to Chemistry than you did," I ramble on.

"Yeah, but you hated chemistry, and that was the one and only science class you took in college," Jenny reminds me. "What's this really about, Robin? Because I know it isn't that you wish you were a first-year resident checking vital signs on eighty-nine-year-old cardiac patients and averaging four hours of sleep a night."

I sigh and look around the living room - Jenny's living room –and I feel like I might cry. "I don't know. It's nothing and everything at the same time."

"Tell me more," Jenny says in her soothing, reassuring best-friend voice.

"I feel lost at work right now. None of the decent, eligible men in Manhattan who *I* want to date, want to date *me*. And the ones who want to date me are beyond awful. It's weird in the apartment without you. I like Tory, but I'm not sure I *get* her. There's something I can't figure out about her. And I don't think she ever has a bad hair day, lounge around in PJs day, or gross hangover day – it's not human. I miss you," I say and exhale loudly into the receiver.

"I miss you too," Jenny says. "Okay, don't kill me, but I have to go in about five minutes to get ready for my shift. Say more about Tory's not being human thing," Jenny instructs.

"I'm being dramatic. She's really nice. She even did some grocery shopping – although she keeps buying extravagant things from Zabar's that are barely food. But something doesn't fit together. She works as an assistant in publishing. She was desperate for the apartment because she said she was in a bad housing situation and needed to get out. She says she's on a tight budget. And then, if you saw her, you wouldn't believe it. She's gorgeous and has the most beautiful, expensive clothes, shoes, and handbags. Also, you can tell she wants to eat, but she basically only eats salad and works out a ton. Although I guess that's better because if she looked like that and she ate pizza every night and never went to the gym, I'd truly hate her."

"Oh, my God. Maybe she's an escort!" Jenny squeals.

"What?!" I ask.

"You know, a hooker?" Jenny explains.

"I know what an escort is!" I yell back. "But there's no way she's an escort."

"That would explain it all!" Jenny says. "The expensive clothes and shoes are required for high-end escorts. And, of course, she has to be beautiful and in great shape – men expect that if they're paying that kind of money. And she wants to eat, but she can't – you know, because of the job expectations," Jenny adds. "Although I'd think she would have a bigger budget – I hear you can make several hundred thousand dollars a year doing that – maybe you could ask her for some connections...."

"You're crazy!" I say to her.

Jenny starts laughing, and I get the giggles and laugh right along with her. "I'm sure she's not a prostitute, but it does explain a lot of your unanswered questions," she jokes. "Did you call any of her references?" she asks, her tone has become slightly more serious.

"I did. She gave me a reference from work, and I called and talked to her. Her name was Ann or Anna or Annie or something like that. She went to Columbia," I say.

"I thought you said she went to Tulane?" Jenny questions.

"No. I mean, yes, Tory went to Tulane, but Ann or Anna went to Columbia," I say.

"I'm confused," Jenny says.

"Sorry, it's irrelevant. I did talk to Tory's reference, and she seemed nice and normal and had good things to say about Tory, *and* she went to Columbia," I add.

"Gotcha," Jenny says. "Sorry, I really do have to go, but we can talk more tomorrow or the next day – especially if you use your cell phone," she chides. "And I'm sorry I can't help with work or the lack of men in New York, but I'm sure things will be great with Tory; it will take a little while to get to know her better," Jenny says.

"You're right," I agree.

"Or maybe she *is* an escort, and she can open your mind to new job opportunities and help you meet some "eligible" men – you could solve all your problems at once," Jenny says before dissolving into a fit of giggles.

"You're the worst!" I yell into the phone, but I'm laughing so hard my words are barely comprehensible.

I'm grinning ear to ear as I hang up the phone. Nothing about my situation has changed in the past fifteen minutes, but I feel so much better after talking to Jenny. It was just what I needed to pull me out of my bad mood. I realize I'm still wearing my heels and coat since I was so rushed to answer the phone when I got home. I'm halfway down the hall on my way to change into sweatpants and an old t-shirt *and* contemplate what to make with the meager ingredients in the fridge - eggplant, ground turkey, green pepper, and left-over rice, when Tory bursts through the door calling my name.

"Robin, are you home?" Tory says.

"Yes, I'm here," I call back. "I'm getting changed, and then I'm going to figure out what I'm making for dinner. Do you want me to make any for you?" I offer.

"Don't get changed!" she commands.

"Why?" I reply. I take a few steps back down the hall in my now bare feet so we can talk face to face.

"Sorry. I didn't mean to yell like that. A friend gave me

two tickets to this thing tonight, and I was hoping you'd come with me. But it starts in like thirty minutes, so we have to leave now," Tory says.

"Oh wow. Tickets to what?" I ask.

"It's a movie and then some cocktails," Tory says nonchalantly.

"Sure, I'd love to," I reply. Then I look down at my white blouse and tan Banana Republic skirt and look at Tory's black crepe mid-thigh dress, which looks like she just put it on moments ago, not ten hours earlier. "I can't wear this. I don't know what to wear," I say helplessly.

"That's fine. Or just throw something else on. We'll be sitting in the back; it doesn't matter," she says.

I hurry back down the hallway and throw open my closet doors. I don't know what I'm expecting, but I look frantically through the hangers as if something new will have miraculously appeared since I was last here this morning. I don't have anything that will match Tory's effortlessly chic look, and certainly nothing I can put together in the next five minutes before we need to leave. I settle on a black deep v-neck short-sleeve shirt that displays my best assets and a pair of black flared pants that balance out my hips – or at least that's what I tell myself when I look in the mirror. I throw my hair into a neat, high ponytail and put on a few coats of mascara before declaring myself ready and returning to the living room.

"You look great. You ready?" Tory asks.

"Yeah. Thanks again for inviting me," I say.

In the elevator, I ask, "Where is the movie? Should we take the subway or a cab?"

Tory opens her quilted clutch with the interlocking C's and pulls out an envelope. "Let me look," she says. "It's at The Ziegfeld, so West 54th Street," Tory says. "We should take a cab," she adds.

In the taxi, I catch a glimpse of the paper in her hand, and it looks like it's meant to be a copy of a movie ticket, but clearly much fancier. I see the words "World Premiere" and "VIP," but that's all I can make out. I try not to let Jenny's comment get in my head, but there's something that doesn't add up about Tory. What kind of publishing assistant who needs a roommate also gets tickets to film premieres?! I know I'm missing something, but I attempt to put it out of my head – after all, I'm going to a movie premiere as a VIP! I also try to overlook the realization that I am woefully underdressed, but as we pull up outside the Ziegfeld behind rows of limos and crowds of photographers, I determine that fact is going to be harder to ignore.

Chapter 24

Zach

It's quiet when I put my key in the apartment door. A sense of disappointment overwhelms me as I realize that Jessica might not be home. Spending the evening together has become my new normal in the span of a few short weeks, and I'm not looking forward to a night alone with my laptop. Although it's quiet when I walk into the foyer, all the lights are on, and the knot in my stomach, which had developed instantaneously, disappears just as quickly.

I don't see Jessica in the living room or the kitchen, but I know she must be home because of the lights. Although I guess it's possible that she came home to change and left again. Before I can get worked up about it, I hear her voice coming from the direction of her bedroom. "Zach, is that you?"

I poke my head into her bedroom and see her sitting on her bed with a book open on her lap. "You're being pretty casual about it if you think it might not be me," I joke.

"Huh?" she asks, giving me a puzzled look.

"I just meant that I'm the only other person who has a key, so if it wasn't me, then it's probably an intruder. You might want to be a little more upset about it," I say, but I can feel my cheeks getting redder as I explain, and I wish I could make myself stop talking.

"Oh, right!" Jessica laughs. "That's a good point," she says.

"How was your day?" I ask, trying to change the topic.

"It wasn't terrible. Not great, but not too bad. It's work, right? What about you?" she asks.

I quickly scroll back through my day at work. I had a great meeting with the CEO and then another good meeting with my chief engineer. Everyone is excited to roll out the next version of our site, and although I don't focus on the financials as much as others, it's hard to miss the current excitement that people have for the company's success. I want to share some of this with Jessica, but I don't want to gush about my day when she's feeling dreary. "Okay. It's work, right?" I reply, and she rewards me with a laugh.

"You know what we should do?" she says excitedly. She shuts her book and jumps to her feet.

"What?" I say. I have no idea what she's about to suggest, but I know I'll be on board with whatever it is.

"We should get ice cream," she replies.

"Ice cream?" I question.

"Yes! It's practically summer. Memorial Day is next week, and I haven't had ice cream yet. And not that Tasti D-Lite crap; I mean real ice cream. What do you say?" she asks.

"I could definitely go for some ice cream," I reply. I

haven't eaten dinner yet – I was planning on warming up the leftover eggplant parmesan that I had for dinner last night – but that doesn't seem too important; I can always eat the eggplant later or simply have ice cream for dinner.

* * *

After a quick shower to clean up from my trip to the gym, Jessica and I make our way out into the warm spring night in search of ice cream. We've walked five blocks south, making casual conversation about the weather and the difference between springtime in New York and California, when Jessica stops on the corner and says, "Where are we going?"

"To get ice cream," I reply.

"I know. But are you leading us to an ice cream place?" she asks.

"No," I say, shaking my head. "I was following you,"

Jessica dissolves into a fit of giggles but manages to get out, "I was following *you*!"

"Well, this can't be that hard," I reply, and I can feel the grin stretching across my face. "It's New York City – there must be ice cream on every corner," I say.

"Of course," Jessica replies. "Now that we know, we need to actually *look* for it."

We continue walking south on Columbus, and immediately I spot a deli advertising "FroYo" in the window. I point it out to Jessica, and she shakes her head. This brings our conversation around to the prevalence of delis and bodegas. For the next few blocks, we debate the merits of them, and we wonder who the brave or perhaps crazy people are who actually eat from the delis' hot buffets. I see a sign for Tasti D-Lite and shrug my shoulders as I point in that direction.

"Definitely not," Jessica says. "I've had so much of that garbage in the four years that I've lived here that I'm probably radioactive by now. I want actual ice cream, with cream and sugar and calories," she says emphatically.

"Okay, okay, message received," I laugh.

There's a Mr. Softee truck on the next block, and Jessica sighs as we walk past it. "How hard is it to get good home-made ice cream?" she exclaims. "A couple of places in Providence near school had the most amazing ice cream, which was all made right there in the store. Don't even get me started about the ice cream on Cape Cod. I spent one summer there between my sophomore and junior year, and, shockingly, I didn't gain a hundred pounds!" she says.

I glance at her in her Nike gym shorts and loose tank top, as if I don't know exactly what she looks like. It appears that she has the type of body and metabolism that couldn't gain ten pounds if she tried, let alone a hundred, but I don't think there is an appropriate way to respond to her comment, so instead I ignore it and ask her about Providence.

"You went to school in Providence? Where did you go?" I ask her. I would have thought college would have come up before now, but I guess not. It seemed weird to ask her in our "interview," and apparently, it hasn't come up until now.

"I went to RISD," she replies.

"Oh wow!" I respond excitedly. I knew she worked in graphic design, so I'm not sure why her answer surprises me, but it does. Maybe it's because she's from California, so I assumed she went to school out there. Or it could be my complete lack of creative and artistic skills that makes me so impressed with someone who goes to art school, especially one as selective as RISD.

Jessica gives me a funny look but thankfully doesn't say anything about my awkward response, and then she continues. "Yeah, I really liked it. I think I may be the only Californian that prefers the Northeast to the West Coast – promise you won't tell anyone, or they'll never let me go back to visit," she says good-humoredly.

I want to know more about her thoughts on the east coast, but I don't want to miss the natural opportunity to ask her more about school – I want to know as much as possible about her. "Did you study graphic design at RISD?" I ask, deciding to go for the school angle first.

"Not really. I got my BFA in photography. That's what I went there to study," she says quietly. I almost have to strain to hear her over the street noise.

"You're a photographer?" I ask.

"No. I mean, technically, I have a degree in it and some experience, but that's not what I'm doing," she says, and I detect a note of sorrow in her voice.

"Why not?" I prod.

"It's too hard to make a living," she replies. "I was silly to think I would be able to do it. Thankfully, I took a few graphic design classes my senior year and picked up enough of it that I was able to get a job right after graduation. Although, I don't think you need any real graphic design experience to edit PowerPoint slides all day," she says.

"Do you take pictures in your free time? Is it something you still think you would want to do?" I ask her.

"Can we talk about something else?" she says. Her voice isn't unkind, although her tone makes it clear that she's serious.

"Of course. I'm sorry to badger you about it," I apologize. We're quiet for a moment, and I look across the street and see the sign for Ben & Jerry's Ice Cream. I point to it, and Jessica turns her head to see what I'm pointing at, and she sighs.

"Is that the best we can do?" she asks.

"We've been walking for over half an hour, and that's the best option we've seen so far," I say.

"I think you're right," Jessica laments. "New Yorkers are so strange – I can get ten different types of Asian food within three blocks of our apartment, but we have to hunt for ice cream."

I want to make a comment about cuisine in Manhattan because it feels like there should be an easy joke with this material, but I can't think of anything to say – this type of thing isn't my strong suit. Instead, I settle for, "Do you usually get a cone or a cup?" and I want to sew my mouth shut to prevent any further inane comments from escaping.

"In the summer, I usually get a cone," Jessica says, and she has once again saved me from my own idiocy.

Jessica orders a cone of Phish Food, and I get a cup of Chubby Hubby. The suspiciously young-looking clerk rings up our order, and I hand him a twenty-dollar bill before Jessica can even reach for her wallet.

"You don't have to pay for mine," she protests. "I'm the one that suggested it – I feel like I should treat."

"It's the least I can do," I blurt out, and she gives me a puzzled look. "I feel bad that the Upper West Side let you down on ice cream options – this is your new neighborhood, and I feel responsible," I say, and I cringe yet again as I hear the words come out of my mouth.

"I guess that only seems fair," Jessica laughs. Just then, the clerk hands over her cone, and she licks the ice cream in a slow, circular motion that causes me to momentarily turn away. Even in middle school, when boys had no control over their bodies, I was never the kid who had to stay at his desk until things "calmed down," but watching Jessica run her tongue over the ice cream is getting me aroused – what is wrong with me?!

We walk back uptown in companionable silence, enjoying our ice cream and the perfect seventy-degree night air. I risk a glance at her and note two things. The first is that she is thankfully almost done with her ice cream – she is biting the last bit of the cone now, which has the opposite effect. The second is that she doesn't look like Cassie anymore. Obviously, she still shares some common features, but when I look at her, I see Jessica; I don't see Cassie. That might have been what drew me to her initially, but now I see that she's beautiful in her own way, easy to talk to, and fun to hang out with. I wonder if I could be lucky enough that she might feel the same way about me.

Chapter 25

Tory

"You're still here?" I say to Robin, the surprise evident in my voice.

"I know. I know. I'm running late," Robin laments.

I don't want to be presumptuous or make her feel worse since she already seems distressed, but I feel like saying, "This isn't like you – are you alright?" We've only been living together for about a month, but in that time, I've never seen her late for work, let alone frazzled, which she clearly is right now.

Instead, I try a gentler version and say, "Is everything okay?"

"Yes, well, not really. I mean, it will be fine - I think," Robin says. Her outfit looks a little more casual than what she usually wears, and she currently has a sandal on her left foot and a flat on her right, and she's rifling through papers in her work bag.

"Are you sure?" I ask. I glance at my watch and realize that if *I* don't leave in the next minute, I'll also be late for work.

"I'm supposed to present this thing today at work, and it's not very good, to begin with, but now I can't even find it," she says, and I can hear the panic creeping into her voice.

"What does it look like? I can help you look for it," I offer.

"You don't have to do that," Robin says, but then she adds, "It's about ten pages that are clipped together with a purple binder clip. I was looking through them last night before I went to bed. I can't imagine where they would be!"

I put my purse down on the couch next to her bag, and before I can stop myself, I ask, "You looked in your bedroom?" My dad would ask this type of question to make me feel like a complete moron. "Of course, you looked in your bedroom; sorry," I apologize. "Let me take a turn looking in your bag with fresh eyes – you can change your shoes while I do this," I offer.

Robin looks down at her feet and then lets out a sound that is a laugh mixed with a cry. "Oh my God, Tory, what would I have done if you weren't here!" And then she hurries to her bedroom to change her shoes. I'm hoping she goes with the sandals and maybe even decides to change her shirt, but I don't feel like I can suggest that.

"I found it!" I cry out when I locate the purple binder clip.

Robin rushes out of her room to inspect my discovery. She takes it from me, flips through it, and then tucks it neatly back into her bag. "Thank you! Thank you so much! I can't believe it was in there – you must think I'm crazy," she moans.

"Not at all," I laugh.

"Oh God, and now you're going to be late to work too, aren't you?" she asks.

"Not that late," I assure her. "If we leave right now, and I have good taxi luck."

We rush out the door and down the hall in time to hear the rumble of the finicky elevator doors beginning to close. We are still several apartments away when Robin calls, "Hold the elevator!" I don't expect this to work because this isn't the type of thing that happens in real life, but then I hear a ding and see a hand extend from inside the car to hold the door open. We arrive seconds later to find Jessica waiting for us.

"Good morning," Jessica says as we get into the elevator.

"Thank you so much," Robin gushes. "I'm already so late to work. And I made Tory late too," she adds.

"I'm late too!" Jessica adds. "My alarm didn't go off."

"What are the odds that we are all late?" Robin asks although I assume it's rhetorical.

"Are you both in Midtown?" I ask them.

"I'm at 54th and Park," Jessica says.

"I'm at 57th and Park," Robin says, giving Jessica a curious look. I'm sure there are at least ten giant office buildings in that three-block radius, with thousands of people in each building, so it's not *that* much of a coincidence.

"I'm at 50th and 3rd Ave," I tell them. "I'll drop you guys on my way there, and that should be faster."

"You're taking a cab?" Jessica asks.

"I always take a cab," I reply nonchalantly and then wish I could take it back. I see Robin and Jessica exchange a look that confirms my fears, but I can do nothing about it now except try and gloss over it.

Our luck continues when we get outside, and a taxi has just dropped someone off in front of our building – it's like he was waiting for us. We scoot across the backseat bench, and the light turns green as soon as the cabbie puts his foot on the gas – it seems like another good omen.

"Do you want to go out for drinks tonight?" Robin asks, directing the question at both me and Jessica. "We can either celebrate if my presentation goes well or drown my sorrows if it doesn't, which I think is more likely."

"Sure!" Jessica replies enthusiastically.

I'm about to reply that I'd also love to join when I remember that I have to go to dinner with my parents tonight. I've backed out of Sunday brunch two weeks in a row, and my father made it clear on the phone last night that I would regret it if I didn't show up.

"I can't. I have something," I reply.

"Oh. Okay," Robin says, sounding slightly deflated.

It would be easy enough to tell them that I'm having dinner with my parents – I'm sure neither of them would ask any questions, and it's a perfectly normal activity for most people. But I don't want to bring these two worlds together. If I talk about my parents or how I grew up with my new friends, they'll think about me a certain way. But if they don't know about that, then I can be anyone I want to be – or at least I can try.

* * *

The cab pulls up outside of the brownstone on the quiet tree-lined street at seven twenty-five. Dinner is served at seven-thirty, and I know better than to be late. I left work shortly before six, went to a bar on Lexington Avenue, and nursed a glass of wine to kill time. While I don't want to be late for dinner, I certainly don't want to be early. Now that I've finally gotten out of this house, I can't believe that I stayed here for so long. I feel the tension starting to build in my neck and shoulders merely standing outside on the sidewalk, and I know it's going to be ten times worse once I get inside.

I suggested we go to the new restaurant, Per Se, for dinner because I know my dad loved it when we ate there this spring. He replied, "No more Michelin-starred restaurants for you on my dime – you'll have to find your own sugar daddy." I'm sure his real reasoning is that he can't berate my mom and yell at me in public nearly as easily as he can in our own dining room, and he had no desire to be on his best behavior. As the cab drives away, I take a deep breath and walk up the grand staircase, steeling myself for what's to come.

There's no one there to greet me when I walk inside. It's not unusual. I know Lorraine is gone for the day, and Roberta is upstairs in the kitchen working on dinner. Still, it makes me realize how different it is to enter this cold monstrosity than it is to come home to my apartment, where Robin is always happy to see me and has taken to leaving me notes on the kitchen counter if she's not home.

I trudge up two flights of stairs to the dining room and note that the massive table is set for three, and I'm the first to arrive. I debate if I should look around the house for my mom or simply take my seat and wait for my parents to arrive – I decide on the latter.

This room is so memorable and yet unfamiliar at the same time. My earliest recollections of eating all take place in the kitchen, where I was hidden away with a nanny or a maid until I could learn proper table manners – according to my father, finger foods and highchairs did not belong in the formal dining room. I was still relegated to the kitchen for breakfast and lunch for most of elementary and middle school, but I did join my parents for family dinner in the dining room once I was in first grade. I remember being so excited about the big promotion until the third night when I spilled béarnaise sauce on the tablecloth, and my father called me a moron.

My dad's loud voice interrupts my unpleasant walk down memory lane. "Tory, so glad you could find time in your busy schedule to squeeze us in," he chides as he enters the room. He swirls the amber liquid in his glass so the ice rattles against the side, and I wonder how many drinks he's had so far this evening.

My mother follows closely behind him, wearing a peacock blue silk dress, which is way too fancy for a week-night dinner at home but not out of character for her. Even though she does attend a plethora of social functions, I suppose she has to "dress for dinner," or she would never have a chance to wear the piles of new items that arrive in her closet each season. "It's so nice to see you," she says quietly, and if I didn't know better, I'd swear that she missed me.

The next twenty minutes are occupied with the usual logistics of the meal. Roberta serves the meal and the wine, and then my father requests additional seasonings even though the food tastes perfect exactly as it's been prepared. I watch my father cut into his lamb chop in the pretentious European style he insists on using, and I'm convinced he's going to complain that it's overcooked, but he merely sniffs and takes a bite and chews thoughtfully – before turning his gaze on me.

"How is everything in your new apartment?" he asks.

The question seems benign, and I exhale before I reply – maybe this won't be as bad as I thought. "It's good. Everything's going really well," I say.

"That's great," my mom replies before my dad cuts her off.

"How long are you going to keep this up?" he asks.

"What do you mean?" I inquire.

"We all know you aren't going to stay in a crappy little apartment with a roommate, pretending you're in college again or whatever it is you're doing over there," he scoffs.

"It's not a crappy little apartment. And I'm not pretending I'm in college. This is what girls, I mean *women* my age, do," I say.

He shakes his head and drains half his glass of wine in one long sip. "So, you're going to keep working for minimum wage and playing house until you're past the age when anyone would want to marry you? Is that your grand plan?" he says callously.

I'm not sure how he turned this around so quickly, but I shouldn't be surprised because this is his routine. I know it will only provoke him, yet I decide to say it anyway. "Who says I want to get married? Why does that need to be part of my plan?"

"How are you possibly going to support yourself?" he scoffs. Before I have a chance to reply, he plows ahead. "I've got a meeting with my lawyers next week to review the terms of your trust again. Now that you've moved out on your own, I think we should revisit whether it makes sense for you to get full control in four years or not," he says, tenting his fingers in front of his face like the villain in a Disney movie.

"Alan, what are you talking about?" my mother says tightly, which are essentially the first words she's spoken during the meal. He gives her a look that I've seen him give her a hundred times before, and I can see her shrink back into her chair.

I cannot believe that he will actually go through with raising the age that I can access my trust, but I think carefully about my reply before I respond – he did it once, and he might not hesitate to do it again. I'd love to tell him that I don't need the fucking money, and I'll be fine on my own. That's what I should say, so I won't have to answer to him any longer. But why is it fair that he gets to keep the money my grandparents made and left for me? Especially since he did nothing to earn it!

I take a moment and try to remember some of my yoga breathing — in through the nose, out through the mouth. I'm simply going to ignore his comments and move on. "I've been working on some editing recently, and I've got some ideas of my own for a book. I've also been thinking about getting back into the violin again." I force a smile onto my face and try to steer the conversation back to the type of dinner table conversations normal people have.

It's instantly apparent that my efforts have failed. My father is also smiling, but his smile is more of a demonic glare. It's as if he knows he wants to say so many mean things, and he can't get the insults out of his mouth quickly enough. "Writers and musicians are really known for making the big bucks. Not that I can see anyone paying *you* to write anything," he laughs. "And I'm pretty sure you peaked at the age of twelve with your violin – after we threw away all that money on years of private lessons, you decided to quit," he says as if he's reminiscing.

I'm speechless for the first time all night. My cheeks are on fire with a mix of anger and shame, and I can feel the tears building, but I refuse to give him the satisfaction of watching me cry. He's made me doubt myself about so many things over the years – my intelligence, my attractiveness, and my overall self-worth, but I was objectively good at the violin; hell, I was *great*. I chose to stop playing because I was a lazy teenager and wanted to spend more time with my friends, not because I wasn't good enough. Although suddenly, I flashback to that concert at Carnegie Hall, a night I haven't thought about in fourteen years. We were in the cab on the way home, and I was so proud of myself. I hadn't made a single mistake, and a professor from Julliard had even complimented me. I relayed that to my father, and he laughed in my face and told me I was average at best, and the only reason someone from Julliard spoke to me was because they were after his money. Now his exact words come back to me. "When you play, all I hear is nails on a chalkboard." He laughed a little after that as if he had made a joke. That was the last night I played my violin.

I know that he's an asshole, and he's always been an asshole; however, remembering this and listening to his tirade tonight feels like an entirely new level of cruelty. Has it always been this bad, and I just don't remember? Or has it gotten markedly worse? I want to catch my mom's eye to see her reaction; although I'm worried if I look up from my lap, the tears will flow. I never know when she will choose to fight with him, defer to him, or simply slip into her own world and pretend like nothing's wrong.

"Well, whatever you do, you can't keep sponging off of us for much longer," my dad says, casually continuing with his tirade while drinking his wine.

"Shut up, Alan! Just shut the hell up!" my mother suddenly yells. She pushes her chair back from the table, stands up, and throws her napkin on top of her barely-touched plate of food. "If anyone should know about sponging off of people, it's you!" she yells at him; her voice is even louder now, and I find myself trying to remember the last time I saw her like this.

I wait on pins and needles for my father to reply, but it's silent for what feels like ten minutes. It's probably only thirty seconds, and then my mom storms out of the room and up the stairs. My dad leaves shortly thereafter, only he goes down the stairs, and I hear the door to his office slam loudly.

I could stay and finish my dinner in peace – although I love Robin's cooking, it's nothing compared to Roberta's. But my appetite is gone, and I really want a drink and to get the hell away from here.

A cab pulls up as soon as I get outside, even though I didn't hail it, and I send it away. I rarely elect to walk when there is a vehicle available – I prefer to exercise in the gym – but I need some time to clear my head. It's a beautiful evening, and I happily remember that I have a pair of sturdy flip-flops in my purse that I used for a pedicure a few days ago. I change my heels for the flip-flops and start walking.

The most direct route from here to my apartment is through Central Park. I may be sheltered, but I do know that a single woman shouldn't walk through the park alone at night. It's definitely a lot longer to go around the park – south down Fifth Avenue and then across 59th Street and back up Central Park West; however, tonight, it sounds perfect. Maybe if I walk for long enough, I can erase some of this evening.

I stop for a drink at a bar near Columbus Circle. It's touristy, and I'm sure I've walked or driven by here dozens of times but never noticed it until tonight. I take a seat alone at the bar and order a vodka martini, and when it's done, I order another.

By the time I get back to the apartment, it's after two in the morning. I'm sure Robin went to sleep hours ago, so I try to be as quiet as possible as I sneak into my room to sleep off the vodka, and hopefully, when I wake up tomorrow, I'll realize that tonight was all just a bad dream.

Chapter 26

Jessica

Walking east on 34th Street, I try to remember if I've ever gone this long without seeing Katie, and I'm convinced I haven't. Even when I went back to California for Christmas, I was only gone for six days, and now it's been over two weeks since we've seen each other. I pick up my pace as I get closer to Third Avenue and the prospect of catching up with my friend.

I see Katie through the window of The Joshua Tree, one of the first bars we came to after we met and, thereafter, one of our favorite bars in the city. She looks up, and waves when she sees me, and her smile almost reaches her ears – I know the giant grin on my face matches hers. I wrap my arms around her as soon as I reach her table, and I'm sure the couple at the table next to us thinks we haven't seen each other in years, not weeks.

"How are you? You look great!" Katie says, at the exact same time I say, "How are you? You look amazing!"

We laugh at how in sync we still are, and I gesture with my hand for her to proceed – giving the somewhat universal signal for "after you."

"I'm okay. I'm adjusting to the new apartment. Three roommates are *a lot*. Especially when we all have the same crazy schedules, and they like to party seven nights a week," Katie sighs. When she says that, I notice for the first time that she has faint circles under her eyes, and she looks a bit tired. She's still stunning, but I don't remember her ever showing signs of fatigue before, even when she worked back-to-back nights until three in the morning at the club. She must notice me staring or the look of concern on my face because she quickly perks up and says, "It's great, though. It's a lot of fun. Now tell me about you and about *your* new roommate!"

I want to press Katie for more details and ensure she's doing okay, but I'm excited to talk to someone about Zach – I'll come back to her issues in a few minutes. "The apartment is great. I can't believe I got so lucky to find something this nice for such a reasonable price."

Katie clears her throat loudly, and I laugh. "Okay, fine. I can't believe *you* found somewhere this great. Although *you* found Robin's apartment. *I* found Zach because I was the total loser that was crying in the hall," I remind her. Before she can say anything, I keep going. "Did I tell you that I hung out with Robin and her new roommate? The girl who actually got to the interview on time. Her name is Tory. I can't quite figure her out," I pause and think about going into more detail, but then I'm not sure what to say, so I simply say, "But she seems nice."

"I'm so happy for you," Katie says. "And what about Zach?" she asks suggestively.

I hesitate before I reply. I'm unsure where to begin, and then I just blurt it out. "I think I like him."

"Wait, you like him, as in you want to have sex with him?" Katie questions, and her eyes are practically bulging out of her head.

"Yes. No. I mean, I think so." I reply, feeling flustered and excited at the mere idea of it.

"You need to back up and start from the beginning," Katie says. "Oh, and I was going to ask about Brian and see if you had heard from him and how that was going, but it sounds like that isn't an issue anymore." She takes a sip from the drink in front of her that looks like a large glass of ice water, but I'm pretty sure it's vodka. I've been so busy talking that I haven't even ordered a drink yet, and the waitress service here is pretty spotty – once I've told her about Zach, then I can worry about a drink.

"I have not heard from Brian – he's such a dick. Although I think I don't care anymore. I dodged a bullet, and I'm better off without him," I tell Katie, and I've almost convinced myself this is true too.

"Wow! Good for you. You're way too good for him," she says. "Now tell me about Zach," she demands.

"He's so different from any of the other guys that I've known. I know that sounds trite, but it's true. He's super smart and really cute, but unlike most attractive guys, it's as if he has no idea that he's good-looking. He talks about current events, and he reads for pleasure, and he's nice. We went on a walk last week to get ice cream, and we have special movie nights," I tell Katie, but I can tell from the look on her face that she isn't able to appreciate how unique it is.

"Won't it be weird to get involved with your roommate? What if it doesn't work out? Where will you live?" Katie asks.

"I'm sure you're right," I concede. "Although something tells me it wouldn't be that way with him. He's nothing like Brian. He would never be an asshole or cheat or anything like that," I say confidently.

"Jess, you've known this guy for a month," Katie chastises.

"It's been more than a month," I say like a petulant child.

"Fine. Five or six weeks, or whatever it is, but still! I just want you to be careful. I know I'm the one that convinced you to move in with him, and I'm so happy it's working out – really, I am. It just seems like it could backfire," Katie says, shrugging her shoulders.

I hear what she's saying. I'm sure that if our positions were reversed, I would be saying the same things to her. However, she doesn't *know* Zach. And she doesn't know how I've felt the past couple of nights when Zach's thigh is millimeters away from mine on the couch – it's as if my entire body is one giant erogenous zone, and one look or point of contact could push me over the edge. I don't ever remember feeling this way with Brian, and I'm pretty sure Zach feels the same way about me.

Rather than arguing about it, I agree that she has a point, and I shift the conversation to Katie's recent auditions. She fills me in on the callbacks that went well but unfortunately didn't lead to any roles, and then she regales me with hilarious stories from the club of drunken bachelor party guests. Then I tell her about work, even though there isn't much to say. My job pays the bills and slowly sucks the life out of me as I draw meaningless graphs and charts for MBA grads who can't manage PowerPoint on their own. By the time we finish our drinks and walk out into the warm early-June night, our conversation about Zach is a distant memory. We hug goodbye and try to make plans for the following week. It's such a nice evening that I decide to walk across town and then catch the bus uptown rather than navigate the humid subway.

My cell phone rings moments after I've left the bar, and I don't even look at the caller ID display because I assume it's Katie calling to tell me something she forgot to say while we were together. "Hey, what is it?" I say as I pick up.

"Hey," the deep voice on the other end sighs, and although it's been almost two months since I've heard it, I recognize it instantly. "Can we talk?" Brian asks.

Chapter 27

Robin

"Can you stop by my office this morning? There's something I want to go over," Frederic asks abruptly as he walks by my desk. He looks polished as always in tight black suit pants, a fitted pink button-down, and a purple and pink tie. There are few, if any, American men that could pull off his wardrobe, but everything he wears looks like it was custom-made just for him, and he never looks out of place.

"Of course," I reply. I'm desperate to ask what he wants to talk about, but he's down the hall and disappears inside Janet's office before I can get the words out. I assume he wants to talk about my ideas for the re-launch. I gave my mini-presentation at the team meeting a few days ago, and Janet and Frederic got called out because of an emergency shipping issue in China, and I haven't heard anything since. I'm sure that's what it is, but his tone makes me nervous. He didn't sound like his usual bubbly self. My armpits start to sweat as I watch Janet's door and wait for him to emerge. He didn't mention a specific time for our meeting, but I figure I'll wait until he comes out of her office and then corner him – I don't think I can take the suspense of waiting for the rest of the morning.

As if Frederic can hear my thoughts, he opens the door to Janet's office. I grab my notebook and hurry down the hall to catch him before he has the chance to get caught up with anything else.

"Is this a good time?" I ask Frederic. I practically corner him next to the row of filing cabinets outside of his office.

"Sure," he replies curtly. My heart sinks at his tone, but I keep the smile plastered on my face, follow him into his office, and close the door behind me once I'm inside.

"Have a seat," Frederic says, gesturing to the chairs in front of his desk. I oblige and suddenly wish I hadn't been so anxious to have this meeting. In hindsight, it would have been much smarter to avoid Frederic all morning, fake a headache, and go home early. Then I could at least put off getting what will certainly be bad news. All I've done now is speed up its delivery!

"Robin, you've done a great job here the past couple of years," Frederic begins.

Oh my God – I'm getting fired! I've never had a panic attack, but as my breathing speeds up and my chest starts to hurt, I'm positive this is my first one. I wonder if this is like a breakup where you get to save face if you are the one calling the shots - should I quit before he has the chance to fire me?

I realize I've totally lost focus and stopped listening to Frederic when he says, "Robin, did you hear what I said?"

It's incredibly embarrassing to admit that I didn't hear him, and at the same time, if he did just fire me, I should probably know when I'm supposed to clean out my desk and turn in my ID card. "Could you repeat it?" I say, my face hot with shame.

"I said we've been very happy with your work here, but Janet and I were a little underwhelmed with your presentation last week. If you're going to get this promotion, we need to see more," Frederic says.

I exhale a sigh of relief, which must seem quite odd to Frederic based on the news he delivered. He gives me a quizzical look and then continues. "We were hoping you would come up with something *bigger*. It needs to have more panache. And we also need to see a detailed work plan and timeline for the brand relaunch that we could put into action," he says.

"I can do that," I say with as much confidence as I can manage.

"I know you can," Frederic says. "Let's circle back next week." Then his office phone rings, and he picks it up with his right hand and waves to me with his left, which is the clear signal that I'm being dismissed.

Back at my desk, I replay the conversation with Frederic, and my initial sense of relief disappears. Obviously, I'm happy that I'm not getting fired, but now that it's off the table, I'm thinking about what he actually said, and it's definitely not good news. My promotion depends on my ability to get this right. And if I don't get promoted now, how many more chances will I get before I *do* get fired? I stop thinking about it before I go any further down the rabbit hole and decide to take action.

I open my Yahoo account, even though personal email is forbidden at work, and I send off a quick email to Kendra. She graduated from Duke with Jenny and me. Although we weren't super close friends at school, we all moved to Manhattan simultaneously and occasionally hang out. Kendra worked at L'Oréal and then quit six months ago to take time off to "relax," as she put it before she starts business school in New Hampshire this fall. I never thought about asking any of my friends for work advice before now, but I know Kendra knows a lot about marketing for a beauty company, and she had to study for her B-school interviews, so she could probably offer some good tips. And it's not like anyone here has any advice to give me; they just keep telling me that I'm doing it wrong.

Chapter 28

Jessica

Considering that I've been obsessing over last night's exchange with Brian the entire day, it's amazing I've gotten all of my work done *and* that it's almost five-thirty! I assumed today would be one of those days where it feels like time stands still. Miraculously, every time I glanced at the clock, another couple of hours had flown by, and now it is time to shut down my computer and go home. Although, even as I say those words in my head, I know that I'm lying to myself – I'm not going home, or at least not *straight* home.

As I pack up my bag and straighten the papers on my desk, I replay Brian's initial phone call, subsequent emails, and tearful midnight voicemail in my head. I was shocked to hear his voice after almost two months of silence. By this point, I assumed I would never hear from him again, and I had almost accepted that I would never get the apology I deserved or find out why Brian cheated on me.

He was sheepish on the phone at first and asked if I would meet him so he could explain. I had the presence of mind to laugh at his suggestion and told him to "go fuck himself." Annoyingly, he seemed pleased with my response and said that I was "exactly right." I didn't want to listen to any more of his nonsense, so I hung up the phone and went home, feeling immensely proud of myself. And I would have stayed that way if only things had ended there. Instead, Brian started an email campaign shortly after nine o'clock, pouring his heart out in a series of letters sent every thirty minutes for three hours. He began with an apology for cheating on me. He blamed his fear of the intensity of the feelings he had for me and an attempt to sabotage our relationship rather than take the leap on true love – which he now knows was a terrible mistake, and he would do anything for a chance to have me back, etc., etc. When I didn't reply to his emails, he started calling my cell phone, and shortly after midnight, he left a three-minute-long message and cried the entire time. Finally, he sent one final email, begging me to see him in person. He said I could set the time and place, but he did say that he would be home every night this week from six o'clock onward waiting for me, just in case I decided to come over.

Although I didn't respond to his emails or messages, I've known all day that I'll be going to his apartment after work. I've tried to lie to myself and pretend that I'm still mulling it over, but somewhere deep inside, I made the decision as soon as Brian first suggested it.

* * *

Waiting for the elevator in Brian's apartment building, I use the mirror in the lobby to check my hair and makeup and experience an eerie sense of deja vu. The last time I stood here, I had no idea what was in store for me at the other end of the elevator ride. On that chilly April day, I was calculating if I could fit all my stuff in the regular elevator or if we would need to book the service elevator for my move. It's quite the juxtaposition – where I thought things were going and what actually happened.

I'm still lost in comparison when the elevator doors open, and I walk down the familiar taupe, carpeted hallway the same way I've done hundreds of times in the past. However, when I reach Brian's front door this time, I don't use my key to open it, even though it's still perversely on my keyring. Instead, I knock loudly and pray this isn't a terrible mistake.

Brian opens the door and envelops me in a hug before I even have a chance to say hello. Over his shoulder, I see a cheese plate and bottle of wine with two glasses on the coffee table, as if he knew I would show up tonight shortly after six o'clock. I wish that I weren't predictable or that I'd waited more than twenty-four hours to come over, but I was too curious to hear what he would say.

I return his hug with lukewarm enthusiasm and try not to notice how warm and solid the muscles in his back feel through his expensive dress shirt. I pull away before muscle memory leads my face to nuzzle the stubble on his jaw and inhale his familiar aftershave – the perfect mix of spice, musk, and something impossible to name that makes me instantly horny.

"It's so good to see you," Brian says. "You look more beautiful than ever – it doesn't seem fair that you keep getting prettier."

It's such a horribly cheesy line, and I still fall for it. I've always been a sucker for Brian's praise. "Thank you," I reply awkwardly.

"Would you like me to pour you a glass of wine?" Brian asks as he settles himself on the sofa. I hesitate for a minute as an image of Brian's naked lower half and Natalie's curly blonde hair pops into my head – there's no way in hell I'm touching the couch where *that* happened. It's obvious that Brian can tell what I'm thinking because he says, "It's new; I got rid of that one." Then I look more closely and realize that although it's still gray, it *is* a brand-new sofa. This one is a bit darker and has a nubby texture; most importantly, I don't have to fear sitting down.

Did he get a new couch because something really disgusting happened to it? Did they have so much sex on it that it was covered in bodily fluids and couldn't be cleaned? Did he feel guilty about what the couch symbolized and didn't want me to feel uncomfortable on the off chance I ever came back here? Or did he simply get tired of the old couch and want a new one? I desperately want to ask him all of these questions about the couch, but I'm not sure I want the answers.

"Would you like some wine?" Brian asks again as I sit down. "It's your favorite," he adds. "Or at least, I hope it's still your favorite."

"It's only been two months; I haven't changed my taste in wine," I say to him. He takes this as a "yes" and pours the Fume Blanc into a glass and hands it to me.

"Jess, I've been going crazy without you," Brian begins.

"You have a funny way of showing it," I reply.

"I know, I know," he says. Then he puts down his glass and buries his face in his hands, and the next thing I know, his broad shoulders are shaking. At first, I think he's laughing, but then I realize he's crying, or rather sobbing is a more accurate description. He can barely catch his breath, so I do the only thing I know how to do; I put my hand on his back and make shushing noises to try and calm him down.

"I'm so, so sorry," Brian wails. "I was so stupid. You were the best thing that ever happened to me, and I messed it all up," he says through tears and ragged breaths.

I'm caught off guard by his display of emotion and ill-prepared to respond. I continue to rub his back, and I hear myself say, "Shhh, it's okay," the same way I used to say to my little cousin when I would babysit for her, and she would scrape her knee and need to be soothed.

Brian tentatively moves his hand, looks up at me with a hopeful smile and his cornflower blue, lightly red-rimmed eyes, and says, "Is it really?" At first, I'm not sure what he means, but then I realize that he thinks I said everything's going to be okay. I don't reply, which he must take as an encouraging sign, so he plows ahead. "I promise I will make it up to you, Jess. I was scared that we were moving too fast, but I'm not scared anymore – I'll show you," Brian says.

"Wait, that's not quite what...." I begin to say, but Brian leaps up from the couch and runs into his bedroom before I can finish my sentence. He returns momentarily with a small blue box and hands it to me. All traces of tears are gone from his face, and now he just looks excited and undeniably handsome. I can't believe this could be happening right now, but it's hard not to think he's about to propose to me right now. How could one day, or even one hour have so many ups and downs – I can't wrap my head around what is about to happen!

"Open it!" Brian implores, and I open the robin's egg blue box with shaking hands. Slowly, I open the small black interior box, and I can hear my heartbeat in my ears as the tiny click of the hinge opens to reveal a small pair of gold heart earrings with a tiny diamond in the corner of each one.

"They're the Elsa Peretti hearts that you liked," Brian beams. "The ones you pointed out didn't have the diamond, but I thought you should have the more expensive ones," he adds, clearly very pleased with himself.

"They're beautiful," I say, and my stomach is in knots trying to process the simultaneous relief and disappointment that it's not an engagement ring, as well as the thrill that he remembered the earrings I showed him over a year ago. I knew it was a long shot after only mentioning them once, but I was still desperately hoping for them. First at Christmas, then on my birthday, and now here they are.

"Try them on," he gushes.

I'm not wearing any earrings at the moment, so it's simple to take these out of their black velvet home and slip them into my ears. Brian holds my face in his hands and says, "They look gorgeous, but not nearly as gorgeous as you," and then leans in to kiss me softly on the lips. It all feels so normal that it takes me a second to process what's happening and pull away. "One second," I say to Brian.

I've been in Brian's apartment for thirty minutes, and it's

like I have whiplash from going in so many directions. I can't get a grasp on my feelings or my emotions with everything happening so quickly. I try to find the right words to explain this to Brian, but nothing comes out when I open my mouth.

Brian looks at me expectantly, but when I don't say anything, he closes the distance between us once more, and this time his kiss is more urgent, and when he wraps his arm around my waist and pulls me close to him, I can feel that he's already hard. My brain is telling me to take it slowly and not rush back into anything, but my body is on a different page. When Brian picks me up and carries me to his bedroom, my libido doesn't even have the decency to protest. In fact, I hear a small sigh escape my lips as he slides my pants off, and I know what's about to happen next. Brian whispers in my ear, "I knew you'd get over it. And don't worry; I remembered to get new sheets too." Although I still orgasm twice because it's been two months, and Brian knows exactly how to touch me, I know at that moment that I'm going to regret this. As I'm falling asleep, it's not Brian's face that I picture – the only person I see is Zach, and I wish I were anywhere but here.

Chapter 29

Zach

I have no right to be upset, and that's making me even more upset! I assumed Jessica would come straight home from work around her usual time, but we didn't have plans, and she never said she would be *home*. That's another thing I'm furious with myself about – my brain calls this her home like we are some couple playing "house," when she's basically just staying here because she has nowhere else to go. I'm sure she doesn't think of this as her *home,* and she's not deflated and sad if *I* make plans and don't tell her about them.

I finally fell asleep last night around midnight, and Jess still wasn't home. I think I heard her come in around three-thirty, and I could tell she was trying to be quiet even though she kept banging into things. Since I have no rational reason to be mad and I'm not great at disguising my emotions, I decided to get up early this morning and get out of the apartment to eliminate the chance of running into her. The idea of making small talk, asking about what she did last night, or even worse, hearing about what was most likely a date, is excruciating.

The morning at work passes slowly, but there are enough meetings and distractions that eventually, it's lunchtime, and I duck out to grab a sandwich and regroup. The cashier at Cosi yells "Next" loudly, and from the exasperated way he says it, I'm guessing it's not the first time he's tried to get my attention. I order the turkey and brie because it's the first thing that catches my eye, and I don't want to piss off this guy or anyone else in line any more than I already have.

When I get my sandwich, a small, slightly sad bag of baby carrots and Snapple iced tea, I head over to the empty table in the corner and determine that I'll use the next fifteen minutes to shake off my problems and clear my head.

"Zach, is that you?" an excited and high-pitched voice asks.

I've just taken the first bite of my sandwich, and my mouth is stuffed with turkey, brie, and honey mustard. I place the thin paper napkin over my mouth to cover the chewing and look up to see who's found me in the back corner of this busy, budget sandwich shop.

"I knew it was you!" Mallory says. "May I join you?

She asks, but she doesn't wait for a reply before putting her brown paper bag on the table and unpacking her lunch, which looks almost identical to mine.

"I didn't know you were in New York," I say to Mallory. "I thought you were out in California."

"I am," she laughs. "I mean, not right now, of course. I'm

still at Intel, still in Santa Clara. I'm out here for a few days for some meetings."

"It's really good to see you," I say to her. This is definitely the kind of distraction I need today. Mallory was in my class at MIT, and although we've lost touch, I considered her to be a good friend at school, especially after what happened with Cassie. There seems to be an unfortunate stereotype when it comes to engineers, especially female engineers, and even more so when people think of female engineering students at MIT. However, Mallory does not adhere to any of those ridiculous stereotypes. She's tall, blonde, and objectively attractive – although not my type. She comes off as a little spacy or ditzy when you first meet her, but that's only until you've sat through an electrical engineering discussion section with her or any class on any subject matter. It didn't take long for me to realize that she was one of the smartest people in my class, if not *the* smartest, and her carefree, friendly nature made her even more unique.

"What have you been up to?" Mallory asks. "Other than the whole Expedia thing – I mean, congrats on that," she adds.

"Yeah, thanks," I reply. "Not too much. There are many more meetings and planning sessions and less innovation and creation now that I'm on this side. I've been thinking that it might be time to move on...." I trail off.

"You should come out west!" Mallory says excitedly. "That's where everything's happening. Of course, there's a ton of pretentious assholes, but you find those everywhere," she smiles.

We continue to talk while we eat our sandwiches, we catch

up on people we know from school, and she fills me in on her current project working on processors for a new kind of mobile phone that's like a handheld computer – she swore me to secrecy after she told me, but the whole thing sounded so out there, it wasn't like I was going to tell anyone about it anyway.

Shortly thereafter, when we've moved on to talking about the latest trends in microchip manufacturing, my cell phone buzzes in my pocket. I'm surprised to see my assistant Amber's name pop up because she rarely calls me, and certainly not when I step out for lunch.

"Sorry about this; let me just see what it is," I say to Mallory as I pull the phone from my pocket to answer it. "Hello?" I say quizzically into the phone, even though I know who's calling.

"Hi Zach, sorry to bother you. I wanted to make sure everything was all right," Amber says hesitantly.

"Of course, it is. I just stepped out for a quick bite to eat," I tell her.

"Okay...it's just that it's one forty-five, and you had a meeting that started at one-thirty. They want to know if you'll be able to join or if they should reschedule," Amber says.

I glance quickly at my watch as if to check her accuracy, and amazingly it's one-thirty! I completely lost track of time sitting here with Mallory. "I'm so sorry, Amber; I didn't realize it had gotten so late. I'll be back in the office in ten minutes. Please ask them to wait and apologize for me," I say as I abruptly end the call.

"I take it you're late getting back to the office," Mallory says and shoots me a smile.

"I'm so sorry! It was great catching up with you. I can't believe we've been sitting here for over an hour," I tell her.

"Don't worry about it. And I'm sorry I made you late," she apologizes. "I'm heading uptown also, so I can walk with you."

As we drop the remnants of our lunch in the trash, I notice the empty sandwich shop. I must have been so engrossed in our conversation that I didn't notice the lunch crowd clearing out. As bad as I feel about being behind for the meeting, I'm in a much better mood overall, and I've stopped stewing over Jessica's late night – it's amazing what talking with an old friend can do for your spirits.

I hold the door for Mallory, and she looks at me with a raised eyebrow, and I can tell she's trying to stifle a laugh. Our friendship back at school was closer to a brother-sister bond than anything romantic. It's almost more likely that I would have pulled her hair than held the door for her, so it makes sense that she finds this amusing. "I can't be chivalrous?" I joke. Mallory laughs, playfully hits me on the arm, and then puts her hand around my waist.

As we approach the corner, I hear a woman's voice say, "Zach? I thought that was you!" It's the second time I've heard this in less than two hours. It takes me half a second too long, but then I realize that it's Tory – my neighbor from down the hall. She's wearing a fancy sundress and has on oversized sunglasses, so I didn't recognize her right away.

"Hey, Tory," I say quickly. Then I add, "This is my friend Mallory," and gesture to my left, where Mallory still has her hand around my waist.

"Hi Mallory, really nice to meet you," Tory says. "I just moved into Zach's building a few months ago."

"Nice to meet you," Mallory says.

"I guess I'll be seeing you around," Tory says to Mallory with a smile.

"Right, yeah," I reply, barely hearing what Tory said. "Sorry, we have to run. I'm late getting back to work," I try to explain.

"Don't let me keep you two," Tory says.

"Gotta go. See you later," I call over my shoulder as Mallory, and I hustle across the street together to catch the light.

Chapter 30

Tory

My cell phone rings as I browse the shelves of denim at the Diesel store in Union Square. I'm killing time while I wait to meet Anna for dinner. I'm sure it's Anna calling to tell me that she's running late, but as I slide my new Motorola RAZR out of my back pocket, I wonder if there's a chance it's my mom or dad calling to apologize for dinner the other night. I'm aware that it would be completely out of character for either of them to do this, but there is a naïve (or more likely, stupid) part of me that continues to think it might happen.

Unfortunately, as I pull out my phone, I see that the display reads "Anna."

"Hey," I say when I flip open the phone and press the shiny green button to accept the call.

"I'm so, so sorry – I'm not going to make it!" Anna says.

"What's wrong?" I ask.

"We have bedbugs!" Anna says, and that's when I can tell

that she's been crying, or maybe she's about to start crying – or both.

I pause for a second before I reply so I don't say the wrong thing. My skin already feels like something's crawling on it, and my initial instinct is to tell her how disgusting that is. I'm sure this won't be helpful or well received. "I'm really sorry," I say instead. "What do you need to do? How did you find out?" I ask. I'm careful not to say "bedbugs" for fear that someone in the store overhears and thinks I'm the one with the pest problem.

"It's been the worst day!" Anna says. "One of my roommates got some new furniture from a friend of hers who moved to Arizona. She rented a U-Haul, and apparently, the bedbugs were in the blanket that comes with the truck. I guess this is a common issue, but oh my God, Tory, it's awful!"

I'm not very well versed on this topic, nor do I have any desire to be, but I feel like Anna needs to keep venting, so I try to be a good friend and stay on the phone. "Is the whole apartment impacted? What do you do to get rid of them?" I ask.

"We're trying to figure that out right now. Her dad called some exterminator for us, and he's on his way over here right now. That's why I need to stay here to figure out what we need to do. Her boyfriend said that he knew a guy who had them, and we're going to have to put everything we own in garbage bags for like a month or something," Anna moans.

"A month?" I question.

"I have no idea. He exaggerates a lot, but who knows?

Okay, it sounds like the exterminator might be here now; I've got to go," Anna says.

"Okay, let me know what happens. And let me know if you need help," I offer, but I think she's already hung up. I know it's terrible to think this when Anna is going through it, but selfishly I hope that any help she needs doesn't mean I have to go anywhere near her apartment or the bugs!

My next selfish thought is that it's Friday evening, and now I don't have any plans. I had been looking forward to catching up with Anna, and although we see each other every day at work, it's not the same. And it still seems like things are a bit off with our relationship. I'd been looking forward to having a few drinks, forgetting about my shitty parents, and pondering my future beyond life as an assistant in a way that can only be done while buzzed in a dark bar on a Friday night.

One thing about growing up in Manhattan is that almost all the kids I know from growing up have moved back here. It's unlike moving home to a rural town in the middle of Ohio or Nebraska, which would certainly be a sign of defeat. When Manhattan is your home, moving back is expected and celebrated. I haven't done a great job of keeping in touch with friends from high school, but for better or worse, I was one of the most popular girls in my class, and if my five-year reunion is any indication, my classmates are still enamored with me and with a single phone call I could have my pick of "friends" to hang out with. I sigh at the tiresome thought of catching up with my high school crowd. Most of them are working in banking or consulting or in law school. Or they are doing something else that makes good use of their Ivy

League educations and that their parents can brag about at dinner parties. I squash the idea as quickly as I come up with it. I'm not in the mood to be the *fun party girl*, which is what would be expected. I can still play that role on occasion, but I'm getting a little tired of pretending to be a trophy wife in the making without any substance or real ambition or whatever it is that everyone thinks I am – dinner with my parents this week may have been the proverbial last straw for me.

I stop at the list of contacts in my phone when I get to "Jessica Barlowe" – the latest addition to my list. I forgot that she'd given me her cell phone number when we hung out the other week, but I'm suddenly overjoyed to see it. I know that Robin has a date tonight, or I would have called her, but maybe Jessica is available! She picks up on the second ring, and from her tone, it doesn't seem like she's saved my number, or else she isn't very happy to hear from me. "Hello?" she questions.

"Hi Jess, it's Tory. From the apartment down the hall?" I say, and it comes out in the form of a question.

"Hi, Tory!" she says excitedly, and I instantly relax. "You don't need to clarify that you live down the hall," she laughs. "What's up?" she asks.

"Do you have plans tonight? Like right now?" I add.

"Nope. I just left the office. I was going to walk home since it's such a nice night," Jessica says.

"Come meet me near Union Square for dinner," I tell her. I hesitate but then decide it's best, to be honest, and besides, it would be weird if I was waiting in Union Square with a dinner reservation and my plans *hadn't* been canceled.

"I was supposed to meet a friend for dinner, and she just called to cancel. Can you come meet me?" I say.

"So, I wasn't your first choice?" she says, but her tone is playful.

"You were definitely my second choice," I say.

"I appreciate your honesty," Jess laughs. "What type of restaurant? I'm not dressed up."

"It's really casual - whatever you're wearing is fine," I say. I realize we may have different definitions of casual, but Jess always looks nice, if a little understated, so she'll be fine. "It's called Craft – on Park Avenue South. Just take a cab down Park from work; it'll be quick." I can hear the sharp intake of breath on the other end of the call and realize that I keep making the same mistake. "Or take the subway, whatever's easiest. Oh, and I have a gift certificate," I lie, "So, dinner is totally my treat."

"Are you sure?" Jessica says. "Isn't that place expensive?"

"Totally sure! The gift certificate expires next week. I got it from work, so I really need to use it." I say. Now that I've started, I have no trouble getting into my lie. It would be better if I did have a gift certificate since I need to stop spending so much money. I'm trying to be more budget conscience, but a lifetime of excess is hard to unlearn.

"If dinner is free, maybe I'll take a cab," Jessica jokes. "See you soon!"

After a couple of cocktails and a shared arugula and apple salad, we both relaxed back in our seats to wait for our main courses. The waitress convinced us to get these elaborate drinks made with gin and about ten other ingredients, but she didn't lead us astray on their delightful taste or potency. While Jessica and I don't know each other well, the alcohol has reduced the barriers, and it's quickly gone from feeling like a slightly awkward first date to dinner with an old friend – albeit an old friend that I don't know much about. When the server brings our third round of drinks, I decide I'll switch to wine for my *next* drink. My buzz is so perfect right now that it doesn't sound weird at all when I say, "Jess, what's your life story - tell me everything."

Jessica's buzz must match mine because she laughs and takes a sip of her fresh drink. "I'll give you the condensed version. Although, until recently, my life's been pretty boring, so the unabridged version won't take that long either."

"Start with the boring stuff and work toward the juicy stuff," I request.

Jess leans forward and puts both of her slender arms on the table. I'd never noticed how delicate and attractive her wrists and hands were before now, like the kind you see in photographs at the nail salon or, better yet, in high-end jewelry stores displaying rings and watches. I'm about to mention it, but thankfully I'm not that drunk yet.

"I grew up in Sonoma, California. And before you ask, yes, my family owns a vineyard, and yes, I literally grew up making wine, and no, it isn't glamorous at all." I laugh because of her deadpan delivery, but I don't interrupt her story. "My grandparents bought the land a hundred years ago or a million years ago – it depends on how they tell the story. Eventually, they turned it into two separate vineyards, and my parents run one of them, and my aunt, who is my mom's twin sister, runs the other one. They are down the road from each other, and my mom and my aunt really do everything together. The vineyards just have separate names because it's good for business or something like that," Jess says and pauses to take a drink.

I am dying to tell her how cool I think this is and how much I wish I had grown up on a vineyard, but I can tell from her tone that it won't be well received.

"Unlike normal kids who played sports or musical instruments or even played with their friends after school, my cousins and I were always working in the vineyard. My mom and her sister have such crazy twin powers that they met their husbands at the same time and then even had a joint wedding – isn't that so twisted and bizarre?" Jess asks, but she doesn't wait for me to answer. "They assumed they would each then have a ton of kids to keep working in *the fields*, but that only worked out for my aunt. She had four kids within the first five years of her marriage. And my mom couldn't get pregnant. Eventually, they had me, but I'm their one and only miracle baby, and unlike my older cousins and the rest of my family, I never wanted anything to do with wine, soil, or grapes. I swore I would get out as soon as I could, and that's what I did," Jess says with a satisfied grin.

"And that's when you came to New York?" I ask her.

"Not quite. I went to RISD first for college. I went to study photography. My uncle gave me a camera for my thirteenth birthday. Although he's as dedicated to the family wine business as everyone else, he was the only one who seemed to understand that it wasn't for me. I took that camera with me everywhere. I had a good eye, and the setting gave me a lot of options."

"That isn't what you do now, is it?" I ask cautiously.

"Unfortunately, no. About halfway through college, I realized that I would need to get a job after graduation that would pay the bills if I didn't want to move back to Sonoma. The career counselor at school suggested graphic design, so I squeezed in graphic design classes wherever I could," Jess says.

"Graphic design sounds really cool," I say to Jess. I envision her sitting at a desk designing video games or websites; it sounds so much more exciting than answering phones and getting coffee for condescending editors.

"In theory, it could be cool, but what *I* do isn't. I make PowerPoint slides all day for MBA grads who can't make pie charts," Jessica says.

"Do you still do any photography? What would you want to do with it if you could?" I ask her.

Jess sighs loudly, takes a sip of her ruby-colored drink, and then looks at the now empty glass as if she doesn't understand how it got to be that way. "In my dreams, I would travel the world taking pictures and then open up a fancy gallery in SoHo, and people would pay tons of money for the privilege of having an original Jessica Barlowe on their wall," she says.

"That could totally happen!" I say.

"I don't think so. But that's why they call it a dream, right?" she says. "Hey, should we get another drink? Shouldn't our food be here by now? I might need some water."

"Our food should definitely be here by now," I reply. I

look around to see if I can see our waitress, but it's so packed I can't see her at all. "I think I'm done with these," I say, holding up my glass. "But I might get some wine. Do you prefer red or white?" I ask.

"I don't drink red wine," Jess says, with no trace of humor. "I had enough red wine before the age of sixteen that I never wanted it again," she says. "I know, I know, that's really weird, but I just don't like it."

"It's totally fine," I say. "I like white better anyway."

Miraculously, our waitress appears at our table with our entrees and two glasses of water – she must have known that the gin would be getting to us by now. "Can I get you ladies something else to drink?" she asks.

"We'll get a bottle of the Sauvignon Blanc," I say to her.

"Are you sure we should get a bottle?" Jessica asks me. "Maybe we should just each get a glass. How much is your gift certificate for?" she questions, suddenly sounding less tipsy.

"Don't worry about it. It's a big gift certificate expiring next week, remember?" I ask her, continuing the lie.

"That's so nice that you got this at work," Jess says, and I hear a tiny bit of a slur edge back into her voice as she regains her comfort level.

"So, how did you end up living with Zach?" I ask her once I've finished chewing my first mouthful of poached halibut.

"All I've done is talk about myself. You must be tired of hearing about me. Tell me something about you," Jess requests.

"Finish telling me about how you ended up living with

Zach first – you said that was the juicy part. Then I'll tell you my story – although I promise it's not all that exciting," I say. As I say this, I'm already thinking about how much I want to share. I'm tempted to tell her everything. All about my fucked-up family, tales of high school with the elite girls of Manhattan at Spence, and how I'm a trust fund brat who is currently without a trust fund and trying to be a regular twenty-something. However, I can picture Jess's face when I tell her all of this, and she'll nod and act like she understands, and then she'll tell Robin and Zach that I'm a rich bitch from the Upper East Side and it will be a repeat of the first semester of my freshman year at Tulane all over again.

I quickly realize I've gotten lost in my thoughts and missed the first part of what Jess just said. I snap to attention and catch the second half of her sentence. "...so, we'd been dating for a while, and I thought we are getting ready to move in together, but he was terrified of commitment and too scared to tell me. Instead, he let me find out when I walked in on him getting head from the waitress at our favorite restaurant," Jess says.

"I bet it's not your favorite anymore," I chime in before I think twice. "I'm so sorry," I quickly add. "I can't believe I said that."

Thankfully Jessica is laughing loudly, and I feel better about my foible. "That's exactly what I said! Anyway, my roommate, Katie, had made plans to move out because our lease was almost up, and she thought I was moving in with Brian. And that left me scrambling to find a roommate. I actually replied to the listing to live with Robin, but I showed up too late for my appointment, and you got the apartment," Jess says.

"Seriously?" I ask her. Now that she says it, I think I remember Robin mentioning it, but my head is too fuzzy right now to put all the pieces together. "Sorry about that," I say feebly because it feels like I should.

"No, it was my fault. I'm always running late, and this time I screwed myself. Although fate works in mysterious ways, and when I was crying in the hall because I lost the apartment, Zach approached me and said that he was also looking for a roommate. He seemed so random at the time, but I really didn't have any better options. Katie convinced me to do it, and I have to admit that it's turned out to be so much better than I could have imagined," Jess says with a smile.

"I don't know him very well, but he seems like a nice guy," I say.

"He's *so* nice. He's funny and smart and really thoughtful," Jess says. "And he's cute, right? He's like the kind of guy who doesn't even realize that he's good looking – which is nothing like Brian, who was always stopping to stare at his reflection in store windows," she groans.

"What about his girlfriend – is she nice? She looks like she could be a model – those girls aren't always nice," I say.

"Huh? What are you talking about?" Jess asks.

"I ran into Zach the other day at lunch, and he was with this girl. It has to be his girlfriend – they were way too touchy just to be friends," I say to her.

"Oh, um, wow, I don't know. He hadn't mentioned

anything..." Jess says, trailing off and looking somewhat flustered.

"I feel like guys can be like that, right? Oh, wait! Speaking of dates, Robin had a Match.com date tonight – I wonder how it went," I say excitedly.

"That's fun," Jess says, but the energy in her voice is suddenly gone.

"Is everything okay?" I ask.

"Yeah, it's fine. I suddenly got really tired, and I think the drinks just hit me. It's been a long week," she says.

I'm the tiniest bit disappointed because I initially had visions of us going to a bar after this, maybe even to a club, and staying out until four in the morning. However, the idea of lying on the couch in sweatpants, watching an episode of *The West Wing*, while I wait for Robin to come home from her date suddenly sounds far more appealing. "Definitely a long week," I say to Jess, and that part is completely true. "Let me go find our waitress to pay the bill. I think they have to do something special to process the gift certificate. Then let's get a cab home."

"Thank you so much," Jess sighs.

I weave through the tables to the back of the restaurant to try and find our waitress and surreptitiously hand her my credit card. There's a thought nagging at me about Jess's weird reaction and something she said about Zach, but my fuzzy brain won't let me remember what it is. Oh well, if it's that important, it will come to me another time.

Chapter 31

Robin

I arrive at the Borders bookstore on East 57th Street a few minutes before the time Kendra and I are scheduled to meet. I resist the urge to browse the tables of new fiction, and I take the escalator straight up to the café on the second floor to secure a table for us to talk. I contemplate getting drinks for both of us so that hers is ready when she gets here - it feels like a sophisticated move that Tory could easily pull off. However, I can't remember what Kendra likes to drink, and I'd probably end up embarrassing myself. I settle for grabbing an empty table for two in the corner and lining up all of my materials neatly in front of me.

Kendra walks off the escalator a few minutes later, and it's probably best that I don't have coffee yet, because I would have spit out anything that was in my mouth. The last time I saw her was about six months ago at a bar in the West Village, and she looked about the same as she did in college: medium height, medium build, shoulder-length dirty-blonde hair, kind of cute, but mostly just average looking. I'm not sure what's happened over the past six months, but the girl smiling at me and walking through Borders looks like a Brittney Spears doppelganger from last month's *US Weekly* cover. Kendra's hair is a few shades lighter than it was previously, and it's hanging loosely but covered on top by an oversized Von Dutch trucker cap. She's wearing a cropped black t-shirt that says "Los Angeles" and impossibly short *and* low-cut jean shorts that display toned (and tanned) abdominal and thigh muscles that she never had before. Even though it's a warm Saturday in June and the rest of her outfit screams summer, she's wearing those fluffy Ugg boots that everyone seems to be crazy about, although I don't understand the appeal. Kendra's outfit and overall look should be ridiculous, but she's pulling it off judging by the appreciative glances from several men at the tables around us.

"I'm so glad you called!" Kendra says as she gives me a kiss on the cheek and slides into the chair across from me.

"Thanks for coming. You look different. I mean, you look amazing," I say before I can stop myself.

"Oh, thanks," she says casually. "I was looking for a change. Although I'm not sure this is working for me," she admits. "I'm trying to figure out my *look* before I start at Tuck in the fall," Kendra says.

"You need a *look* for business school?" I question.

"Well, no. But it's a chance for a fresh start, and I feel like I've been a wallflower my whole life. I'm tired of blending in," Kendra sighs. Even with her dyed hair, new makeup, and the trucker hat, she looks exactly like the girl I used to know when she makes that face.

"Well, you definitely don't blend in now," I tell her. "You look great," I quickly add, in case she thinks I was being sarcastic. "Can I get you something to drink?" I ask her.

"I'd love an iced mocha. With fat-free milk, please," Kendra requests.

"Sure thing," I reply as I head up to the counter for our drinks. I decide that Kendra's beverage choice sounds good, and I order one for each of us. The kind-of cute guy at the register tells me he's running behind and will bring us our drinks when they're ready. I return to Kendra empty handed and feel oddly guilty as if I'd let her down by coming back without her mocha.

Kendra barely seems to notice that I've left and returned without the drinks. She's typing something on her T-Mobile Sidekick; she quickly snaps the screen shut and puts it in her bag when I sit down. "Sorry. Just IM'ing with my mom." Once again, I marvel at how different Kendra is and also exactly the same.

"What can I help you with for work? You mentioned some sort of re-branding on the phone," Kendra says.

"Yes, that's exactly it," I say. I'm happy that Kendra brought up the topic, and now we can get to work. It's not that I don't want to chat and catch up with her, but I want to make sure we get the work done first – I have no idea how much time she's allotted for this favor, and I want to make the most of it. "I'm supposed to come up with a complete plan for rebranding skincare at Victoria's Secret. You know I worked at a bank before this. I'm technically in marketing, but up until now, I haven't been allowed or asked to do anything creative. I've only worked on forecasting, inventory analysis, and sales channel management for the past two years. Then, suddenly, they want me to have these great creative ideas about transforming the whole line of skincare, and no one is giving me any guidance!" I exclaim. It feels good to vent, although I might need to rein it in. The guy from behind the counter is placing our iced mochas on the table, and he seems a little alarmed by my emotional outburst.

"That sounds really challenging," Kendra says kindly. She takes a small taste of her drink, licks her frosted pink lips, and continues. "I worked on a few different rebrands while I was at L'Oréal. I was even working on one right before I left. I'm happy to help if I can. Can I look through the material?" she asks, gesturing to the stack of colorful papers I've laid out on the table.

"Of course! I brought all of my notes, some pictures of what the products and packaging look like right now, a list of competitors, and this file I found on consumer research from a few years ago," I ramble on.

"This is great, Robin. We can definitely work with this. Give me a minute to look it over," Kendra says.

For the next fifteen minutes, I stare out the window at the pedestrians on Park Avenue, at people browsing the book-shelves of the travel section, and at customers waiting in line to order coffee – basically anywhere but at Kendra. I don't want her to feel rushed or that I'm watching her while she works. I've run out of places to look that don't make me look super creepy when she announces, "I've got it. I know exactly what you should do!"

"Seriously?" I question. I know she's got more experience than I do and got accepted into a top business school, but it still seems unlikely that she could solve my problem of rebranding the entire skincare line in fifteen minutes.

Then Kendra draws a few graphs she calls "maps," and plots my brand versus the competitors. She says that currently, we are in an area with too many other players and that we need to find a place where there is "white space." She makes several notes on the map and then grabs a blank sheet of paper to show me what she's figured out about our customers and the segment that we should be targeting, as well as the message we should be using and our brand message and position.

Two hours later, I feel like I've taken a crash course in brand management, and I have no idea how I'll ever repay Kendra.

"I'm sorry to rush off like this, but you should have most of what you need," Kendra says. "I'm supposed to meet a friend downtown," she apologizes, pulling out her Sidekick to quickly type a message.

"Are you kidding?" I ask with disbelief. "This was amazing. I don't know how I can ever thank you for all of your help," I say to her.

"It was fun," Kendra says. "We should get together again before I leave for Tuck," she adds.

"I would love that. I need to buy you dinner or drinks, or both!" I say.

"Good luck with the project," Kendra says, pushing her chair back from the table. I wonder for a second if she's going to bend down and give me a hug. It feels like we've gotten infinitely closer over the past two hours, but maybe that's only from my perspective since she's saved my career! But there is no hug. She simply gives me a little wave on her way to the escalator, and I can't help but watch as everyone around me watches *her* walk away.

I briefly wonder if *I* should think about reinventing my look. I wouldn't go in the same direction as Kendra, but it could be time for a haircut or a new style of clothes. The thought is fleeting as I realize the only thing I have time to revamp right now is this line of skincare products. Although there are still a few empty tables in the café, so I'm not monopolizing this one, I decide that I've been here long enough. With Janet out on vacation, I have time to finish up the rest of this over the next several days and then work with the right people at the office to turn it into a presentation before my next team meeting.

I elect to walk back to my apartment from Borders because it's a beautiful Saturday afternoon. I don't remember it being such gorgeous weather a few hours ago, but that's probably because I had my own personal cloud hanging over my head. With this massive weight lifted, I feel like I could float home to the Upper West Side. I walk west on 59th Street along the southern border of Central Park, and other than the sickening smell of manure from the horse-drawn carriages, it feels like a perfect summer day. I'm not even as disturbed by the sad-looking horses today. Usually, I get upset merely at the thought of the glorious animals forced to pull tourists around the park all day in extreme weather. Today I'm in such a good mood that I don't even give the coachman a dirty look as I pass by. When I get to Columbus Circle, I elect to walk north via Broadway instead of going straight up Central Park West. I want to take the long way home today, and sometimes there are even concerts in the plaza in front of Lincoln Center in the summer, and I rarely have a chance to take a leisurely walk to check those out.

There are people milling about everywhere around the various concert halls and performance venues, although I don't get the sense there's a free outdoor concert today. I continue my journey north on Broadway, and as I pass Alice Tully Hall, I happen to look left down West 66th Street, and see Tory. It takes me a second to realize that it's her because it's out of context. I'm about to yell out her name when I notice a much older man hold open the front door of a small apartment building and lead her inside. I know that I still don't know her very well, and there could be a dozen explanations for why she's going into that apartment, but my heart still sinks. It's one thing to have a wild theory about something, and it's something else to see the theory confirmed right before your eyes.

Chapter 32

Zach

Jessica opens her bedroom door and walks slowly into the living room as if it's painful to walk. She looks adorably rumpled in pink striped pajama pants and a gray tank top. Her hair is pulled into a messy bun on top of her head, and she has remnants of eye makeup underneath her eyes – I know I'm biased, but I'm not sure she's ever looked cuter. She takes a couple of steps toward the kitchen, then appears to change her mind, walks toward the living area, and collapses on the couch across from where I'm sitting.

"Are you okay?" I ask.

"I will be. It seems I had too much to drink last night," she moans.

I've spent all week getting over my misplaced sense of jealousy, and I hate that I feel the tiniest bit of it start to creep back in. Before I can ask where she went or who she went out with, she answers both questions for me. "I went out with Tory last night. She had a gift certificate to use at Craft.

"Wow, that place is supposed to be really good," I say.

"It was great. It's really expensive. I'm glad she got that gift card from work – that's not exactly the type of place that's in my budget," Jessica adds.

I want to tell her that I'd be happy to take her to Craft or any other high-end restaurant in the city, but I'm not sure how to say it or what she would think if I told her. Before I can think too much about it, Jess changes the subject. "Is there any coffee left?" she asks hopefully.

"Of course. There's plenty left," I say. Jess softly grunts as she attempts to pull herself up from the coach. "Stay there; I'll bring it to you," I laugh.

"Thank you," she replies, slumping back into the couch without protest.

I'm not much of a coffee drinker, but my realtor gave me a ridiculous coffee and espresso maker as a housewarming gift. It looks like something that belongs behind the counter at Starbucks. It's attractive in an industrial way, and I have plenty of counter space, so it lives in a place of prominence in the kitchen. When Jessica first saw it, I thought she was going to faint. I'd never seen anyone so excited about a kitchen appliance before. When she moved in, Jessica assumed that I drank a lot of coffee, which was a very reasonable assumption, and she didn't want to bother me to use the machine unless I was using it too. I still don't love coffee, but after the past couple of months, it's growing on me, and it's a small price to pay for how happy it makes her.

"You should also have some Gatorade," I call out to her. "And maybe some Advil?" I suggest.

"I think I ran out of Advil," she sighs. "It was on my list, but I never made it to Duane Reade. "I'll have water; I don't have any Gatorade."

"I have Gatorade in the cabinet. Sorry, it isn't cold – I can put ice in it. And I have plenty of Advil. Let me grab some for you, and I'll be right back," I say to her, and I rush off to my bathroom to get the medicine.

When I return to the living room, I find Jess stretched out on the couch, wrapped up in the red and gray MIT blanket I got as a thank-you gift for a recent donation. Her eyes are closed, and I worry that she might have fallen asleep, but they flutter open as I put her drinks and tablets on the coffee table.

"You're a godsend," Jess says as she washes down the Advil with half the bottle of Gatorade. Then she props herself up on a couple of throw pillows and gingerly picks up her coffee mug. She inhales the hot steam rising off the top and then takes a small, grateful sip. "I already feel better," she says.

"Glad to hear it," I reply, although I'm doubtful that any of these remedies work that quickly.

"You know what would really make me feel better?" Jessica asks.

"What?" I ask her.

"Blueberry pancakes from Sarabeth's," she announces.

"You look like you can barely get off the couch," I joke.

"That's just because all of this hasn't kicked in yet," she says, gesturing to the supplies I brought her. "Give me one episode of *Entourage,* and I'll be ready to go. Did you TiVo the last episode?" she asks hopefully.

I laugh in spite of myself. "That's a terrible show – you know that, right?"

"I know, but that's why it's so good! We'll watch one, and then we'll go to brunch, and then we can go to the park. Wait, do you have other plans? I shouldn't have assumed you'd be free today; that was dumb of me," Jess says.

"Nope, no plans today. Other than your choice of television show, that sounds like a great plan," I tease her.

* * *

Ninety minutes later, we are seated at our table at Sarabeth's, and Jess is devouring a plate of blueberry pancakes drenched in maple syrup.

"Do you want a bite?" she offers. She stabs a neatly cut pancake bite onto her fork and waves it around in my direction.

"No thanks," I reply.

"Suit yourself," Jess laughs and then adds, "I can't believe you got a grilled chicken sandwich. There are so many amazing brunch options."

"It's too late for breakfast. I was thinking of getting an omelet when we first got here, but after forty-five minutes of waiting in line, I wasn't in the mood for breakfast anymore," I say.

"That's why they call it brunch. You can eat it all afternoon. And besides, there's never a wrong time of day to eat pancakes," she tells me.

"Fair enough," I say. I won't ask her for a bite now, although her buttery, syrupy pancakes make my chicken sandwich taste rather dry and unappetizing – the second half remains on my plate untouched.

After brunch, I turn east on 80th Street to walk toward Central Park, and Jess asks if we can take a slight detour and walk a few blocks up Amsterdam to go to a camera store that she's wanted to visit. I'm intrigued to learn more about her love of photography since she quickly closed up about it the last time it came up. When we walk into the store, her face lights up like the proverbial kid in a candy store. She does a lap around the small store, looking briefly at frames and albums, but most of the real equipment seems to be behind the case, and that's where she goes next. I hang back by a table of acid-free photo albums and watch her talk to the guy behind the counter. The next thing I know, his face is as lit up as hers, and he is pulling a massive camera out of the locked glass case. Jess puts the strap behind her neck and holds her eye up to the viewfinder, and the two of them continue to have a highly animated discussion. Then they change the lens and talk some more, and eventually, Jess gently removes the strap from her neck and almost begrudgingly hands the camera back to the guy.

"Are you ready?" Jess asks me.

"Yeah, I'm ready to go if you are. Are you going to get anything? Are you getting that camera?" I ask her.

"Are you kidding?" she says in a tone of disbelief.

"What? It wasn't good?" I ask her.

"Are you kidding? It's amazing! But it's three thousand

dollars. And that's just for the basic camera. Each lens is like two thousand dollars more!" she exclaims.

"Oh. I had no idea," I say.

We walk in silence for a bit after that. We both veer right at the next block and start walking toward the park, although we still aren't talking. "Do you still use your camera from school?" I ask carefully. I haven't seen her with a camera, but I assume she must have her own camera if she studied photography at RISD.

"I sold it," Jessica says.

"What? You sold it? Why?" I ask, throwing all of these questions at her at once.

Jessica abruptly stops walking and turns around to face me, leaving only a few inches between us. "I needed the money for my security deposit when I first moved to Manhattan. It wasn't like I was going to need it for my job, and I needed a place to live. I don't have the kind of parents who pay rent and buy apartments. My parents wanted me to come back to California to help on the vineyard; if I wanted to do anything other than that, I was on my own," Jessica says. Her tone is hard to read – she doesn't sound angry or sad or resentful; she just sounds matter-of-fact.

I'm desperate not to say the wrong thing. I'm in awe of her strength, determination, and wit, and she's so beautiful that it's difficult to be this close to her and keep my thoughts straight. Instead of saying anything, I reach over, put my arm around her, then bend down and kiss her directly on the lips. I feel her lips part slightly, and I'm overjoyed at this invitation to slip my tongue gently inside her mouth. My mind is racing so fast that I cannot sync my brain and body. I haven't been able to let my guard down for such a long time, but somehow, I knew that Jess would be *the one*. She's the one who will make me whole again and let me trust again – I know now that I'll never have the same issues with sex and intimacy that I've had with other women these past years. I reach my other arm around to embrace her tightly while continuing to part her soft lips with my tongue. I could never imagine being this type of couple, but my body is reacting so strongly that I'm having visions of pushing her against this brick wall on West 85th Street if we can't find somewhere to be alone soon.

The next thing I know, Jess pulls away as if released from a trance. "You're just like the rest of them!" she exclaims. "I thought you were different, but you're not!" Jess yells bitterly and runs down the street.

Chapter 33

Jessica

I wander aimlessly around the park after I leave Zach. I may be upset, but I can still appreciate that it's a beautiful day to be outside. I don't remember when it suddenly became summer; I swear it was only a week or two ago when the trees were beginning to bud, and it was too cold to go out without a coat. Even after four years in Rhode Island and four here in New York, I still haven't adjusted to the temperamental seasons of the northeast. I thought there were supposed to be three months of each season; at least, that's how the calendar always describes it. I knew that we didn't have real seasons in northern California — it was either hot and dry or it was rainy.

I'd pictured three months of winter rolling into a beautiful flowery spring. Then, after several months of that, we'd get a warm and sunny summer from June until August. It's been eight years, and no two years have looked exactly the same. However, every year *has* included a seemingly endless winter, followed by a disappointingly late and short spring, and then without any warning, summer pops up with oppressive heat and humidity that makes most people long for sweater weather.

Miraculously, today is one of those few perfect summer days with just the right amount of heat, no humidity, and plenty of sunshine. Every resident of Manhattan seems to be taking advantage of the weather, and the park is packed; I don't know if I've ever seen it so crowded. The paths are crammed with bikers, runners, rollerbladers, dog walkers, strollers, and a few ordinary pedestrians trying not to get run over. There are couples cuddling on blankets on the lawn next to raucous children playing tag and serious games of frisbee. If I weren't so pissed off at Zach, I would revel in the beautiful scene and imagine the potential for captivating photographs. Instead, I angrily powerwalk along the pavement and chastise myself for my poor taste in men.

I'm beyond furious with myself for sleeping with Brian. I had finally gotten over him, or at least I was in the process of getting over him, and then I went running back the moment he beckoned me. I pound my feet on the ground as if I can stomp out the bad decisions, and it garners curious looks from the couple passing by – it takes a lot to be the "weird" person in Central Park, but I don't care about that right now.

My thoughts immediately go back to the most recent night in Brian's apartment. Deep down, I knew he wasn't sorry for cheating on me. I don't know why I thought it would make me feel better, or wanted, or maybe even loved, if Brian chose me again. When I was lying there next to him after we'd had sex, I knew that we weren't getting back together. I think he even saw this as some sort of perverse conscience-clearing, although it's hard to tell if he even has a conscience. As I listened to him snore, all I knew was that I wanted to get the hell out of there, but on the bright side, I was one hundred percent over him and never wanted to look back.

I spot a couple about my age making out on a blanket underneath a tree, and my surprising first instinct is jealousy – I want to be on that blanket kissing Zach. But that would require Zach to be the guy that I thought he was. The sweet, smart, kind of dorky, and really hot at the same time guy who had a crush on me. Not the kind of guy who has a girlfriend, doesn't tell me about her, and still tries to kiss me!

A second glance at the couple reveals that things have escalated quite quickly. The guy has his hand all the way up her skirt, and because I can't tear my eyes away, I catch a flash of pink underwear being rolled down her thigh. I almost shout at them to "get a room," but this is New York City, after all, and I'm not going to be that pitiful person, even if I am in a terrible mood. Although I no longer wish to switch places with them – I've never been one for hardcore PDA.

I wander aimlessly through the park for another hour or so. I'm still upset with Zach *and* myself, but my pace eventually returns to normal, and my temper has mellowed. I also thought my hangover was gone, but I'm suddenly hot and tired, and all I want to do is take a nap. I'm not ready to talk to Zach, but I refuse to wander around all day just to avoid him. Luckily my meandering has led me close to the park's entrance at West 72nd Street, and I'm only a few blocks from the apartment.

It's cool and quiet when I walk inside. I'd braced myself to see Zach, but the door to his bedroom is wide open, and there's no sign of him. I breathe a sigh of relief that I can put that confrontation off a little bit longer, at least until after my nap. As I'm changing back into last night's pajamas for my nap, I decide to leave Zach a note. I'm still mad, but I think I may have overreacted, and I want to apologize and clear the air to talk later. I glance at my desk and don't see any blank paper, but then I remember seeing a stack of Post-its on Zach's desk.

I've only been in his room a handful of times, and it looks the same today as it has every other time. The room is incredibly tidy, and doesn't look like a guy in his twenties, working at Expedia, lives here. The king-sized bed has an iron headboard and is made neatly with a plaid navy and maroon comforter. There is a large, dark Oriental rug over the parquet floor that is centered in the room and underneath the massive bed. It looks like the kind of rug that belongs in a library or maybe a cigar bar. His furniture is dark and heavy as well. I think it is something like mahogany and looks like a matching set. I remember seeing a pad of yellow Post-it notes right on top of his desk the last time I was here. Now all I see is his closed laptop and a leather cup holding an assortment of pens and pencils. Without thinking, I open the top drawer to see if the yellow pad is there or perhaps something else to write on, and I freeze when I see what's inside.

I've heard of people doing double-takes, but I thought that was a figure of speech. In this case, I literally look in the drawer and then look again because I cannot believe what I'm seeing. At first glance, it looks like a picture of me and Zach. He has his arm around me, and we are both smiling and standing in front of a large building or monument with columns. But then I come to my senses and realize that Zach and I have never been to a building like this, and I've never worn or even seen this pink and white dress, and we've never even posed for a photo together!

I hold the photo closer to my face, with complete disregard for the fingerprints I'm getting on it. Upon closer inspection, it's obvious that it's a picture of Zach and some other woman – but a woman that looks almost identical to me. I get a shiver up and down my spine and drop the photo on top of Zach's desk. I have no idea what's happening, but suddenly everything seems weird and wrong, and I want to get the hell out of here.

As I hurriedly strip out of my pajamas and back into my clothes, I marvel at my change in focus. I could barely keep my eyes open a few minutes ago, and now I'm on high alert. I pack a small overnight bag and call Katie as I'm on my way to the subway. "Can I crash at your place for a few days? I'll explain when I get there."

Chapter 34

Tory

Monday morning feels slow and painful, as always. The past weekend already feels like a distant memory, and next weekend feels so far away. The only bright spots are my violin lessons. I still can't believe I followed through and contacted my old teacher to find a reference. He retired several years ago, but he was thrilled to hear from me and recommended Randall, who currently plays with the New York Philharmonic and teaches lessons for extra income. His schedule isn't particularly flexible, so I had to meet him Saturday late afternoon between his rehearsal and performance. Randall met me outside his apartment building near Lincoln Center exactly as planned. He was older than I expected him to be, but he was extremely professional, and I felt at ease almost as soon as he ushered me into the understated lobby of his non-doorman building. It took me over thirty minutes to find any sort of rhythm, but then muscle memory kicked in, and my body remembered what to do. I have a lot of work to do to get back to where I was before if that's even possible, but I'm thrilled simply to be playing again – especially without any pressure or expectations. Now I just need to make it through the week to my lesson next Saturday.

I'm stuffing padded envelopes with advanced copies of books when a vision of a Garfield comic pops into my head; a fat orange cat sitting on the counter with a thought bubble over his head that says, "I hate Mondays." I never read Garfield comics, so I can't even remember where I've seen it, but I let out a small huff at the absurdity of a cat knowing or caring what day of the week it is, which I suppose is the point of the comic. I might prefer to change places with that lazy cat right about now. It's only Monday, and I'm already done with this week - I'm pretty sure that I'll be stuffing and addressing these padded envelopes every single day; I saw stacks of boxes in the hall, and I think they're all for me.

"Tory, can you come into my office?" my boss, Paula, says, interrupting my daydream of trading places with a fictional cat. I hadn't even noticed that she'd opened her office door, let alone approached my cubicle.

"Of course," I reply. I grab my pink Moleskin notebook and Montblanc pen and follow her into the office. I'm aware that my personal office supplies are excessive for someone with my job description, and likely another reason that my boss doesn't like me, but with so many miserable things about this job, I'm not going to make it even worse by using Bic pens and bulk legal pads.

I follow Paula into her office. Before I have the chance to sit down, she asks me to close the door, which gives me a terrible feeling. I flip through the past several days in my mind to figure out what I could have done wrong. I was late to work last Thursday, but Paula was at a breakfast meeting. I came back late from lunch on Monday, but then I stayed until after six to finish entering her monthly expenses. I spend countless hours each day surfing the Saks and Barneys websites, but I don't think she can check my browser history, so it can't be that.

Before I can think of any additional wrongdoings, Paula pulls a thick manuscript out of her leather satchel and plops it on her desk with a thud. Although most printed manuscripts look identical from the outside, I immediately recognize this as the one I took from the slush pile. I just finished making notes this weekend, and I'm positive that I left it on my desk last night; I have no idea how it ended up in her bag.

"I found this on your desk," she begins. Her tone is cool, and her face is completely blank, making it impossible to discern her feelings on the matter. She hasn't asked a question, yet it seems like she wants me to provide an answer.

I hedge and say, "I got it from the slush pile."

"Really," Paula says. She draws out the beginning of the word, and she doesn't add a question mark to the end, but this single word conveys a hell of a lot of skepticism.

"Yes. I skimmed through the pile a few weeks, or maybe a month ago, and this one seemed intriguing. I've read it a couple of times and made a lot of notes. I was going to check your calendar to see if you had time this week to talk about it," I say.

"Hmmm," Paula says and rubs her top lip with her index finger as if she were applying lip balm. This time I don't take the bait, and I sit quietly and wait for her to speak again. I'm not sure what I'm being accused of, or if I am being accused of anything at all, but nothing about this feels good, and I don't want to risk making it worse.

"I could have sworn this was the manuscript Nathan was talking about," Paula says.

It takes me a moment to remember that Nathan is her nephew. The one who came in was immediately given the title of junior editor and his own assistant. I know I shouldn't complain about nepotism since my father called in a favor to get me this job, but all that did was get me an interview for this crappy assistant position.

I choose my words carefully since she seems to imply that I somehow took this manuscript from Nathan. "I'm not sure about that. I found it in the slush pile in the middle, and it had no notes."

"Hmmm," Paula says again as she flips through the pages of the manuscript. "Looks like you took quite a few notes, or *someone did*," she adds under her breath, but she says it loudly enough so that I can hear it.

My face grows hot, and I ball my hands into fists so tightly in my lap that I feel my nails dig into my palms. I know that Paula never liked me. I'm not the perfect assistant, and I'm sure I don't show the proper amount of enthusiasm for being her assistant, but that's not why she doesn't like me – she's loathed me since my first day of work. It never bothered me too much before now – I foolishly and smugly chalked it up to some sort of resentment of my "youthful good looks." Although Paula is still a very attractive woman, she's the kind of woman you can tell used to be gorgeous and is fighting the aging process every step of the way. My guess is that she's about fifty, and even though I don't like her, I must admit that she looks good for fifty, even if it's somewhat artificial. She gets constant facial peels and fillers and dresses like she's always ready for happy hour. I think she'd look much better if she just accepted her age.

But my thoughts on her unwillingness to age gracefully aren't my priority right now as I seethe at her accusation. I choose my words carefully before I speak. "That manuscript was discarded into the slush pile, and *I* found it. You're always suggesting that we take the initiative and look through there, and this was the first time that I found one that spoke to me." I don't add that this was also the first time I looked through the pile. "*I* believe the book has a lot of potential, and *I* also have a lot of comments and changes that *I* would make, and that's what you see written all over those pages," I say through tight lips, but I am able to keep my voice level.

Paula leans back in her chair and silently thumbs through the pages again. A sigh escapes her lips, followed by, "Hmmm," and it takes all my self-control not to scream an obscenity at her. Instead, I say, "I'd love it if you could take a look and let me know if you also think it has potential."

"I already looked at it. I don't connect with the characters in the way that I require for something I represent," Paula says haughtily.

"But I thought...." I begin to say, but she cuts me off.

"Keep trying. It takes a long time to get a sense of what types of books will sell and what won't." Then she hands me the manuscript, swivels her chair around so she's facing her computer screen, and effectively dismisses me from her office.

Back at my desk, the red light on my phone is blinking angrily at me, accusing me of abandoning my post. I wonder how many of Paula's urgent calls I've missed while I was in her office, being accused of thievery and stupidity. The robotic voice informs me that I only have one new message, and as I sit poised with my overpriced rollerball pen, ready to take down a message, I'm floored to hear my mother's voice.

"Hello, Tory. I hope that it's alright that I'm calling you at work. I was hoping that you could find time to meet me for dinner one night this week. Just me, not your father. Please try to call me back before four today. If not, then tomorrow after ten – when your father will be out of the house. Speak soon."

I press five to hear the message again and then listen to it a third time just to make sure I've heard her properly. I'm racking my brain to remember the last time my mom called me, and I can't recall. I do remember the last time that we went out to a meal together with just the two of us – it was graduation weekend at Tulane. My parents had come down for the occasion. I think it was only the second time they had ever been to visit me at school. Most parents were there for several days to attend all of the graduation events as well as help their children move out of their dorms or apartments. My parents arrived twelve hours before the ceremony. The three of us went to dinner in the French Quarter the night they arrived, and then they attended graduation the next morning. When it was over, my dad got a call and said that it was a work emergency and he had to leave and return to New York. My mom decided to stay, or he told her to stay (I'm not sure which), and we went out to dinner that night together.

Considering that meal was almost four years ago, something must be going on if she wants to share another meal.

I'm sure there are things I should be doing for Paula, but I'm not in the most charitable mood toward her at the moment, and I'm too curious to wait. I dial my parents' home phone number from my desk phone, and after only one ring, a vaguely familiar voice picks up the phone – probably one of the newer maids that I've only met a handful of times. "Hello, Wallace residence; how may I help you?"

"May I please speak with Lizzie?" I ask. It sounds strange to me to say her nickname out loud, although I'm hoping this show of familiarity will cut through any red tape that the household staff may utilize. Only her closest friends are allowed to call her "Lizzie."

"May I ask who's calling? I'm not sure if *Elizabeth* is available at the moment," she says, hammering home the use of her full first name.

"It's Tory, her *daughter*. She asked me to call her," I reply. I may not be a frequent caller, but I'd still like to be able to get through if and when I do call.

"Oh, of course. Miss Wallace, I didn't realize that it was you. I'll get your mother for you immediately. Please hold."

"Sure," I reply.

My mother must have been close by because I hear her voice on the line almost instantly. "Hello, Tory. Thank you for calling me back so quickly – I know we don't often exchange phone calls."

That could be the understatement of the year, although I decide to let this one go. "You want to have dinner? Is everything alright?" I ask her, getting right to the point.

"Yes. There are several matters that I'd like to go over with you. It's long overdue, and it's entirely my fault," my mom says. She sounds contrite and perhaps even guilty, two words I don't often associate with my mother. Angry, bitter, withdrawn – these are words that come to mind first when I think of the woman who gave birth to me.

"When would you be available? I know you lead a very busy life, but time is of the essence, and I'd like to get these things out in the open as soon as possible," she says.

"Should I be worried?" I ask.

"No, no, of course not," she says, although her clipped tone makes it difficult to believe her.

"Can we do tomorrow night?" I ask her. I'm free tonight but need another day to mentally fortify myself. Between the shitty meeting with Paula and this mysterious interaction with my mother, I need time to recover and prepare.

"Unfortunately, I have a dinner with your father tomorrow night that I can't get out of. I can do the night after that?" she suggests.

It's bizarre listening to my mom talk openly about dodging my dad, even though I know that my parents fight incessantly. I'm not sure what my mom wants to share that my father can't know about, but it can't be anything good.

"Sure, that works for me. Do you want to go somewhere near me on the Upper West Side?" I offer.

"That would be perfect. There's no chance we'll run into your father in that neighborhood. Can you email me the address?" she asks.

I'm about to ask if she even *has* email and ask for her address when I remember that we have exchanged a few messages – she has an AOL address that someone set up for her because she needed it for one of her committees. "What kind of food would you like?" I ask.

"You just pick somewhere you'd like to go; I'm fine with anything. See you in two days."

I'm too shocked to even say goodbye. My mouth is still hanging open when I hear the beeping of a dial tone.

Chapter 35

Robin

The meeting with Kendra lifted a giant weight off my shoulders, and my spirits remained high the rest of the weekend and into the beginning of the work week. I hadn't realized how tense this presentation had been making me, and now with that dread gone, I feel like I can breathe again. I want to share my good mood with someone, but other than quick glimpses; I haven't seen much of Tory in days. She was holed up in her room for most of Saturday morning, which I learned later that day was due to a terrible hangover. We hung out briefly Saturday afternoon when I got back from Borders, and I filled her in on my date from Friday night. It wasn't the worst date I've ever had, but certainly, no one I plan on seeing again. The guy talked about himself the entire night, and when he finally asked me a question, it was if I ever thought I'd be interested in a threesome.

Tory was disgusted on my behalf, and after chatting for a

little longer, she excused herself to return to her room. Late that night, when I was about to fall asleep, I heard classical music playing in her room, but when I listened more closely, it sounded like it was a violin solo and that the music was being played live in her room. When I heard the door open and movement in the hall at three in the morning, I chalked the whole thing up to my almost dreamlike state; however, the next morning, it seemed too real to be a dream, and I simply added it to the list of perplexing things about Tory.

Tory went quickly to her room again this evening after returning home from work, but I'm not going to let that dampen my mood. Although my optimism is likely unwarranted, I open the Match.com site and start browsing through potential dates. I've been on enough bad dates to know that guys lie in their profiles and are rarely who they seem to be, yet I look at tonight's list with fresh eyes and hope "Mr. Right" is out there somewhere.

I've been looking for a few minutes when a picture jumps out at me - Ethan. He looks vaguely familiar, but I can't immediately place him. I click on his profile, and it hits me when it gets to the education field; he was in my class at Duke. We were in a study group together freshman year – I think it was for a sociology class. I close my eyes and try to picture those annoying sessions in the library breakout rooms. It's starting to come back to me. He was smart and did all the reading well ahead of time. He was nice enough but kind of immature. Although aren't all college freshmen immature, and some just hide it better than others? He was cute in a dorky kind of way and, if I remember correctly, quite short –

not that it's his fault, but I've always had a thing for taller guys. Although his profile says he's six feet tall, he's either grown or lying. I suppose either one is possible.

I scrutinize the rest of his profile and see that he works as an environmental engineer, likes racquetball, Sunday brunch, and volunteering with a local pet shelter, and he lives on the Upper West Side. He's still a little dorky looking but in a cute way. He has sandy-brown hair that looks like it could use a trim, light brown eyes, and sun-kissed skin. It's difficult to tell, but there's water behind him in his profile picture, and he might be on a boat or on vacation somewhere – either way, he looks relaxed and happy – kind of like a younger Hugh Grant. I don't spend any more time second-guessing my decision, and I "Like" his profile and then immediately shut down my computer.

I log back on twice before going to bed, and my heart sinks a little bit each time. I should have known it was too good to be true. I'm not even sure why I was so excited about Ethan. Something about him felt less like a blind internet match and more like a reconnection with an acquaintance from college. Finally, I realize how stupid that sounds and log back off, wash my face, brush my teeth, put on my soft granny-style pajamas, and go to sleep.

The next morning, I promise myself I'm not going to check my Match.com messages before I go to work. I promise myself in the shower, while I'm brushing my teeth, while I'm making coffee, and while I'm getting dressed. But I break that promise as I grab my bag. I've never had great willpower, and this proves it. I'm prepared to see an empty inbox. I've even given myself a little pep talk. But when I log in and see one new message, my heart skips a beat.

Robin Cromwell – is that really you? What a wonderful surprise to hear from you after all this time. Would you like to get a drink with me after work tonight?

I practically glide all the way to work.

Chapter 36

Zach

I haven't heard from Jess in four days. I don't know what I did to upset her, where she went, or when she's coming back. I've thrown myself into work as a distraction, and that's made my team happy, but I feel awful. I canceled my last two sessions with Dr. Green because things had been going so well, even though she reminded me in strongly worded voicemail messages that psychotherapy doesn't work that way. I'm tempted to cancel my session tonight because the last thing I want to do is talk about my feelings, but I know that's a bad idea.

I spend the day in meetings and even manage to forget about Jess for a few minutes here and there when I'm coaching the developers on the new site functionality. So I have mixed feelings when my calendar alert dings at six o'clock. I'm happy to have made it through the day without breaking down and calling Jess. So far, I've only done that once, and it's not something I'm proud of. On the other hand,

I'm not looking forward to an hour with Dr. Green. I can't sit through another session and continue to bottle everything up. I've been holding it inside for so long; I don't know what will happen when I finally crack.

I thought my appointment was at six-thirty, but when I checked my calendar again, I realized my session is at seven. This gives me enough time to go home, change and drop off my bag before I go to Dr. Green's office. It's not like khakis and a button-down are that uncomfortable, but I always prefer jeans and a t-shirt if I have the option.

I'm waiting for the elevator when I hear a door close down the hallway. I turn to see where the noise came from and see Tory walking toward me. I raise my right hand in a casual wave, and she doesn't wave back to my surprise. Instead, she stops walking in the middle of the hallway as if deciding whether to continue toward me or return back to her apartment. I assume she must have forgotten something inside, but when I squint and see the look on her face, I can tell that she's stopped because she doesn't want to come closer to me.

Confrontation is out of character for me, yet something drives me toward where Tory is frozen like a statue. "What's going on? What did I do? Where's Jessica?" I throw multiple questions at her at once because I'm too impatient to wait.

Tory hesitates, and I'm worried that she's going to turn around and walk away without answering me. I think she considers it but then changes her mind and says, "Are you stalking Jessica?"

"What?" I stammer in reply. "Why would you ask that?"

"How else can you explain it?" she demands.

"What are you talking about?" I ask.

"Don't play dumb. You know what I'm talking about," Tory says. She puts her hand on her hip, starts tapping her foot aggressively, and looks mad.

I have no idea what she's talking about, although I completely believe that Tory thinks I know. I'm unsure of the best approach to make her understand this without pissing her off even more. I try a different negotiating tactic instead. "Look, I know that I fucked up, and I really upset Jessica. But I swear I have no idea what I did wrong."

Tory narrows her eyes and looks at me like she's trying to figure out if she can believe me. She sighs, although I can tell that she hasn't let her guard down. "She found the picture," Tory says.

As soon as Tory says it, it all clicks into place. "Oh shit," I mutter quietly.

"What's going on with that? Have you been following her?" Tory asks.

"It's not what you think. I have to find her to try and explain," I say, turning toward the elevator and repeatedly pressing the call button.

"She doesn't want to talk to you. She's still too upset," Tory says.

"But I can explain it to her," I plead.

"It's not just about the picture. However, she's pretty pissed off about that. She's mad that you were unfaithful to your girlfriend," Tory says.

"What girlfriend?!" I sputter.

"The one I saw you with the other day. The tall blonde," Tory says casually.

"You mean Mallory? She's not my girlfriend! She's an old friend from college. She's more of a sister or lab partner than anything else," I make a sound that's part laugh and part strangled cry. "Did you tell Jess that she was my girlfriend?"

For the first time in the conversation, Tory looks contrite. "I may have told her that," she says. "She was hanging all over you. I just assumed...." Tory trails off.

"I have to go see Jessica right now," I say to Tory. "Do you know where she is?"

"Honestly, I'm not sure. I ran into her when she was running out of the apartment on Saturday with her suitcase. She told me about the picture she found and was shaken up. She said she was staying with a friend, but I don't know any of her friends. I tried calling her yesterday and the day before to check in on her, and her phone went straight to voicemail," Tory says sadly.

"This is such a mess," I sigh.

"I'm sorry if I made it worse," Tory says meekly.

"It's not your fault," I tell her. I'm annoyed that Tory jumped to conclusions about Mallory, but I know that none of this would have happened if I'd been honest with Jessica from the beginning – although if I'd done that, who knows what would have happened.

"Do you want to come in and talk about it?" Tory asks, gesturing back down the hall toward her apartment.

"No thanks. There's somewhere else I need to be. I'll take a rain check, if that's okay."

✳ ✳ ✳

I rarely fidget, but I can't stop my leg from vibrating rhythmically up and down as I sit on the couch in Dr. Green's waiting room. Now that I've finally decided I'm going to talk, I need to get it all out as quickly as possible.

Dr. Green opens the door to her office at precisely seven o'clock. If she's surprised to see me here, she doesn't let on. "Come on in, Zach," she says with a warm smile.

"Thanks," I reply as I walk past her into the office and take a seat on the couch.

"It's nice to see you," she says, and then adds, "I was hoping you would come back."

"Yeah, sorry about the last couple of sessions," I say sheepishly. I paid her in full for the ones that I missed, but I still feel guilty.

She waves her hand as if dismissing my apology. "Things come up, don't worry about it. I'm just glad you're here now. How are you doing? How have things been going? She asks.

I'm glad she has some background, but I wish she was completely up to speed so I don't have to relive it all. Although I guess that's why I'm here now. "Things were great until they weren't," I say.

"I'm sorry to hear that," she says. Dr. Green tents her fingers in front of her face, and I'm tempted to ask why she isn't taking notes yet. "What changed?"

"Remember how I told you about my new roommate, Jessica?" She nods, and I continue. "I didn't tell you every-thing," I admit.

"Okay," she says calmly.

"And the only way that this will all make sense is if I tell you about my relationship with Cassie first," I say. Just saying her name out loud makes my cheeks flush, but it also relieves some of the tension that's been locked away inside for the past seven years.

"Whatever you think would be most helpful," she says. I'm getting annoyed with her inability to steer the conversation when she says, "Zach, tell me about Cassie."

With this simple request, the floodgates open. "Cassie was my girlfriend my senior year of college," I begin. Dr. Green looks up from her legal pad, and I'm guessing she's going to challenge me since I originally told her that I'd never had a real relationship. I clarify before she gets a chance to ask. "I *thought* Cassie was my girlfriend, but I learned later that she never thought of me as her boyfriend," I explain. Dr. Green nods and jots something in her notes.

"She was from Australia and was majoring in architecture. We hadn't crossed paths at any point in our first three years at MIT. We both needed another humanities credit for graduation and ended up in the same introductory anthropology class our senior year. I'm not ashamed to admit that it was love at first sight for me, or at least infatuation at first site. I'd dated other girls in high school and in college before her, but I fell hard for her the second I met her."

Dr. Green makes eye contact with me and nods again, which I assume is a sign to continue. I guess she has nothing to add yet.

"I should have known something was off sooner," I begin, but Dr. Green cuts me off.

"*Should* isn't helpful. Tell me how it was from your perspective." This is her first opinion in our sessions, and I like it.

"We studied together a few times, and then she asked me out on a date. She was way out of my league, but I figured she was just trying to thank me for helping her with her assignments. Cassie needed assistance with the anthropology project, but it turned out that she was also taking an introductory coding class, and I helped her a lot with that as well," I say.

"What do you mean when you say that she was out of your league?" Dr. Green asks.

I always thought this was a common expression, but I explain it to her anyway. "Cassie was beautiful. Tons of guys thought she was attractive," I say.

"I promise this is purely objective, but you are an attractive man Zach. Do you not think of yourself that way?" she asks.

"Honestly, not really. I know that I look a lot better than I did in high school, yet when I look in the mirror, I still see the short, scrawny, acne-ridden kid with bad hair," I admit.

"Hmmm. Well, we can address that another time. Although I think it is safe to say that others likely see you differently. Please continue," she requests.

"Cassie and I started dating a few weeks into the semester – or at least I thought we were dating. Things got physical quickly – much faster than in my previous relationships. We had sex every chance we could get. It was almost all-consuming, and I'd never experienced that type of passion before Cassie. My advisor even had to call me to his office because my professors were starting to notice that I was distant in class and not turning in all my assignments. Luckily, classes were always easy for me, and I got back on track while still dedicating all my free time to Cassie."

I think back on that year and wonder how much I can skip through while still giving Dr. Green the background she needs. "By the time we got to the middle of spring semester, I was completely in love with her. Cassie was busy with an internship of some sort, and I ended up doing almost all her coursework for her. She had an unusual class load. She'd taken all the classes for her major by that point, so she was filling in with math and science classes, which were no problem for me. At first, I was just helping her, but eventually, I was doing everything except taking her in-class tests; and I'm ashamed to admit that I even wrote her papers and did her take-home tests," I confess. I've never said this out loud before, and getting it out in the open feels wonderful and horrible.

"That's terrible that she would ask you to do that for her," Dr. Green says.

"I could have said no," I reply, but I didn't see it that way at the time.

"Anyway, right before graduation, I bought a ring and decided I was going to propose to her. She didn't have any job offers yet, and I had a great job offer from Microsoft. She needed a visa to stay in the country, and I couldn't bear the idea of being apart from her," I say.

Dr. Green nods again, and I swear she's sitting on the edge of her seat, waiting for what I'm going to say next. I would think she's heard a lot of good material over her years as a psychologist, but it appears that my story may be worthy of a top ranking.

"Not to ruin the ending, but obviously, we didn't get engaged," I tell her. I know I need to get through the last part of this, but it's just as painful to say it out loud as it was to hear it seven years ago. I take a deep breath to fortify myself. "When I proposed two days before graduation, she laughed in my face. She thought it was so funny, in fact, that it took her several minutes to calm down from her laughing fit. I thought that it was nervous laughter or that I'd just caught her off guard, but unfortunately, that wasn't the case. Cassie then told me I was the biggest loser she'd ever met. She said that it was pathetic that I thought she'd actually been my girlfriend all this time when I was only her pitiful minion. She told me that no one would ever want to date me, let alone marry me, and she said that I was the worst lover she'd ever had, and if I wanted to do the female population a favor, I'd never have sex again," I tell Dr. Green, staring straight at the floor as I relive the worst day of my life.

"Oh my God, Zach, that's horrible. I'm so sorry that happened to you. That is a traumatic event," Dr. Green says.

"It was terrible, but maybe...." I'm not sure what I was about to say, but Dr. Green cuts me off again.

"But nothing," she says. "No one deserves to be treated like that. You didn't do anything to deserve that, and it wasn't your fault. That kind of trauma causes all sorts of issues with trust and love – I'm not surprised that this has impacted you so deeply," she says.

Her words are so validating that I feel tears spring to my eyes. I've been so ashamed of how Cassie used me, and at my darkest, I even believed the things she said were true. This has kept me from having a normal relationship for the past seven years. Hearing the words now, after all these years, and with Dr. Green's explanations, makes me see everything so differently.

"There's so much to deal with here, Zach. It's going to take a while for you to recover and heal, but the first step is getting it all out in the open. Can I ask how Jessica fits into this equation? What made you ready to talk about it?" Dr. Green says.

I exhale slowly before I say anything. Even if the drama with Cassie wasn't my fault, I know I must own my role in what happened with Jessica, which doesn't feel as good. "Jessica looks exactly like Cassie," I say. "I saw her in the hall a few months ago, and I kind of lost my mind. I lied about needing a roommate and made up all sorts of stories to convince her to move in with me. I thought it was some sign from the universe, even though I don't believe in that. Then I got to know her, and I barely even see the resemblance anymore. She's a completely different person, and she's wonderful, charming, funny, and genuine, and I really like her. She's the first person I could imagine myself completely being with since that horrible incident with Cassie," I admit to Dr. Green. "But now I've screwed it all up, and I don't know if she'll ever be able to trust me," I say sadly.

"We've certainly got our work cut out for us," Dr. Green says. However, the twinkle in her eye and the smile on her face makes me think there might be hope.

Chapter 37

Jessica

I'm lying on the air mattress on Katie's floor, watching her get ready for work. She obviously gets dressed in the changing rooms at the club since hot pants, and her string top would be a bit much to wear on the subway, but she says she prefers to do her hair and makeup at home. Katie is stunning no matter what she has on her face or how her hair looks. I think she looks best without any makeup and her hair up in a simple ponytail, but that's not the look they are going for at the strip club. I'm mesmerized as she uses tiny brushes and sponges to make herself glamorous.

"I wouldn't know what to do with half of that stuff," I say.

"What do you mean?" she asks. The words come out a little funny because she is using her hand to pull down her eyelid, and the contortion of her face somehow impacts her voice.

"I barely know how to use mascara and lip gloss. I'd never

be able to put on false eyelashes or face gel or whatever it is you're doing," I say to her.

"This is highlighter. And you don't need any of it because you're a naturally beautiful farm girl," she insists, glancing over her shoulder to blow me a kiss before turning back toward the mirror.

"Hardly," I laugh before turning over on the air mattress and then rolling off and onto the floor.

Katie lets out a laugh and quickly follows it by saying, "Oh shit, Jess, are you okay?"

"I'm fine," I reply, rubbing my hip and sitting up on the floor.

"Not to bring up a sore subject, but when do you think you'll go back to your place? Of course, you're welcome to stay here. It's just that you're stuck on that air mattress when you have a nice bed and your own room across town. *And* I know that isn't the first time you've fallen off. I keep hearing the thuds," she adds.

"I know I need to talk to Zach. I'm not sure what's going on; it's all so weird."

"You won't know until you talk to him," Katie advises. "Maybe there's an explanation."

I sigh and hoist myself back on the bed. I've been staying here for five days now, and Katie and I have a tacit agreement only to discuss Zach once a day. I assume that we are now done for the day, but I also know that I am overstaying my welcome, and I need to do something soon. I grab my cell phone from my bag and power it on for the first time since I arrived here. I haven't charged it, but since it's been off the whole time, it still has almost a full charge. Katie looks at me and nods at my accomplishment, but thankfully she doesn't say anything. I wait for the cell signal, and I'm shocked when the little icon informs me that I have nineteen new voicemail messages.

"Nineteen messages!" I blurt out.

"That's what happens when you go off the grid," Katie says.

"Oh my God, I hope there's nothing wrong at home. I didn't even think that my parents could be trying to get in touch with me," I say sullenly.

"It's probably people worried about you," Katie says, and then quickly adds, "Did your parents call?"

"I don't know. I'm listening right now," I tell her.

"Just look at the list of calls. You don't have to listen to all the messages first," she chides. "How long have you had a cell phone?" she chuckles.

"You know I'm not good with these things," I tell her. Meanwhile, I seem to have figured out how to find the list of voicemail messages. "Okay, it looks like there are twelve messages from Tory. Four from Brian. One from my cousin. One from my dad. And one from Zach."

"There's only *one* message from Zach?" Katie asks, not trying to hide the surprise in her voice.

"Looks like it," I reply. "The calls from Brian are all super late at night, all four right in a row. Ugh, he's so gross. I can't believe I went down that path, and now he thinks I'm a booty call – I'm so mad at myself," I say and shake my head. "There's a lot from Tory - I hope there's nothing wrong with her. Let me listen to the ones from my cousin and my dad first."

I use the tiny down arrow to scroll through the list to select the message from my dad and then hold the phone up to my ear. Some of the message is garbled, and it's hard to tell what he's saying. I hear the words "slip," "minor," and "just wanted you to know," but he's talking so fast, and there's so much background noise that I can't make out anything else.

"What does it say?" Katie asks. She is looking at me intently with one eye completely made up and one eye makeup-free – it would be comical if I didn't have a pit in my stomach.

"I can't tell. It's really hard to understand him. I'm going to listen to the one from my cousin and see if that helps."

I put the phone back up to my ear and hear the familiar voice, clear as a bell, of my oldest cousin, Greg. "Hey Jess, sorry to be calling you like this, but your mom's had a little accident. She's okay, so don't freak out, but I thought I should tell you. I overheard your dad's message, and I think he underplayed it, so you wouldn't worry. I don't want you to worry, but you're not a little kid anymore, and I think you should know." I let out a little gasp as I wait for the news, and Katie walks over and grabs my free hand with hers. I squeeze her hand and listen to the rest of Greg's message.

"She fell while she was getting out of the truck, and she broke her ankle and tore something in her knee – a ligament, I think. She's going to be fine, but she's going to be laid up for a while, and you know how she can't tolerate any pain medication, so she's just making the best of it with a little vino. Anyway, I know there isn't anything you can do about it, but I thought you deserved to know. Give me a call if you want to talk. And hey, we miss you out here, kiddo," Greg says, and then the message cuts off.

I don't realize that tears are streaming down my face until Katie starts blotting them with a tissue. "What is it? What happened?" she asks quietly.

"It's my mom. She's hurt. And I'm the worst daughter ever. It happened days ago, and I didn't even know about it because I'm shut in here whining about my own stupid problems," I sob into Katie's shoulder.

"You're not a terrible daughter; your problems aren't stupid. Is your mom going to be okay?" Katie asks, looking worried.

"I think so, but I don't know," I moan. Then I blow my nose into the already soggy tissue that's in my hand and quickly pull myself up. "I have to go home," I say.

"Okay. I think it's good that you want to sort things out with Zach," she says.

"No, not *that* home. I need to go to California – I have to see my family," I explain to her.

"Oh right, of course," Katie says. "Do you have the money for a plane ticket?" she asks candidly. Finances were one thing that we were always brutally honest about, and we both know that a last-minute plane ticket to San Francisco doesn't fit into my budget.

"I can put it on my credit card. I was actually getting close to paying it off, but I guess that will have to wait," I sigh.

"When are you going to go?" she asks.

"As soon as I can. I'm going to go back to the apartment now and pack, and I'll look at my computer and see if I can buy a ticket for tonight," I tell her.

"What are you going to do about Zach? And what about Tory? Don't you want to see what all of those calls were about?" she asks. "I'm not even going to ask about the calls from Brian." She says, rolling her eyes. I told Katie about the horrible mistake I'd made going to Brian's apartment, and she gave me a well-earned lecture, but it felt good to share.

"I'll try to give Tory a call later. If I see Zach at the apartment, then maybe we'll try and talk. If not, I'll figure it out when I get back. My mom is much more important," I say.

"What about work?" Katie asks.

"I've got vacation days saved up. I'll call Max as soon as I know when my flights are. My parents said they'd finally gotten basic internet at the vineyard, but I can't imagine the dial-up speed will be fast enough for me to get any work done from there."

"Good luck," Katie says as she wraps her arms around me in a bear hug. "I'm here if you need anything," she reminds me.

"I know," I say to her. "And I'm so thankful for that."

I should be counting every penny, but I can't bear the thought of three subway rides and two transfers to get back to the Upper West Side. I hop in the first cab I see outside of Katie's apartment and try not to think about my mom in a hospital bed with broken bones. I flip open my phone and stare at the messages from Tory and Zach. I have time to listen to them now but choose not to. I just want to get to the apartment, buy my plane ticket, and pack my bags. I can't focus on anything else right now.

There's minimal traffic, and I'm in the elevator and back on the ninth floor before I know it. I hesitate momentarily when I get to the front door; my hand hovers above the door handle with my key suspended in midair. Then I summon my courage and enter the apartment, only to find it completely empty.

Zach has high-speed internet, which I took for granted at first, but I'm incredibly grateful for now. Regrettably, I haven't been back to California in years, and the last time I flew, I had a voucher that came with my student American Express card. I know there are a ton of new travel sites, but I haven't used a single one of them, and I don't know much about them. I know that Zach works at Expedia, and although I'm angry with him, it doesn't mean I shouldn't use the one travel website I've heard of. I'm impressed by the site's usability, and I find a round-trip ticket for five hundred and thirty dollars, which is a lot less than I thought I would have to pay for a last-minute ticket. I enter my credit card information and accept that this trip will likely put me back into debt. I shake those thoughts aside and think about getting out to see my family.

I stare at my closet and try to figure out what to pack. My New York City attire is completely inappropriate for the vineyard, especially if I'm going to be assisting with summer pruning. My clothes are all wrong even if I'm only helping around the house or in the shop. There's not much I can do about it now, so I grab tank tops, cutoffs, and a few pairs of jeans and shove them into a duffel bag. It's been forever since

I've been to Sonoma in the summer, but I did spend every year there until I went to college, and I remember enough to know that it's brutally hot and dry during the day and can get chilly at night. With that in mind, I throw in a couple of sweatshirts and bathing suits.

I give the apartment another look around and try to figure out if I'm missing anything. I know my return plane ticket is in a week, but something makes me wonder if I'll really be coming back here. On that note, I debate leaving a note for Zach to let him know where I'm going and then decide to check Tory's apartment on the way out instead. She left me all of those messages that I still haven't had a chance to listen to, so if she's home, I can see what she wants and tell her where I'm going. Hopefully, I can even ask her to pass the message along to Zach, so I can avoid that confrontation for a little while longer.

I'm about to knock on Tory and Robin's door when I notice that it's been left open a crack. This is the type of situation where I realize I'm still a Northern Californian and not a true New Yorker. If I were, I'm sure I would be alarmed and suspect foul play. Instead, I assume one of the girls had their hands full and didn't close it properly when they came in. I drop my heavy duffel and backpack in the hall and knock lightly as I simultaneously push open the door and announce my presence. "Hello? Robin? Tory? It's Jess. Is anybody home?"

No one immediately answers, and I take a few steps into the now-familiar foyer until the living room comes into view. I've heard the phrase, "My eyes must be playing tricks on me," but this is the first time I've understood it. Zach and

Tory are sitting on the couch, and they are locked in a tight embrace. I can't see Zach's face, but Tory has her eyes closed. "What the hell is going on?!" I yell. The noise startles them, and they jump apart and both start talking at the same time.

I hear them calling my name, but I don't bother to listen to any of their pathetic excuses. Instead, I run out of the apartment, slam the door, grab my bags and race down the hall as fast as my legs can carry me. The elevator is waiting with the doors open, and I say a little prayer of thanks as I jab the door close and lobby buttons simultaneously. In the taxi, I delete the message I haven't listened to from Zach and every single message from Tory. Then I look back at the beautiful pre-war building that was my home for a few short months and burst into tears.

Chapter 38

Tory

"Oh my God, what just happened?" I say to Zach.

"I have no idea," he replies, cradling his head in his hands

We had just returned from our frantic run down the hall, trying to chase after Jess, but she was already gone. I called down to check with the doorman, and he told us that she had gone straight from the elevator to a cab and was nowhere in sight. We've each tried calling her, but the calls go straight to voicemail.

"I left her like a dozen messages over the past few days. I explained to her that I was wrong about your friend from college. Even though I didn't have all the details yet, when I left her the message this morning, I told her that you were coming over this afternoon and you were going to explain the picture. I don't know why she freaked out like that," I wonder aloud.

"Did you see her face? She looked so hurt and angry," Zach says sadly.

"It just doesn't make any sense," I say.

"I wonder where she went," Zach says.

"I don't know. Maybe she went back to wherever she was staying before?" I hypothesize. "I'll try to call her again later. I'm sure it will be fine," I tell Zach, although I don't feel as confident as I sound.

"Are you sure?" Zach asks.

"I hate to do this, but I have to get ready for dinner with my mom. Can we talk more later?" I ask.

"Sure. That's fine," Zach says halfheartedly.

"Hey, thanks again for sharing all of that with me. That couldn't have been easy for you. I'm really glad that you trusted me enough to tell me about Cassie," I say as I reach out and squeeze Zach's forearm.

"Thanks for listening," Zach says. "I hope that Jessica will be as understanding."

"I'm sure she will. She'll probably just need time to process it. It's kind of a lot to take in," I say.

"Yeah," Zach agrees. "Have a good time at dinner with your mom. I guess I'll talk to you later. Let me know if you hear from Jess," he says.

Clearly, Zach has no idea what dinner with my mother entails, or he wouldn't have phrased it that way. "Of course, I'll let you know if I hear anything," I assure him.

As I'm blowing out my hair to prepare for this mysterious dinner with my mother, I keep running through my conversation with Zach. I was pleasantly surprised when he followed up and told me that he wanted to talk and share some information that would clarify his behavior. I was not expecting him to unload a traumatic story about an evil girl from college who stole all his self-esteem and basically ruined him for seven years. And if that was a shocker, then I certainly wasn't prepared for him to tell me that he's actually one of the founders of Expedia and current Chief Technology Officer and not just some random database guy, which is what we all thought he was.

I have no idea how Jessica will receive any of this news, and I'm unsure if she'll be able to get past the creepy factor of his initial attraction. However, I do understand why he would choose not to share his financial information with our group because it's the same reason I haven't been honest about mine. People are funny about money, especially when some people have it, and some don't. They jump to conclusions and make judgments based on what you have, not who you are. I have a feeling that Jessica won't be quick to forgive him for that, either. I push aside the nagging feeling that I'm not much different than Zach as I continue to lie to Robin and Jessica but convince myself that they've never come out and asked me, so it isn't truly a lie.

* * *

I'm meeting my mom at Jean-Georges. She said I could pick anywhere that I wanted to go, but I didn't believe her. She's used to eating in a certain type of restaurant, and it's not the kind that has paper placemats. I'm the first to arrive, and the maître d' shows me to our table. I order a vodka martini with extra olives and stare at the menu while I wait for her to appear.

I'm debating between the steak frites and the sole with vegetables (like the battle between good and evil) when my mom slides into the chair across from me. She's dressed simply in a plain sheath dress and pearls, but I know the dress is Chanel, and the pearls are Mikimoto Reserve and cost over fifty thousand dollars.

"What are you drinking?" she asks as her greeting. I tell her, and she motions for the waiter and orders one for herself as well as a basket of bread. My mother only drinks wine, and I've rarely seen my mother do more than pick at a roll. Even when I was a child, she would admonish me for eating more than a few bites of bread. I was lucky enough as a kid to get fresh croissants in Paris and warm scones in London, but I knew from the age of six that carbs weren't good for me and that I should only have "a taste." I try to hide my shock at her order and wait instead for her to say something.

"Thank you so much for making time for me," she begins.

"No problem," I reply hesitantly. "What's going on?" I ask.

"I'm not sure where to start," she sighs.

I rarely worry about my parents, but she's being so obtuse that I'm getting quite concerned. "Seriously, what's wrong?" I ask again.

"Oh, good, here's my drink," she says as the waiter puts

her glass down in front of her. "Thank you," she says to him. "Okay, a little Dutch courage here, and I should be good to go." She takes a huge gulp from her glass, not even noticing when a little bit spills on the napkin in her lap, and then looks at me and nods once. I swear it's like I've never met this woman before.

"First, I want to apologize for being such a terrible mother," she begins.

It must be instinct because I automatically say, "You're not a terrible mother," even though I've complained of this very thing to anyone who would listen for years.

"Tory, it's true, and we both know it. I'm not here to make excuses for myself. Well, maybe a couple of excuses. Although, I think they're more like explanations. I'm not asking for your forgiveness, as I think that's more about my need for absolution, but I want you to have all the information you deserve. And most importantly, I want to set things straight going forward," she says firmly.

After my afternoon with Zach, I'm not sure if I can handle more confessions and revelations, but I may not have a choice. Also, my curiosity is killing me, and I'm on pins and needles waiting to hear what would explain years of neglect and distance.

She takes another sip of vodka, smaller this time, and begins to talk. "Let's begin with some facts that I don't think you know. Your father didn't grow up wealthy." She must see the look of confusion on my face, so she shakes her head and continues. "He had money, of course, but not *serious* money like he always led you to believe. All the real money comes from my family."

"O-kay," I reply, drawing out the word. Although it's somewhat interesting to learn that the "generational wealth" I've heard so much about is from my mom's side and not my dad's, I'm trying to figure out why this is such a big revelation.

"Let me tell you a story," she says by way of reply. "In some ways, my childhood and adolescence were very similar to yours; in some ways, they couldn't have been more different. Growing up as a child of Manhattan society in the Fifties did not leave much room to deviate from the norm. I know how it sounds to complain, poor little rich girl, but meeting my parents' expectations wasn't easy, and I constantly disappointed them. I was sent to Bryn Mawr for college. And when I say sent, I mean that I have no recollection of even applying; it was simply understood that I would attend," my mother says.

"I didn't know you went to Bryn Mawr. How did I not know that?!" I ask her. The disclosure of my father's money is not nearly as surprising as this.

"That's because I was only there for one year, and it's not something I like to think about," she sighs.

"What happened?" I ask. I'm leaning forward with both hands on the table, and I'm quite sure this is the most genuinely interested I've ever been in my mother.

She spears one of the vodka-soaked olives from her glass and pops it in her mouth. Once she's done chewing and has patted her lips, she continues her story – she's still my mother. "I was initially reluctant to attend Bryn Mawr. To be honest, I had secret hopes of going to a co-ed school like Cornell, but that was never an option. However, after the first few weeks, I began to enjoy it and loved the freedom it gave me. I made real friends, and there were constant opportunities to socialize with boys at The University of Pennsylvania, Villanova, and Haverford. It was such a different time back then. You probably can't even picture what it's like to have girls' and boys' colleges and to have the boys calling on the girls for dates." I think she's going to say more, but her voice trails off, and then she changes direction.

"Anyhow, I met a boy from Penn that first semester of school. He was still from an *important* family, which is what my parents wanted, but he was different than the boys I knew previously. I wasn't the most beautiful girl in high school, and I started blossoming in college, but my classmates were much prettier. However, this boy didn't see me that way. Instead, he thought I was wonderful and beautiful, and we had a special connection," my mom says.

My dad went to Harvard, *not* Penn. I know this because he rarely misses an opportunity to name-drop. Until right now, I've never given my mom's dating life much thought. I have no illusion that my parents love or even like each other, but it's bizarre to hear my mom talk about dating someone other than my dad!

She must not see a weird look on my face or notice if I've zoned out because she continues right along with her account. "I brought him home over the Christmas holiday to meet my parents, and they both liked him. When I went back to school in January, my dad took it upon himself to get to know this boy's father – he was from the Main Line – and they struck up a correspondence. By the time I came home for spring break, they were almost giddy with excitement about uniting our families," she says.

"Wait, did he propose?" I ask.

"I'll get to that; let me just finish my drink." Then she swallows the last of the vodka from her glass and gives a satisfied sigh. "He proposed on the last day of finals, as I was preparing to return to New York for the summer."

"You were engaged to someone else?" I exclaim. I quickly put a hand over my mouth when I realize how loud I'm being.

She waves a hand to dismiss my question and incredulity and continues. "I was ecstatic; if possible, my parents were even happier. My mother started planning the wedding as soon as I got home."

"So, what happened?" I ask. I'm getting impatient with all of the details, and I want to find out what happened with this guy who isn't my dad!

"We set a wedding date for that December. My mother thought summer weddings were overdone and wanted a Christmas-themed wedding at The Plaza. The summer was a whirlwind of planning and occasional train trips back and forth to visit each other."

"What about school?" I ask.

"What do you mean?" she replies.

"I mean Bryn Mawr. Why were you going to get married in the middle of your sophomore year of college? You were going to get married at nineteen, live in a dorm, and go to separate schools?" I question her.

"It was a different time," she sighs. "I wouldn't have returned to school for the spring semester. We were going to get a house near the Penn campus. He would have continued at school, and I would have started setting up our lives. I would have gotten the house decorated and planned our social life. Probably have even had a baby," she says.

"At nineteen? What was the rush? This wasn't the dark ages," I say, and then I remember that none of this happened. "Why didn't you marry him?"

"It was August, and the invitations for our massive engagement party had just gone out. The party was going to be at the house in Newport – it would have been silly to have a party in Manhattan on Labor Day Weekend because all my parents' friends were in Newport. *He* was coming to visit that next weekend, and the moment he arrived at the door, I knew something was wrong," she says. Her face has clouded over, and it looks like she's reliving that day rather than sitting in a restaurant with me.

"He didn't hug or kiss me. He simply said that we needed to talk and went directly to the sitting room. I knew what he was going to say before the words were out of his mouth, although I didn't get them exactly right. He told me that he couldn't marry me because he was marrying someone else," she says sadly; it's as if the retelling is breaking her heart all over again.

"Who was he going to marry?!" I demand, and I don't care that I'm raising my voice this time.

"A girl he knew from high school. It's the oldest story in the book. He got her pregnant, and so they were going to get married," she tells me.

"Wait, he cheated on you?" I ask. I'm now angry at this mystery man from thirty years ago on her behalf.

"He did. I honestly wasn't so upset about that. I know I should have been, but things were different. I wanted to wait until marriage to lose my virginity, and he was fine with that, but it was almost expected that boys from our circle would find girls willing to *put out* who weren't "marriage material" while they were waiting to get married," she says.

"That's so fucked up," I say, not even caring about my language.

"You're absolutely right," she replies. "And most of the guys would have refused to claim paternity or insisted on a back-alley abortion, but he did what he thought was right, and he married her."

"Is that really doing the right thing? Did she even want the baby? Did she want to get married?" I ask.

"We didn't think about it that way back then," she says. "We're getting distracted. The point is that he broke off the engagement."

"So, why didn't you just go back to school? You said you only went for one year?" I push.

"Ah, yes. That's where the story goes downhill," she declares.

"Seriously?! The story hasn't gone downhill *yet?*" I ask her.

She ignores my remark and signals for the waiter, who appears instantly beside our table. "We'll have two more of these," she requests, pointing to our glasses. "And please bring out the bread; I'm famished." Then she turns to me. "My parents were furious with the broken engagement. They blamed me for humiliating them in front of all their friends and turning our family into a laughingstock. I was miserable and embarrassed, but I didn't understand why his infidelity was my fault or why people would blame my parents for it. I planned to go back to Bryn Mawr that fall and move on with my life, but my parents wouldn't let me," my mom says.

"They wouldn't *let* you?" I ask.

"I wasn't headstrong and confident like you. When they said no, I didn't even think to challenge them," she admits. It's hard to focus on the story now because I can't believe that she just gave me two unprompted compliments in a row. I know that isn't the point, but it's hard not to take a moment and bask in this unfamiliar glow.

"I'd never had much confidence to begin with. *He* was the one that made me feel good about myself for the first time, and when he dumped me, he took all of that with him. I spent the next few years living back at home, working on DAR luncheons, and sitting in at my mother's bridge games when they needed a fourth. Meanwhile, my parents spent that entire time telling me a variety of horrible things that made me feel continuously worse about myself: I was too plain for any man to want me; I'd never find a husband; I was damaged goods; they'd be stuck with me forever; I'd end up a spinster, and other things such as that," she says.

"That's horrible, Mom. I can't believe they said that to you."

"I didn't realize it at the time, but it was pretty horrible. It's only been over the past year or so that I've finally realized how badly they treated me. And, in turn, how badly I treated you," she says, and I see tears start to form in the corners of her eyes. "But we can't get into that yet. I need to get all of this out there so you'll understand. I want you to finally know *everything*," she says emphatically.

"I was twenty-three when my parents took a sudden

interest in me again. They'd convinced me that I'd never get married because no one would ever want me, and I'd accepted that as my fate. But then, one night, my mom got all excited and insisted that I get dressed up and ready for dinner. She made me do my hair and makeup, and she was particularly nice to me, which was rare. When I went down to the dining room that evening, your father was there to join us. He was introduced as the son of one of my father's friends who was in town on business, but it was clear that we were being set up," she says.

"Why were they setting you up?" I ask.

"I didn't find out the real reason for several years. At the time, I took the whole thing at face value." She clearly notices the look of annoyance on my face because she says, "Tory, I promise I will tell you; just be patient." I nod, recross my legs and wait for her to continue.

"Where was I? Oh, right, your father came to dinner. He was perfectly fine. I wasn't particularly interested in dating him, but he *was* interested in dating me. My mother was over the moon, and it was the first thing I'd done that had made my father happy in years. We dated for about six months, and the whole time my parents told me how lucky I was that someone was finally interested in me and that he would be my only chance. When your father proposed, I knew that there was only one possible answer," she says quietly.

"You were twenty-three, and you thought that if you didn't marry Dad, you didn't have any other options?" I probe. I'm not trying to sound mean, but I genuinely don't understand.

"I'm sure it must sound crazy to you, Tory. But I didn't

have a college education, and all my friends were engaged, married, or having babies. My family was incredibly wealthy, but none of the money was actually mine. And I'm embarrassed to admit that I felt lucky that someone finally wanted me. I had come to believe everything my parents told me."

"So, you married Dad in 1973, and then I was born in 1976. Is that it?" I ask her.

"It's hard to convey a lifetime in one evening," she says with a dry laugh, "but there's still a little more to it than that. I'm almost done, I promise." Just then, the waiter slides a thick wooden board onto the table bearing a loaf of freshly baked bread and a slab of herbed butter. My mother bypasses the serrated knife and pulls a hunk of bread from the loaf, but she does utilize her butter knife to spread a pat of freshly churned butter.

"We got married in 1973 and moved into an apartment on Park Avenue. Things were fine at first. I wasn't sure what to expect from a marriage. The only example I had was my parents, who didn't have a particularly loving relationship. After a few months, he told me the same things my parents told me. He said that he was doing me a favor by marrying me and that if he didn't do it, no one else would," she says.

I gasp upon hearing this, although I have no idea why I'm surprised. Maybe I thought that he only became a bastard later on.

"Then you were born in 1976 when I was twenty-six years old. I wasn't ready to be a mother, but then again, I don't think anyone ever truly is. I had plenty of paid help because that's how it was. I had a nanny, housekeeper and lots of staff to care for you. I can barely remember what I even did because no one would let me do anything *motherly*. Then, as you know, my parents both died in that plane crash in 1978. Even though I had a strained relationship with them, it was still heartbreaking. Your father took charge of everything at that point – it was what men did, and I didn't expect him to do anything different," she tells me.

Now she takes another bite of bread and, finally, a sip from her water glass, and something about her determined body position tells me that the next thing that comes out of her mouth is going to be huge. "Your father told me that my parents had left all of their money to him. He told me that they left me with some money in a trust and that they provided you with a trust as their only grandchild, but that he was the sole heir of their estate."

"You can't be serious?!" I practically yell. My voice draws the attention of the guests at the tables on both sides of us, and I don't care.

"Unfortunately, I believed him," she says, shaking her head. "I knew my parents were never happy with me, and I had no reason not to trust him. He told me that he handled everything with the lawyers and our financial advisors, and he's been in control ever since."

"Wait, are you saying that he lied? That your parents didn't leave the money to him?" I ask. My head is swimming as I try to absorb all of the information I've learned tonight, as well as this new version of my mother.

"That's exactly what I'm saying," she says, and she shows the first hint of a smile I've seen all night. "I know I should have left him years ago. He's a terrible person, and he's horrible to you. There's no way I can change that, and I'm sure you'll never forgive me. I want you to know that any time I suggested it, or he could even sense that I was thinking about it, he would threaten me. He led me to believe that he had complete control over every penny, even both of our trusts and that if I ever left him, he would make sure that you never got a penny," she sighs.

"You stayed with him so I would get the money?" I ask, feeling dazed.

"Yes. And No. But, yes, that's one of the reasons. I always felt that I didn't have control over my own life because I didn't have any money of my own, and I didn't want you to be in that situation. I was going to stay until the day you got your trust and then get out, no matter what he did to me."

I look at my mom, and it's like I don't even recognize the woman I'm sitting across from. I've thought so many things about her for my entire life, and it appears that all of them were wrong. "Mom, you didn't have to do that," I say, and my voice cracks on the last word.

"Fortunately, that's neither here nor there anymore," she says.

"What do you mean?"

"It's just too much to get into tonight. But let's just say that I finally made a friend outside of my circle, and she introduced me to some other great women. Over the past nine months, I've realized that *I'm* not the problem. Once I got to that point, I got up enough courage to go see the head of our financial management team, and I learned something very interesting," she says with a wry smile. Now I know that she's just drawing it out to tease me.

"Come on. You have to tell me," I beg her.

"I learned that *all* the money is in my name. The entire estate. Everything. Your father has been lying to me for the past twenty-four years since my parents died. *That's* why he didn't want me to leave. If I divorce him, the prenup that I didn't even know we had, leaves him with one million dollars, not a penny more."

Chapter 39

Robin

I'm not sure what to expect walking up Amsterdam Avenue toward West 79th Street to meet Ethan at Blondies for our first date. I'm not really a 'sports bar' kind of person, although I have been here a few times over the years. Jenny used to love coming here to watch Duke basketball games, and I occasionally came with her. I would complain that most people in the bar had a Peter Pan complex and were only here to relive their college days, and then Jenny would laugh and tell me that I was a curmudgeon. We've exchanged a few emails since our online reunion, and from what he's told me about himself, Blondies doesn't seem like the type of place he would pick.

I brace myself for the screaming fans and wall-to-wall bodies, but when I step inside the bar, that's not what I find. There's a low-level hum of voices, and only half the tables are occupied. The televisions are split between Yankees and

Mets games, and the patrons at the bar are intently watching the games but not screaming at the players the way it was when I was here back in March during the Final Four tournament. I glance to the left and immediately spot Ethan sitting at a table with his hands wrapped around a full pint of beer. He stands up as soon as he sees me and offers a shy wave. I'm ashamedly relieved that Ethan is even more attractive in person than he is in his Match.com profile picture – and he looked great in that. I don't want to be shallow, but there is something irresistible about immediate physical attraction. I've also had enough experience to know that when guys misrepresent themselves with their pictures, that's not the only thing they are lying about.

I slide into the seat across from him, but before I have a chance to say as much as the word, "hi," Ethan announces, "I'm so sorry for picking this place. I was thinking of a coffee place near here with a similar-sounding name. After I sent the email, I knew it wasn't quite right, but it wasn't until I looked up the address when I was coming to meet you that I realized my mistake. Do you want to leave and go somewhere else?" he asks, looking mortified.

The tension seeps from my shoulders as I shake my head. "It's totally fine," I reply. "We already have a table, and it's not nearly as crowded as I thought it would be. Although, I'd be lying if I said I wasn't a little bit relieved that you chose this by accident," I say, and let out a small laugh.

Ethan exhales and visibly relaxes, although it doesn't look like he's at the point yet where he's ready to laugh about it. I almost say, "Don't worry, this will be a funny story someday," and I clap my hand over my mouth to keep the words from escaping. We're five minutes into our first date, and I'm already thinking well into the future – what is wrong with me? This isn't like me at all. Although, even in the banter of our emails over the past few days, there's been a unique ease and comfort that I've never experienced with anyone else.

I command myself to focus on what Ethan is saying and not the noise in my head. "What would you like to drink?" he asks. I pray that this is the first time he's asked the question, and he hasn't been trying to get my attention while I've been lost in my thoughts.

"This probably isn't a great place to order wine, right?" I joke with him.

"I think beer is your best bet," Ethan says. "They have a huge list on tap."

Beer is never my first choice, even though I'll occasionally drink it. It might be because I had my fill of cheap keg beer in plastic Solo cups during college, and I've never developed a taste for good beer. Whatever the reason, the only beer I ever order is light beer in a bottle. I like it if it's really cold – it barely tastes like beer and is refreshing. I hesitate before I order because I always overthink my decisions on dates. I worry that he's going to judge me for ordering a flavorless light beer when he just told me how many options they have on tap. Then I force myself to order what I want and not what I think I'm supposed to get. If I'm ever going to be in a real relationship or even enjoy dating, I must be myself.

"I'll have a Bud Light, please. And I'd rather have it in the bottle; I don't need a glass," I say.

"Coming right up," Ethan smiles.

He returns a couple of minutes later, holding two bottles of beer. He places one in front of me, puts the other in front of his seat, and moves his barely touched pint glass out of the way. "Cheers," he says, holding up his bottle in a toast.

"Cheers," I reply, raising my bottle and lightly tapping it against his. "You didn't have to get one just because I did," I say, indicating my bottle of beer.

"Oh, I know. I should have ordered it in the first place. This is going to sound so stupid. I'm not much of a beer drinker, but whenever I order a light beer, my friends give me a hard time. I ordered that pint of IPA when I got here because I thought that's what I should get, even though I just wanted a cold bottle of light beer. Isn't that crazy?" he asks.

"It's not quite as crazy as you think," I reply sincerely.

The remainder of the evening flies by with easy conversation, several more rounds of light beer, and too many buffalo wings to count. We talk about college, work, family, roommates, racquetball, and cooking until after midnight. I have to check my watch twice to confirm the time; the first time I look at my wrist, I'm sure I've gotten it wrong; there's no way we've been sitting here talking for over five hours!

"I've got to get home," I say reluctantly. "I have to get up for work tomorrow."

"Me too," Ethan replies. "I can't believe it's so late."

"Thanks. This was fun," I exclaim too loudly as soon as we get outside. I'm not ready to say goodbye, and I'm not sure if we should shake hands or hug or kiss, but my nerves are getting the best of me, and I'm certain that I'm about to ruin the best date I've ever had.

"I'll walk you home. If that's okay with you," Ethan quickly adds.

"You don't have to do that," I say to him, although the prospect of another few minutes together makes me giddy, so I amend my statement and say cautiously, "unless you were going to walk anyway."

Ethan smiles at me and replies, "I'd love to walk. And it's right on my way."

I don't put up more of a fight, and we walk the few blocks together until we arrive in front of my building. Ethan stops walking and turns to face me, adjusting his glance downward so he's looking into my eyes. "I had a great time tonight, Robin."

I love the way he says my name and that it sounds heartfelt and not cheesy when he says it. "I had a great time, too, Ethan," I reply, copying him.

"I'll call you tomorrow," he says, leaning down and kissing me on the cheek.

It's such an innocent gesture, the cheek kiss. Parents, friends, siblings, and even strangers kiss on the cheek, but there is something about the way Ethan leans into me and breathes before kissing me softly on the side of my face that feels sensual and certainly not platonic. "Okay," I whisper back, feeling almost lightheaded from the mix of excitement and beer coursing through me.

I watch Ethan walk down West 78th Street and then turn north on Columbus Avenue, and that's when I remember he mentioned in his first email that he lives on West 87th Street and Broadway - my apartment is definitely not "on his way."

* * *

I've been counting the hours since my first date with Ethan, and now that it's finally time for our second date, I get stuck in a meeting, and I'm running late! I rush into the apartment and hurriedly throw my bag on the couch, narrowly missing Tory. "Oh my gosh, I'm so sorry! I didn't even realize you were there. You're sitting so still and didn't say anything when I came in." I say this to explain *and* apologize.

"It's okay. I'm reading this manuscript, and I got sucked in. I feel like I haven't seen you in days. Do you want to order dinner and watch *The West Wing?*" Tory asks hopefully.

"Sorry, I can't. I have a date," I say, trying to hide my eagerness. I don't want to get my hopes up for my second date with Ethan, but I can't seem to keep my enthusiasm under control.

"Oooh! Who's the date with? You seem excited." Tory comments. She sits up straight and puts the massive document she was holding on the cushion next to her to give me her full attention.

"It's a guy from college. I barely knew him freshman year. But we still know several of the same people. It feels less like an online date and more like a date with an old friend. Does that sound stupid?" I ask her.

"Not at all!" Tory assures me. "Where are you going? What are you going to wear? These are the important questions." I laugh at her faux dramatics, and she takes this as a sign to jump off the couch, march me into my bedroom, and start sifting through the clothes in my closet.

Although living with Tory is entirely different from living with Jenny (and I miss Jenny all the time), I feel incredibly grateful that the universe brought Tory into my life. Of course, she's still a complete mystery to me most of the time, but I think she's a good person, and she's proving to be quite a good friend.

"You still haven't told me where you're going. I need to know that to figure out what you're going to wear," Tory says.

"We're going to Blue Smoke for dinner. It's in Murray Hill. Ethan says it's really good," I tell her.

"He's taking you for barbeque on your second date?!" she asks incredulously.

"He said the food is good and that they have great drinks, too," I add.

"I've been there. The drinks are great, and the food *is* good, but that's not the issue. You can't eat barbeque on a second date! You're going to be a mess," Tory insists.

"I'll be fine," I reply, although now I'm second-guessing if this is true. "If you've been there, then you know what kind of place it is. What should I wear?" I ask her.

Tory shakes her head but turns her attention back toward my closet. "Definitely dark colors," she mutters, but I think she's talking to herself. "Put on those bootcut True Religion jeans you had on the other day," Tory instructs.

I do as she says and grab the pair from the top of my shelf. These are my only pair of "fancy" jeans; I'm not surprised that these are the ones she picks for me to wear. I almost had a heart attack when I saw the price tag and handed over my credit card at Bloomingdales last month.

"I'll be right back," Tory says.

I don't know if she's giving me privacy to get dressed or if she has something else to do – maybe she just has to go to the bathroom, but I wriggle into the jeans and take a moment to admire myself in the mirror in her absence. I don't magically have Tory's body when I put these pants on, but they do make my butt look pretty damn good and make my legs look several inches longer. I tried on about thirty pairs to get the right ones, and these were the perfect fit. They weren't too low cut to make me uncomfortable or self-conscious; they hit at just the right place to make me look curvy and sexy.

"Yes! Those are perfect," Tory exclaims as she comes back into the room. "Put this on," she says as she throws a piece of clothing at me.

"What is it?" I ask.

"It's a shirt. It will look perfect," she declares.

"One of your shirts?" I ask stupidly.

"Yes, of course, it's one of mine. Who else's shirt would it be?" Tory laughs.

"Your clothes would never fit me," I say to her.

"Yes, they will," she argues. "Just put it on. It's the perfect shirt for your date."

Reluctantly, I shrug off the blouse I'd worn to work that day and slip Tory's shirt over my head. It's a simple black tank top and quite possibly the nicest fabric I've ever felt against my skin. It hugs my body perfectly, but it isn't clingy or tight. It also has a dip that shows the perfect amount of cleavage. As I slipped it on, I saw that the label said Dolce & Gabbana. I can't begin to imagine how much this top costs, and yet again, it creates questions I can't answer, such as how can Tory afford clothes like this?

"Oh, my God! That looks perfect on you!" Tory squeals. "That shirt never looked that good on me. It's like it was meant for you. You can keep it," she says casually.

"What? I could never keep this. I'm not sure I even feel comfortable borrowing this," I stammer.

"It's done. It's yours now. I would never be able to wear it again, knowing how much better it looks on you. Now that I think about it, I have a couple of other Dolce shirts that would be perfect for you! I'll grab them later and throw them on your bed. Your hair looks perfect because it always looks perfect – ugh, I'm so jealous. You just need a little makeup touch-up, and you're ready to go," she says as she spins me around and points me in the direction of the bathroom.

I emerge a few minutes later, and Tory is back on the couch, this time with a plate of food in front of her on the coffee table.

"What'd you make?" I ask quizzically.

"That's funny. It's leftovers from last night that I'm going to pick at while I read this. It's from Jean Georges," she says nonchalantly.

"Oh," I reply, at a loss for words. Tory left me a message that she was going out last night and would be out late, but I thought it seemed casual. I've obviously never been to Jean Georges and know nothing about it, except that it is the top restaurant in Manhattan. I wouldn't think eating dinner there would be a non-event!

As I wait for the elevator, I can't stop thinking about all the things I know about Tory and what I don't. Now tonight, she's throwing luxury clothes at me and talking about opulent dinners like they're nothing, and the pieces finally add up.

I'm not sure if she's required to keep it a secret because her agency makes her or if she's just embarrassed to tell me. I want to find a way to tell her I'm here for her and can help her. I'll try my hardest not to judge her for being an escort – I just need to figure out the best way to let her know.

Chapter 40

Jessica

The best thing about the vineyard is that there's always work to be done, and I never have long to dwell on my own problems. When I start to think about that crazy picture in Zach's drawer, or Tory and Zach secretly hooking up, or my dreams of being a photographer never coming true, someone yells my name and needs my help. It may not be a long-term solution to deal with my issues, but it's not a bad fix in the short term.

Ordinarily, my parents would ask tons of questions, but thankfully they don't know that there's anything wrong. Instead, they think I came home to help because of my mom (out of guilt or obligation) and assume that I'm dying to return to my great job, roommate, and friends in New York. If I hadn't had to explain my new address, I'd probably let them believe that Brian and I are still together. I think it works best for all of us this way, and I have no interest in filling them in on the disaster that my life has become.

"Jess, you almost ready to shut it down for the night?" my cousin Greg calls out.

"Almost," I call back. I'm in the back room, which my mom uses as an office, and I'm attempting to go through the paperwork from the past week. When I checked with my mom this morning, she was visibly anxious that things were already starting to fall apart in her absence. My dad tried to assure her that he'd been checking the mail and keeping up with the orders and the bills, but everyone knows that my dad is more of a big-picture guy when it comes to numbers, and his real place is out in the rows or in the cellar. I promised her that I would spend the day in her office making sure everything was up to date. She looked somewhat calmed by this but not entirely relieved, and now that I'm here, I can see why. She may be current on the bills and orders, but she has an obscure, antiquated system of Post-it notes, tiny scraps of paper, and three-ring binders that haven't been updated in twenty years.

"You ready to walk back over to the house for dinner?" Greg asks as he pokes his head around the corner of the room.

"Almost," I reply, "Hey, does this computer even work?" I ask. I point to the hulking piece of machinery that takes up half of my mom's desk.

"I'm not even sure," he laughs. "She got it a few years ago because my mom told her she needed a computer. She tried to use it, and it didn't go so well. I don't even think it's plugged in anymore," he says.

"Oh, my God! That's why I couldn't turn it on! I didn't even think to look at that," I say, shaking my head and laughing.

"I'm not sure it would have done you any good if you had plugged it in. Aunt Kelly does everything on paper," Greg says, referring to my mom.

There are so many things I want to say, but I bite my tongue and don't say any of them. I've been home less than a week, and although it's surprisingly wonderful to be with my family and be able to help out, it's clear that they view me as a bit of an outsider, and my opinions aren't always welcome. I think of myself as extremely low maintenance and laid back, but it turns out that's only by New York standards. I received side-eye stares and exasperated sighs over my first few days back on everything from my preference for seltzer over tap water to my inability to remember how to drive a stick shift pickup truck. So now, I ignore the comment about my mom's refusal to use a computer and simply say, "Let's get back for dinner; I'm starving."

After a lively dinner with my entire family, my dad, uncle, and cousins offer to clean up while my mom and I sit on the back porch. My mom is quite agile on her crutches now and barely needs help getting around. Although she still can't put any weight on her leg and can't use the crutches on uneven terrain, so it will be a while until she can resume her normal role here. I bring two glasses of wine outside, and we sit on rattan chairs next to each other, and she puts her leg up on the ottoman.

We don't say anything for a few minutes; we simply sip our wine and stare out at the beautiful vista in front of us. I've missed this view - perfect rows of vines as far as the eye can see, backlit by a multicolor California sunset. If I wasn't seeing it with my own eyes, I wouldn't believe that it was real. In Manhattan, I convinced myself that I preferred the "concrete jungle" to northern California's mountains, meadows, rolling hills, and flat plains. But now that I'm here, I'm not so sure.

"Penny, for your thoughts?" my mom asks, breaking the silence.

"I was just thinking," I say.

"That's pretty vague. Care to be more specific?"

"I don't know. I was thinking that maybe I won't go back to New York," I say. I don't realize I'm thinking it until the words are out of my mouth.

"Huh," my mom replies. I'm not sure what I expected, but I thought she would be more excited than that!

"You don't want me to come back?" I question her.

"Of course, I want you to come back. *If* that's what you want to do," she says without changing the volume or tone of her voice.

I hesitate before sharing, but then I decide it's the best thing to do. "I know you think everything is great back in New York, but things aren't going all that well," I admit.

"I know," she says casually.

"What?! What do you mean? How do you know?" I say, exasperated and confused by her response.

"Jessica, darling, you've never had much of a poker face. I don't know exactly what's happening, but I knew from the second you got back here last week that you were running away from something. I was just waiting until you were ready to talk about it," she says.

I'm the tiniest bit annoyed that my news isn't a shocking revelation, though a feeling of relief quickly overshadows it. No matter how long I'm away from home and how distant I feel from my family, they still know me and are here for me when it matters.

For the next hour, I pour my heart out and tell my mom everything. I give her the details about Brian and tell her about Zach and Tory, my unfulfilling job, my worries about money, and my fear that I'll never realize my dream as a photographer. She occasionally interjects to ask a clarifying question or clucks sympathetically, but other than that, she just lets me vent and weep. When I'm all done, I feel empty and a bit better.

My dad comes onto the porch just as I've finished, and I'm guessing he's been monitoring the scene from inside the house and was waiting for the "all clear" sign before he came out. Instead, he says, "Hey, Jess, you've got a visitor."

"Someone's here to see me?" I ask quizzically. I wrack my brain and wonder if there's a friend from high school who found out I was in town and stopped by – I didn't do a great job of keeping in touch with people after I left for college, so that would be surprising.

"Can I send him out?" my dad asks.

My mom replies, "Sure," before I have a chance to respond.

I'm glad I'm still sitting down because otherwise, I might have fallen over from shock when Zach walks out onto the porch and says, "Can we talk?"

Chapter 41

Zach

Jess looks like a bucolic version of the person I've known in New York. She has a pinkish tint to her cheeks, and her hair is in a loose braid and is a lighter color than it was a week ago. The woman next to her with the bandage on her knee and cast on her ankle must be her mom, but she crutches surprisingly quickly off the porch without introducing herself.

"What are you doing here? How did you find my parents' house?" Jess asks.

"You told me the name of the vineyard," I remind her.

"Oh, right," she says. "Did you bring *Tory* with you?" she says bitterly.

"No," I reply. "Why would I bring Tory?" I ask.

"Let's just get this over with," she says, sounding annoyed.

I knew she was going to be mad. Tory and Dr. Green prepared me for this, but part of me was hoping her anger would dissipate with her time away – unfortunately, that doesn't seem to be the case. "Can I sit down?" I ask as I point to the rattan chair across from her.

"I guess so," she shrugs and then folds her arms protectively across her chest.

I've gone over this speech a hundred times in the past week. And then I rehearsed it at least a dozen more on the drive here from the airport. Still, now that I'm here sitting across from Jessica, it doesn't feel like it will be enough. She's looking at me expectantly, and I'm worried that if I don't say something soon, she'll ask me to leave, and I'll lose my chance entirely. "I understand that you're upset," I begin and cringe as the words leave my lips. This lame opener was never part of the plan.

"Upset?" Jessica says sarcastically. "You could say that. I'm also confused, hurt, and angry," she fires off.

"Right. Of course. I didn't mean to say it that way. I have a lot to explain. Will you give me the chance to tell you all of it?" I beg her.

Jess crosses her arms even tighter over her body and raises her eyebrows in a gesture that screams "whatever," but she doesn't say "no," and I take that as an invitation to keep going. I start at the beginning and tell her everything I told Dr. Green and then Tory about my relationship with Cassie in college. Jessica's body language is unreceptive at the beginning, but when I arrive at the painful retelling of the "breakup," Jess softens, and her face looks sad and almost sympathetic.

"That's terrible. I'm sorry that happened to you, Zach. But I don't understand the rest of it. Were you searching for someone who looked like Cassie to be your roommate? What's going on with your girlfriend? What's happening with you and Tory? I still have so many questions, and I don't feel like you've been honest with me," she says.

I exhale loudly and wish I could ask for a glass of wine or even a glass of water before I keep talking; however, I sense that it wouldn't go over well. I don't think Jess is going to have much sympathy for the rest of my story, especially since I haven't been honest with her, but I've come this far, so I need to tell her everything, and then she can decide what she wants to do after that.

"I don't have a girlfriend. Tory ran into me when I was with an old friend from college, but Mallory is definitely not my girlfriend. And there is nothing going on between me and Tory. I was only talking to her to try and find out how to get in touch with you. I told her about Cassie to help her understand the bigger picture, and you happened to come over right after I told her. She was simply hugging me."

Jess doesn't look entirely convinced, but the pained expression on her face relaxes ever so slightly. Unfortunately, I know that the worst is yet to come. I tell myself that it's like ripping off a band-aid, and if I do it quickly, it will be less painful. In limited mouthfuls, I attempt to explain a few key facts. First, I own the apartment outright and never needed a roommate. Second, I'm one of the original developers of Expedia, and I made a lot of money when I sold the company. Third, I initially asked Jess to be my roommate because I was so drawn to her physical resemblance to Cassie that I couldn't think straight, and I needed to find a way to be around her. And finally, I can't believe that I ever thought Jess and Cassie were anything alike, and I like Jess only for who she is, and I hope she might someday forgive me.

When I'm done talking, Jess stares at me but doesn't say anything or alter her posture or expression. I'm desperate to know how she feels about everything I've just unloaded onto her, yet I can tell that she's not ready to respond. So, instead, I get up and walk back through her parents' house, where everyone has disappeared behind closed doors, get in my rental car, and drive back to my hotel room to wait and see what happens next.

Chapter 42

Tory

Paula has ignored me for the third day in a row. I don't miss her nagging requests or condescending tone, but I'm certain that I'm going to get a call from HR any moment that tells me to pack up my stuff and leave. Now that I've learned all about the financial situation from my mom, I'm not really concerned about needing the paltry salary from this job, but I still don't want to get *fired*. And I especially don't want to get fired by Paula!

As a precaution, I took the manuscript I've been editing home with me and left it there. I'm not sure if I'm supposed to do that or not, but Paula made it clear that she wasn't interested, and I feel like it has real potential. I don't know yet what I could do with it on my own. However, it has the author's contact information inside, and I want to keep it in a safe place, which means far away from here.

My desk phone rings, and I wonder if my negative thoughts actually had the power to summon a call from HR, but then I see it's from an external line. "Hello, Paula Smith's office," I answer robotically.

"Tory, it's your father," the man's voice on the other end says.

"Hello, Dad," I say.

"We need to talk. Right now," he says gruffly. My dad's voice is usually strong and commanding, but it almost sounds hoarse and gravelly today, as if he's sick.

"I'm at work right now," I say calmly.

"Come to the house immediately after work, or there will be consequences," he demands.

A couple of weeks ago, this comment would have made my blood run cold, and I would have agreed to be there as soon as I could leave the office. Instead, I reply, "That's not going to work for me today. If you want to tell me something, we can find a good time to meet."

"What kind of bullshit response is that!" he explodes. "I know you've been talking to your crazy mother. She doesn't know what the hell she's talking about," he rants.

Unfortunately, I've listened to my father speak badly about my mother for years, so this isn't a surprise. I'm ashamed to admit that I believed some of the terrible things he's said. I'd like to think that I wouldn't have needed any proof from my mom after our dinner last week to show that my dad is a manipulative liar and my mom is telling the truth. But after years of living with their volatility, it did help when my mom's attorney sent over copies proving that she is in complete control of the estate, with the exception of my sizable trust, which is mine and mine alone.

"I've got to go, Dad," I reply coolly. I can still hear him shouting as I hang up the phone.

* * *

I'm meeting my mom again for dinner after work. She made me swear that I would pick a *local* restaurant this time, but I still can't picture her eating somewhere that wouldn't qualify for Michelin stars. I pick DB Bistro for us because it's more casual, not too far from work, and still has the legitimacy of being a Daniel Boulud restaurant.

My mom is already sitting at the table when I arrive, and she is engrossed in conversation with the woman at the table next to her. Manhattan is a small town, which happens to have millions of residents, and I sadly accept that we will sit beside one of her society friends for the evening. I slide into the chair across from my mom, give her a smile and wait for her to notice that I've arrived.

"Hi, Tory," My mom says warmly. "Tory, this is, oh, I'm so sorry. What did you say your name was again?" she says, looking at the woman to her left.

"It's Evelyn. Nice to meet you, Tory," the woman says as she extends a hand to shake mine. "I'm meeting a friend, and your mother and I got to talking while we were both waiting. I'll leave you to your dinner now."

"Nice to meet you," I reply automatically. My mother is decidedly unfriendly and never talks to strangers. I don't think I've ever seen her strike up a conversation with someone at a neighboring table, and if someone were to try and speak with my mother, she would shut them down immediately. I barely know what to make of this new version of my mom – the one that isn't weighed down by criticism and cruelty.

"I should warn you that your father is going to call you," my mom says.

"He called today," I inform her.

"I filed papers today and told him to move out," she says proudly.

"Wow, does it happen that easily?" I ask her.

"I'm not sure I would call any of this easy, but he doesn't have a leg to stand on, and he knows it," she says.

"Because of your parents' will?" I ask.

"Yes. Because of that. And he also violated the prenup. Of course, I didn't even know that my parents had us sign one, but they wanted to protect the family," she says, taking a swallow of her wine.

"So, he gets one million dollars, and everything else is yours?" I question.

"That was only if we got divorced and he held up his end of the marriage. Technically, he shouldn't get anything, but I haven't decided what I'm going to do. I just want this to be over and done with as quickly as possible," she says.

"What do you mean?"

"I hope this doesn't upset you or come as a shock. I debated whether I should even tell you, but I think you can handle it," my mom says. I notice that her small hand is trembling slightly, and in a completely uncharacteristic move, I reach over and steady it with my own.

"Mom, I'm fine. You can tell me whatever you want. I doubt that anything will shock me at this point."

"Your father has had many affairs over the course of our

marriage. I was devastated by the first one, but slowly I became numb to them. He thought I would never be able to divorce him, so he became increasingly blasé with each woman – he barely bothered to hide them the past several years, which is how I have detailed proof of every relationship."

I'm not shocked when she tells me this. I mean, *of course,* my dad cheated. It's exactly the kind of thing he would do. I shouldn't expect anything different from him. But for some reason, it still stings a little bit. I think it's mostly on my mother's behalf, but I also feel oddly betrayed. "I guess that fits," is all I say.

"I am so sorry to have to tell you this. Please know that I didn't make the connection initially, and by the time I knew, I didn't feel there was anything I could do about it," my mom pleads.

"What are you talking about?" I ask irritably. I'm starting to get frustrated with her cryptic messaging.

"Your father was sleeping with Paula," my mom says with a forlorn sigh.

It takes a minute for this to sink in. "My boss, Paula?!" I cry.

"Yes. That's how he knew her," she says.

"He got me a job with his mistress?!" I say. I know my voice is way too loud for the tight surroundings, but I can't control the volume as the realization sinks in. "And you knew?" I ask.

"I didn't know at the time. I didn't find out until after he stopped seeing her," she says. "I didn't know what to do at that point. I was sure he would be furious if I told you. He also told me that he'd changed your trust, which made me concerned about you losing your job, although now we know it was all a lie. I'm sorry, Tory."

"That's why she hates me so much!" I say as this new reality settles in.

"I'm sure she doesn't hate you," my mom says.

"No, she does. She definitely hates me. But at least it makes sense." I've gotten a lot of unexpected information so far tonight, and we haven't even placed our main course orders! Still, I feel better about my situation at work than I have in months. Paula is never going to like me, but it's not my fault. And now I can ignore everything she's said about that manuscript and trust my gut; she didn't want me to succeed with it, and I think it has potential.

We spend the rest of the meal discussing my mom's early notions for starting a charity that could help educate women of all socioeconomic levels about emotional abuse and the importance of self-confidence. I trade ideas with my mom, but the entire time I'm thinking about the manuscript on my coffee table and what I'll be able to do with it if I'm not affiliated with an agency or publishing house, and also sitting on a lot of money.

I hail a taxi for my mom, which is a big change from the car service that usually ferries her and my dad around the city, and just as she's about to pull away, I remember something. "You never told me the real reason your parents invited Dad over for dinner."

She gives me a curious look, and then it's clear that she understands. "I'll tell you next time," is all that she says, and the cab pulls away.

Chapter 43

Robin

I *know* it's a cliché, and I hate people who say things like this, but I feel like I've known Ethan forever, not just for a few hours over three dates. This thought plays on a loop over and over in my head as I ride up the elevator to my apartment.

"You're glowing!" Tory gushes as soon as I open the door. "How was it? Tell me everything!" she demands.

I can feel the smile stretched across my face, and I know there is no hope of containing it, so I don't even try. "It was amazing. It was perfect and comfortable, and it felt like our twenty-third date, not our third date. But not in the way that dull couples stare at each other because they've run out of things to say. It's like we finish each other's sentences, and yet we can't stop talking because we want to learn everything about each other." I feel bad gushing like this, especially since I know Tory sat home the past few nights and went to bed early. I don't even know how to begin the conversation and ask if something happened to her at *work*.

"That's wonderful. I'm so happy for you," Tory says thoughtfully. "When's the next date?" she asks.

"The day after tomorrow. We made plans before he even kissed me goodnight." I beam at her, remembering his eagerness to see me again and his passionate kiss at the door. I toyed with the idea of inviting Ethan upstairs because most guys are anxious to get to the bedroom. I'm sure he would have been interested but he seemed just as happy to move at a slower pace.

"What are you watching?" I ask as I kick off my shoes and plop down on the couch next to Tory. Ethan and I went to dinner right after work, so it's still relatively early. Watching mindless TV for an hour or two before bed sounds perfect – especially with my big presentation tomorrow afternoon.

"It's *Survivor All-Stars*. I think the season is over now, but I still have to watch the last three episodes on TiVo. If you know, don't tell me who wins," she says.

"You don't have anything to worry about. I don't think I've watched an episode since the first season," I assure her.

We watch in companionable silence as I struggle to make sense of something called a "Tribal Council" happening with the disheveled, scantily clad men and women on the seemingly deserted beach. Tory is paying rapt attention, so she must know what's happening, but I don't care enough to ask her to fill me in. At the commercial break, Tory begins to fast-forward through the ads, but I notice that it's a L'Oréal ad, and I ask her to press play. She doesn't question why I want to watch the commercial, and soon the living room is filled with ethereal music. A beautiful model on the screen showcases a new bottle of lotion that looks identical to the one Kendra and I discussed, with the exact benefits and talking points that I'm presenting to Frederic and Janet tomorrow.

"Oh, my God! Oh my God! Oh my God!" I yell over and over again because they are the only words that will come out of my mouth.

"What's wrong?" Tory asks. She's visibly concerned and confused, which is understandable.

"That's my campaign!" I shout.

"What?" Tory asks.

"That's what I'm presenting tomorrow to my bosses!" I exclaim.

"L'Oréal stole your idea?" Tory asks, looking back and forth between me and the television.

"No. Oh no. God, no. I think I stole *their* idea! Shit! I have to call Kendra," I say. I don't give Tory a chance to comment, and I pull out my phone and dial Kendra's number, praying that she will pick up.

"Hey Robin, what's going on?" Kendra says when she answers the phone.

I try to keep my voice calm, but it's difficult. "I just saw an ad on TV for a L'Oréal lotion that looks exactly like what you helped me with. The packaging, brand positioning, and even the tagline," I say through tight lips.

"Oh wow, really?" Kendra says.

"Yes! How is that possible?" I ask her.

"Sorry about that. The stuff I told you was all from a

L'Oréal campaign that I was working on before I left. I was *pretty* sure that they decided they weren't going to launch that product, but I guess they changed their minds," she says casually.

"Kendra, I'm supposed to present that idea to my bosses tomorrow!" I tell her.

"Oh wow, that's rough," she replies. "I wish I could help, but I'm on my way out for the night. I know you'll think of something. Good luck," she says, and then she's gone.

"That didn't sound good," Tory offers quietly.

I'm too stunned to reply. Instead, I simply stare at the television, which is now showing a Honey Nut Cheerios commercial. I know Kendra was doing me a favor, but I can't believe she would help me by giving me a *stolen* idea! "I'm so screwed," I say aloud.

"What happened?" Tory asks. I'm guessing she already knows the gist of it from listening to my end of the phone call.

I summarize the situation as quickly as I can for Tory. I'm already starting to perspire as I count the hours left until my presentation and realize there's no possible way to redo everything in time. "I'm going to get fired," I exclaim and hide my face in my hands.

"What would you need to do to fix it for tomorrow?" Tory asks.

"I don't think it's possible," I sigh. "My meeting is tomorrow right after lunch. There's just not enough time – it's impossible."

"Nothing's impossible," Tory says. "Okay, there *are* things that are impossible, but maybe this isn't one of those things. I've got a lot of experience with cosmetics, and I know a lot about skincare. I've also been doing a lot of writing and editing at work, so I could probably help you – if you want," Tory offers.

"Really?" I ask. I turn to look at her and try to hide the look of shock on my face.

"Yeah, is that hard to believe?" Tory asks.

"No, of course not," I say, stumbling to cover for my unfortunate faux pas.

"Let me look at what you have," Tory says.

I reach over to where I left my work bag less than a couple of hours ago, although it feels like a lifetime at this point. I grab my laptop and one of the many hard copies of the presentation that will now go straight to the recycling bin, and I hand a copy to Tory. She immediately starts to flip through the presentation. "Wow, this *is* exactly like that ad we just saw," she says. I know she's right, but it stings to have it confirmed.

"I think you can still use a lot of this," Tory says when she's done looking at the handout. "You can keep all the background information and your competitive landscape analysis. That part hasn't changed."

"You're right. I hadn't thought about that." I was so shocked initially that I didn't stop to think about all the work I put into this that could be salvaged. Kendra did give me the idea for the rebranded skincare, but she also explained how the whole process works. I used her guidance and did a lot of my own work on the competitors and on Victoria's Secret historical brand performance as well. I know I'm still totally screwed on the actual recommendation that I owe Janet tomorrow, but at least the entire thing isn't garbage.

Tory slides gracefully off the couch so she's sitting directly in front of the coffee table. She pages through the document again, reading each page carefully, and then flips to the middle, produces a pen from somewhere I can't figure out, and starts writing. "What about two different lines of skincare – a premium line and a lower-priced line that's a little more fun and aimed at younger women?" Tory says.

"Did you *just* come up with that?" I ask her.

"It's basically all there in your background pages. It seems like you are almost suggesting that, but then in your recommendation, you go ahead and suggest that L'Oréal idea – the one your friend gave you."

I grab the paper from her and read through it again as if I'm looking through it with fresh eyes. "It does kind of read like that, doesn't it?" I ask Tory. "I think a lot of companies use that strategy – they have a premium brand and then more of a mass market brand. But now I need to figure out what that looks like in detail. And I have less than twenty-four hours!" I moan.

"Let's think about some ideas," Tory says. I find her optimism oddly reassuring, though I can't believe it's actually going to work. I'm not sure why Tory is so interested in helping me out, although I'm not going to question it – I know I have no chance of pulling this off by myself.

"That sounds good," I reply. We spend the next forty-five minutes writing down ideas, most of which are bad. Tory knows a surprising amount about skincare, and I wonder if she learned any of it from being in so many hotel rooms. I instantly hate myself for thinking this of my lovely roommate, who's dropped everything to help me tonight, and I try to erase those thoughts from my head. Just when I think we might need to give up, Tory turns over the page and writes out a description for a premium line of skincare revolving around "effortless beauty" and a "glow" line of products focusing on fun, fruity flavors for younger consumers. The ideas need a little tweaking, but as soon as I see them, I can already picture the new packaging and the advertising! I know it will be a scramble to get the changes incorporated tonight and then get the new packaging images put together tomorrow morning at the office, but I think I might be able to pull it off. With minimal sleep and a lot of coffee, I think it's possible.

"This is amazing! How can I ever thank you?" I ask Tory.

"Don't worry about it. I'm happy to help. That's what friends are for, right?" she asks tentatively.

"Yes, of course," I reply, and I feel a cheesy smile spread across my face. I didn't realize that I was worried about Tory reciprocating my feelings of friendship until I heard her refer to me as her friend.

Sensing that her role in the project is done, Tory gets up, says good night, and walks toward her room. "Tory, can I ask you something?" I call after her, and she turns around. I wasn't planning to say anything tonight, but the recognition of our friendship emboldens me. The words get twisted as I think about the right way to phrase them, and I end up saying, "I know that your job probably isn't what you always imagined. If you ever want to talk about it, or any problems you're having there, or with anyone that you're forced to work with, I'm here to talk."

Tory doesn't look surprised or upset at all; she even looks

a bit relieved. "Thanks so much, Robin. That's really nice of you. It's late, and I know you have a lot to do tonight, but I would like to talk about it sometime. You know I'm even thinking about changing jobs – I might even go out on my own," Tory says.

Chapter 44

Jessica

I assumed Zach was already on his way back to New York. I wasn't particularly hospitable, and he has no good reason to stick around here. This makes it quite startling when I come into the kitchen late in the morning and find Zach at the breakfast table, sandwiched between my mom and dad.

"Good morning, sleepyhead," my mom says. I don't think she's called me this since high school, and I wasn't overly fond of the nickname then, either. She always claimed it was a term of endearment, but it felt more like a condemnation of my lazy work ethic. "Your dad gave Zach a tour of the property this morning, and now he's been telling us a little bit about himself while we have breakfast."

I try to catch my mom's eye to give her a death stare that conveys how betrayed I feel, but she's busy buttering her toast and doesn't meet my eye. After I poured my heart out to her last night and told her what Zach did to me, I can't believe she would sit here now and make small talk with him!

"I'm going to head over to the office," I say as I fill a mug with what's left at the bottom of the coffee pot.

"Don't you want anything to eat?" My dad chimes in.

"I'm not hungry," I reply. Then I awkwardly pull my boots on without bothering to untie them and escape out the back door before there are any more questions.

By late morning my stomach is growling, and I'm getting a headache from looking through the unfamiliar paperwork. I don't dare go back to the house for fear of running into Zach. I'm trying to match up two bills that don't look like they've been paid and also appear to be duplicates when my dad knocks at the open door. "Can I come in?" he asks.

"Of course," I reply, thankful for the interruption.

Then he pulls a paper bag out from behind his back, and I almost groan in delight as I see the logo on the bag and recognize the familiar greasy smell. "I thought you could use a little treat," he says as he places the bag down on an empty spot on the desk and sits down in the empty chair across from me.

I carefully unwrap the slippery paper that contains my favorite sandwich – bacon, egg, and cheese on waffle bread. It seems like it should be simple to replicate, but this tiny restaurant in Sonoma makes it better than anywhere else on the planet, and I love my dad so much right now for remembering this fact. "Thank you," I mumble through a mouthful of food.

"How's it going with all of this?" he asks, gesturing to the papers strewn all over the desk.

"It's okay," I shrug.

"Your mom's accident has me thinking that we really do

need to bring this place into the twenty-first century. It's time we take advantage of technology," he says.

"What does Mom think about that?" I ask him.

"She's not thrilled," he sighs, "But she realizes that it's time. She's known for a while, and now that she's injured and won't be able to work for a while, it's inevitable. Besides, it's not like you can stay here and try to make sense of her paper-work for much longer," he laughs.

"I've been thinking about it, and I'm going to move back here. That way, I can help out with whatever you guys need." I wasn't sure I was going to say it, but now that it's out there, I feel calmer. I wouldn't say that I feel *better*. I'm not excited about the decision, but it feels like the right thing to do. My family needs me, and I've tried now for several years to make it as an artist, and clearly, that was a bust, so it's time for me to come back home and do what I'm supposed to do.

"Jess, what are you talking about?" he says.

"I'm going to move back here to work with the rest of the family," I explain, although I don't know why I have to explain myself.

"No, you're not," he says, and he shakes his head.

"You don't want me here?" I ask him. I know I let everyone down when I left for college, but I can't believe they won't take me back.

"Of course, I want you here, Jessica. But this isn't where you want to be," he says. "Your mother and I would love to have you here. Having you home this week has been a gift, but we know you won't be happy here. And the only thing we want is for you to be happy," he says with a mix of acceptance and tranquility.

"You aren't mad at me for leaving to go away to school and moving to New York?" I question.

"Of course not," he replies. "Why would you think that?" he says, looking genuinely confused.

"Because everyone else is here, and *I* didn't want to be here. And because I had to get loans to go to school," I say, and I know I sound like a petulant child as soon as the words are out of my mouth.

My dad lets a tiny smile escape from the corner of his mouth before he replies. "Not everyone is going to be happy living and working on a vineyard. Some people are meant for bigger things. I'm not sure all of your cousins want to make their whole lives about wine, but none of them were brave enough to try anything else. And as far as your RISD tuition goes, we would have loved to help you with that, but we just couldn't afford it. We didn't *not* pay for it because we didn't support you. Is that what you thought?" he asks.

I can't reply right away; I need time to absorb everything he's just said. I've spent the past eight years thinking my parents were upset with me and that they didn't support me, and it turns out I was completely wrong. I'm also pretty sure my dad called me *brave* for following my dream. "I don't know what I thought," I reply. I don't think I can bear to tell him the truth. "Sometimes I get stuck in my own head and can't see the forest for the trees. You know what I mean?" I ask him. This doesn't even come close to explaining away my situation or apologizing for how badly I've misjudged things, but one of the benefits of the parent-child relationship is that it doesn't need to.

My dad doesn't say anything for several minutes, and I

finish chewing my sandwich in the overwhelming quiet of the room. I think it's his turn to speak, so I wait it out. Finally, he speaks, but it's not what I thought he would say. "I think Zach can help with our tech issues."

"What??" I ask, and I turn to look at him like he's gone crazy in the past three minutes, which perhaps he has.

"I talked to Zach this morning about the business and these back-office problems, and he had some good ideas. He's a smart guy," my dad informs me like I didn't know this already.

"Did Mom tell you what happened with him? Did she tell you that Zach lied to me?" I demand of him.

"Your mother told me all about it last night. And then Zach told me this morning," he says simply.

"He did? What did he say?"

"I would say that he told me pretty much everything. He told me about that girlfriend from MIT. He told me that he lied to you about needing a roommate and how he wasn't honest with you about why he initially asked you to be his roommate," he says.

"Did he also tell you that he lied about his job?" I stress.

"Yes and no. He said it was more a lie of omission. He wasn't upfront about his job or past success, but you never asked him any questions about his job that would have caused him to lie."

I'm about to object, and then I think about it for a second. I spent so much time talking about my own job and what I wanted to do that I rarely asked him about what he did at work. Once I knew he worked at Expedia, I assumed I knew about his job and left it at that. "I guess I do make assumptions sometimes," I say quietly, but it's loud enough that my dad can hear it.

"I just met the guy, and I'm not defending him. However, he did come all the way out here to talk to you and try to make things right. And he was upfront and more than forthcoming with me and your mom, which counts for a lot in my book. Also, Jess, I know he lied to you, and that's wrong. But he also helped you when you needed help. His initial motivation was certainly questionable but ask yourself if he's done anything since that point that's been anything but kind and genuine."

My dad kisses me on the top of my head and makes his way out of the office; it's clear that he's not looking for a response. He's given me so much to think about this morning that my head might explode. I need to rethink my relationship with my parents, I need to reconsider if I'm going to go back to New York or stay here, and most urgently, I need to reexamine my entire situation with Zach and determine if *I'm* the one who's fucked it all up.

Chapter 45

Zach

I was surprised and relieved when I got a call from Jessica. After spending the morning with her parents, I came back to the hotel. I did some research on small business technology systems and then called a friend at Oracle to figure out what would be the simplest and fastest to implement for the vineyard. I obviously hoped Jess would call, but it didn't feel right to leave without helping her parents, even if she never wants to speak to me again.

"Hey, it's Jessica," she says when I answer the phone; caller ID already informed me of that.

"Hi. I'm glad you called," I say.

"Are you still in town?" she asks. "Where are you staying?"

"I'm still here. I'm at the Mission Inn."

"Wow, you're fancy," she says. I think her comment sounds more playful than judgmental; at least, I hope it does.

"It's not too shabby," I reply. Then I jump into more practical matters to ease some of the tension. "I don't know if your dad mentioned this to you or not, but I believe I can help them transition their office to a newer system."

"You mean one that doesn't require an ink pot and a quill?" she jokes.

"Something like that," I reply good-humoredly. "Is there a good time for me to come over and look at the current setup?" I inquire.

"There's really not much to look at. But you're welcome to come by. I'm here right now if that's convenient for you." I swear I can hear her holding her breath as if she's nervous to hear my reply – maybe it's just wishful thinking.

"I'll be there soon," I say.

I've been out in Sonoma now for five days. It feels disloyal to my East Coast roots to declare my love for California this quickly, but I definitely have a strong crush on the thirty-first state.

"Is it working *now*?" Malcolm calls out from the back corner of the room. Malcolm was a classmate of mine at MIT who now works at Oracle. He doesn't customarily make house calls to set up systems, especially two hours north of his office in Silicon Valley, but he's doing me a favor.

"I think it's all good," I reply. I look over the screen on the oversized monitor again and am pleased with what I see. I'm even more pleased by the lack of paperwork and clutter on the desks, resulting from transferring everything for the vineyard's bookkeeping, records, and systems to an electronic format.

"That should be everything," Malcolm says as he shuts his laptop with a flourish.

"Thank you so much," Jessica gushes. "This is so impressive."

"It's not a big deal," Malcolm says, but I can tell he's happy with the praise. "Tell your parents that they can always call or email me with any questions. AT&T put the DSL line in at their house and here in the office the other day, and I noticed your mom's gotten comfortable with it in a short amount of time," he says to Jessica.

"My mom has been *emailing* you from the house?" Jess asks.

"She still has a lot of questions. Although she seems relatively at ease with the laptop Zach got her," Malcolm adds.

"I can't believe it. I honestly didn't think she knew how to use a computer," Jess says.

"I guess she just needed a few lessons," I say.

"And some *really* nice gear," Malcolm says, giving a low whistle. I wince as he does it, as this has been a tiny sticking point with Jess, and I would prefer not to dwell on it.

Jess gives me a sideways glance, but she doesn't say anything, and I take this as a good sign. I honestly didn't get much; it was only a couple of new computers and a laptop for Jess's mom, and I cleared the equipment purchases with both of her parents before I ordered anything. I felt like it was the least I could do, especially since I still have connections with Dell, and the equipment is practically free for me.

"I'll get out of your hair then. You guys have a great afternoon, and let me know if you have any issues," Malcolm says. Then, he zips up his bag and disappears, leaving me and Jess totally alone for the first time in days. We've had a couple of unaccompanied moments together since we made up, but we knew those were always finite – Malcolm, her cousin, or her dad were always due back momentarily. Now, it's just the two of us, and no one is on the way.

"What now?" Jessica asks.

This question could have unlimited meanings. She must know how vague and simultaneously leading this question is. I believe we are on fairly solid ground right now, yet I still worry about saying the wrong thing, and this feels like the ultimate opportunity to go astray. "What do you mean?" I ask her. It may be a cop-out to throw it back at her, and still, it seems like a better option than getting it wrong.

"My mom is getting better. And this place practically runs itself, thanks to you, and she can manage things from the house if necessary, so she doesn't need us anymore," Jessica says.

Her clarification is helpful since I know now that she's talking about the vineyard. I'm about to add my thoughts when she starts talking again.

"I've been able to do a little work here now that we have DSL, although my boss is pretty tired of my inconsistent schedule. If I don't get back to work in the next few days, I may not have a job to get back to," she says.

This broadens it a bit more, but now I know that she's referring to work and planning her trip back to New York.

"I'm not sure if I want to go back to that job. I don't think that I want to work at a vineyard for the rest of my life, and I no longer feel guilty about that, but I also don't want to make PowerPoint slides forever. And if I do go back to New York, I don't have anywhere to live," Jess says.

I see that her "what now?" question is quite far-reaching. I wasn't sure how to respond initially, but at this last part, I have to interject. "Of course, you have somewhere to live. Nothing's changed. That's still your apartment," I say confidently.

"Everything's changed, Zach. I know that we've talked things out, but I can't go back to living in your apartment when I know you own the place and don't need a roommate," Jess says. We went through our apologies, and we've been polite and even friendly the past several days while working on getting her parents' office put together, but this is the first time we've talked about our living situation.

"I don't think that should make a difference," I say to her.

"But it does. I wouldn't feel right about it," she says sadly.

I hate the idea of her moving, although I understand why she feels it's the right thing to do. There's also been a tiny undercurrent of flirtation this morning. I didn't think we would ever regain that dynamic, and I worry that it will slip away if we don't get to spend more time together. "What does that mean? Are you going to stay in California?"

"I've talked to my parents about it a lot, and I think I will go back to New York, at least for now. As for an apartment, I'm not sure what I'll do. It's like I'm back at square one - like when I met you," Jess sighs.

I want to tell her that it doesn't have to be this way. I want to ask her to live with me again like we did before and convince her that it won't be weird. In my craziest fantasy, we start dating, and she moves in with me, and we live happily ever after, but even I know enough to keep that type of thing to myself.

The high-pitched sound of Jess's cell phone pulls me out of my daze. "Hey Tory, what is it?" she says. Then there's a long pause while she listens to Tory talk. I know that Tory and Jess patched things up shortly after I got to Sonoma. Since then, they've spoken every day, and at least I can wipe that concern off my conscience. "No way! That's incredible! You can't be serious!" Jess says, and I find myself doing that annoying thing where I whisper, "What is it?" because I'm too impatient to wait for her to get off the phone.

"Oh, my God! That's amazing! I can't believe that really happened! I can't wait to see you and Robin. I'll be back tomorrow," Jess says and ends the call.

I give Jess a puzzled look, and all she says is, "I'm moving in with Robin; I'll fill you in on the rest later."

Chapter 46

Tory

When I hang up from my call with Jessica, Robin stares at me, anxiously awaiting my report. "Well, what did she say?" Robin asks. She's kicked off her heels but still has on her work clothes and is impatiently bouncing on the balls of her feet on the parquet floor of our living room.

"She said she's coming back tomorrow. *And* she's going to move in with you!" I say excitedly.

"That's great," Robin says. "Did she sound surprised? Was she excited?"

"She sounded a lot more surprised that you thought I was a *hooker* than she was that I was getting my own apartment," I say to her, but my tone is playful.

Robin slumps to the couch and buries her face in her hands. "Did you really have to tell her that part? I cannot believe I thought that. I'm never going to be able to live that down, am I?" she asks.

"Maybe someday," I joke, "But I think it's unlikely., I admit I didn't find it quite as funny when Robin first confronted me. But after letting it settle for a few days, I think it's hysterical. A lot has happened this past week for both Robin and me (and apparently, for Zach and Jessica, too), and I take a moment to think back through it all.

After the second dinner with my mom, where I learned about my dad's affair with Paula, things moved quickly. My mom filed for divorce the next morning and kicked my dad out of the townhouse. She'd worked with her attorney to get the paperwork in order, and once she was assured my father had no path for retaliation, she went to work. I'd never seen this side of her, and from what she told me of her subservient upbringing, I believe it was new for her too. My mom suggested I move back into the brownstone to keep her company. She hasn't changed so much that she doesn't think a massive brownstone on the Upper East Side would be everyone's preferred address. I thanked her for the offer but told her I wanted to try living on my own. As much as I've loved living with Robin, I'd like to have my *own* apartment. It also helps that I now have complete control of my trust fund. I didn't go crazy, but I *did* rent a beautiful one-bedroom apartment in a newly constructed building – no more pre-war apartments or brownstones for me.

The craziest part of the week was when I told Robin I was moving out. I tried to cushion the blow as best I could. I told her that I would pay rent for the next few months until she found a new roommate. I wasn't sure yet what Jessica was going to do, especially since we had just made up and started talking again, but I intimated to Robin that she would be a good roommate option if she did decide to move back to New York. I expected Robin to be surprised by the news and likely upset, but what I never expected in a million years was for her to say, "Tory, I know that you're an escort. I know that you may be making good money, but I don't want you to feel like you have to do this. Why don't you stay here, and we'll figure out a way to make it work."

I must have stared at her for a solid five minutes with my jaw hanging open before I could even muster a reply. I think she took my silence as some sort of confession because she moved closer, took both of my hands in hers, and told me that she was "there for me." Once the initial shock wore off, I wasn't sure whether I should laugh or cry. Instead, I said, "Robin, what the fuck are you talking about? What would possibly make you think I'm an escort?!" Then she was the one to look taken aback and started babbling about my late nights, the man she saw me with at Lincoln Center, mysterious bottles of toiletries from the Ritz Carlton, and unexplained luxury goods. She capped it off by telling me that I was beautiful enough to be a high-priced call girl, and I hated myself for taking it as a compliment. Robin admitted that Jenny was the one who initially suggested it, and then it was stuck in her head.

I'd be lying if I said it wasn't a bit tense that first night. Jessica had just started talking to me again once Zach explained that we were only friends, and then I found out that Robin had been making incorrect assumptions about me as well. I wasn't used to using her as a sounding board, but I called my mother to vent, and she pointed out that none of it would have happened if I'd been honest and open with my new friends from the beginning. I immediately pointed out the irony in her statement, given how much she'd hidden from me. But she stressed that I should learn from her mistakes, not fall into the same traps, and offered other platitudes that didn't make sense.

I decided to take my mom's advice, at least as far as being honest with my friends, and by the next day, I started to see Robin's mistake as comical, not tragic. When I sat down with Robin to tell her about my parents, my childhood, and my dad's control over me (and my mom), she listened with rapt attention. When I got to the part about my mom's recent revelations, I thought Robin was going to fall off her chair. "This is like a *Lifetime* made-for-TV-movie!" she exclaimed.

When I talked to Jessica just now, I gave her a shorter version of the story, and I let her know that Robin thought I was making money by selling my body to lawyers and investment bankers, which she got a big kick out of. I knew from our conversation earlier this week that she wasn't sure about coming back to New York and was nervous about her current living situation. I didn't want to say anything until I was positive, so I waited until I signed my lease this afternoon and then called Jess as soon as I got home.

"Did she say anything else?" Robin asks. Her question pulls me out of my recap and back to the present.

"Not really. She sounded happy about coming back, and I think she's excited about staying in the building," I say.

"Do you think it's going to be weird with her and Zach? Is she going to need to move in right away? When is your new place going to be ready?" Robin asks, firing questions at me in rapid succession.

"I guess it might be a little weird between her and Zach at first. But, I want them to remember that they each have a crush on the other one and were on the brink of dating, although I'm sure it won't happen overnight."

"And the apartment?" she presses.

"I think she'll want to stay here starting tomorrow when she gets back," I say.

"What about you?" Robin asks.

"My apartment won't be ready for a little while. I'm going to take a few weeks and go away. I found this writing retreat in Vermont that looks interesting, and then I may stay with my mom or go out to the Hamptons until my apartment is ready," I tell Robin.

"What about your job? Are they going to let you take that much time off?"

"That's the last thing I was going to tell you about. I'm on my way into the office to sort that out right now."

* * *

Most of the office has cleared out by the time I arrive at five-thirty. Paula is sitting at her desk typing on her computer, and she's barefoot and wearing her reading glasses. It's clearly hit that point in the day where she feels comfortable enough to let the cracks show. I don't bother to knock on her door or announce my presence; I simply walk into her office and make myself comfortable in her visitor's chair. It's funny that this is the same spot where I was almost in tears a week ago, and now I feel like I own the room.

Paula makes an exaggerated show of looking down at her

watch and then looking up at me. "Isn't it a bit late to be starting the day? You wouldn't want me to report that to HR?" she asks.

"That's fine with me. I came in to give you my notice and clean out my desk," I tell her.

"You're quitting?" she says, obviously surprised by my news.

"Yes. I don't think this is working out," I tell her. "I know that you only hired me because my dad asked you to. It's clear that you didn't want me here to begin with, even when you were sleeping with my dad. But I have no desire to be here now while you take out your misplaced rage on me."

Paula squints her eyes slightly and purses her lips. It's clear that I've pissed her off, and I'm not sure how she's going to respond. She must decide that I'm not worth a raised voice. Instead, she lays on sickly sweet faux concern and says, "You'll be missed – have you been able to find another job? I'm guessing that it won't be easy for you to be unemployed for long." This means that my father must have filled her in on the status of my finances, or at least what he falsely assumed those were. This makes it even more satisfying when I update her on my plans.

"I'm going to be doing some writing in the short term," I tell her.

"Writing? What do you mean? *You're* not a writer," she says unkindly.

"You don't know what I can do. I'm working with the author of that manuscript you said you weren't interested in. We're rewriting her book and will be co-authors on the new version. We already have an agent," I say smugly.

"You can't do that," she says defiantly. "You found that book here. It's ours!" Paula cries.

Thankfully I've been over this multiple times with our new agent, as well as an attorney, just to be safe. "You have absolutely no rights to that manuscript. She sent it to you and dozens of other agents and publishers. You discarded it, and I'm the one who saw the potential. And the real potential in the book is only once my edits and revisions have been added. You have no claim to anything," I say firmly.

"I'm going to consult our attorney," Paula says, but she doesn't sound particularly confident.

"Please do," I say flippantly, pushing myself up to a standing position and turning to leave. "I'll grab a few things from my desk, and then I'll be gone. Thanks for such an interesting work experience. It's going to make great material for a book someday," I tell her. I don't turn around to look, but I'm sure her mouth hangs open as I leave.

Walking north up Park Avenue, I call my mom to fill her in. I promised her I would tell her how everything went with Paula at the office.

"I wish I could have seen the look on her face," my mom says gleefully.

"I'm just happy not to work there anymore," I say.

"I'm happy for you, too," she says. "You know, I think I know a few ladies who have some good connections in publishing. I'm going to make a few phone calls, and I can help you get your book going."

"Thanks, Mom, but I'm okay," I say.

"Tory, don't worry; these aren't like your father's connections. This won't be the same as working for Paula. These are powerful women or at least the wives of powerful men, and they could really help you out," she insists.

"I appreciate it, but I don't want to use your connections. We already have an agent who's interested, solely based on the edited manuscript, and I want to try and do something on my own," I say.

"Okay, I understand. I'm here if you want, but I think that's great. I'm proud of you, Tory," she says.

"Thanks, Mom." I wonder if the pedestrians around me on the corner of Park Avenue and 56th Street think I look crazy with the massive smile on my face. But of course, it *is* Manhattan, and there is a tacit agreement that we all ignore each other, so I shouldn't worry about it. "Hey, Mom, I keep meaning to ask you. What was the reason that your parents invited Dad to dinner that first time – what's the story there?"

"Oh right," she laughs. "I still haven't told you. There's nothing funny about it, but by now, I've decided to see humor and irony in the situation because we are where we are." I have no idea where she's going with this story, and I'm intrigued. "One of your grandfather's friends owed him a favor. As you remember, my parents were quite certain that I would never find a husband after my broken engagement. So, when his friend owed him something, my father had him send his son over for dinner to meet me. I'm not entirely sure of the details, but it seems that he was promised a large inheritance if we got engaged and then married."

"That's terrible!" I exclaim. "It was like an arranged marriage?" I ask.

"I suppose you could think of it that way. I didn't know about it at the time. I didn't know about it until years later when your father told me," she says.

"Wait, Mom, how do you know he's telling the truth?" I ask.

"What do you mean?" she replies.

"He lied about your parents will, he lied about my trust, and he's lied to you about almost everything else. Why do you believe this is true?" I ask her.

There's a long pause on the other end of the phone, and I wonder if I've lost her. It's annoying the way that cell phone calls drop all the time – it's so quiet on the other end that I almost press the end button and try to call her back, but then I hear her voice. "I can't believe I never stopped to think about that," she says quietly. "Even when I found out that my parents didn't leave him in charge of the estate, I never doubted that initial part of the story."

"I know I never got to meet my grandparents. And it definitely sounds like they did a lot of hurtful things. But maybe Dad made them out to be even worse," I say tentatively.

"I've been mad at my parents for so long; I can't remember a time when I wasn't mad at them. I felt slightly better when I found out they didn't cut me out of their estate; however, I couldn't get over the anger I felt from learning that they practically sold me to your father," she says.

"When did Dad tell you that?" I gently probe.

"Oh, my goodness, he told me that shortly after my parents died. We'd come back from a fundraiser where I'd been talking to another man, and he accused me of flirting. Then, he abruptly changed course and said he had nothing to worry about because my parents weren't around to trick someone else into dating and marrying me. It was just another one of his tirades," she says, and I can hear in her voice that she's reliving the moment.

"Mom, listen to me. He was lying to you. I know it. He did it to break your confidence. It was another one of his lies. I'm not defending your parents or anything, but I think you've had this hanging over your head for your entire life, and it's not true," I say.

"I don't know what to think," my mom says. "What does it mean if it isn't true? It's not like I can change the past," she says wistfully.

"I know," I say softly. "We can't change the past, but we can change the future. From this point on, you can do things differently. We both have the chance to start over – I will be a writer and work on being a good friend and daughter. What are you going to do?"

"Well, Tory, I don't know. But I guess, for the first time in my life, I'm going to do what *I* want to do."

Chapter 47

Robin

Ethan holds open the door for me at Asia de Cuba, and I happily step into the dark, air-conditioned restaurant and away from the throng of people milling around Madison Avenue on this humid Saturday evening. As we approach the hostess stand, Ethan puts his hand gently on my waist and rests it there while the immaculately dressed hostess peruses her list to ensure we *do*, in fact, have a reservation for two. This simple gesture is comforting and also a huge turn-on. We still haven't slept together, although we've come close, and the sexual tension from merely being around Ethan and feeling his body on mine is driving me crazy. I press myself closer to him and almost explode with happiness when Ethan casually leans down and kisses the top of my head. I notice the hostess glance up at us, and I instantly recognize the look of envy mixed with irritation that passes across her face. I've given this look to countless adorable couples over the years, and I can't believe that

I'm finally on the receiving end of the evil glare – it feels amazing.

"Right this way," the hostess snaps as she grabs two menus and motions for us to follow her all the way through the dining room to a booth two steps away from the kitchen door. I briefly wonder if we would have gotten a better table if we had kept our hands to ourselves, but I don't let it bother me; I don't care where we sit.

We look briefly at our menus, and then Ethan says, "What do you think looks good? You always seem to order the best things – I should let you order for me from now on."

It's such a simple statement, yet it gives me goosebumps. We've only been dating a few weeks, and he's already talking about the future. Ethan also likes that I appreciate good food and enjoy eating it. He says he has no interest in women who don't like to eat or who constantly count calories and grams of fat. At first, I thought it was some sort of line, but I finally believe him based on how he looks at me and touches me.

"The roasted duck looks good. And the chicken empanadas. Or the casaba cakes?" I offer.

"That all sounds delicious," he says. "I knew I shouldn't even bother to look." And he makes a show of putting his menu face down on the table.

The waiter arrives shortly after that and takes our order. The waiter is incredibly personable and outgoing. I have a feeling that he is one of the many talented performers in the city who is waiting tables while they wait for their big break. Ethan and I barely have time to start a conversation before the waiter returns to the table with our drinks, except he seems to have brought the wrong order. I'm about to tell him this when Ethan nods and gives him a look. "Thank you so much."

"My pleasure," the waiter replies. "Enjoy your celebration." And at that, he pops open the cork of a bottle of Veuve Clicquot, pours us each a glass, and puts the bottle in a waiting ice bucket next to the table.

"What is this? We didn't order this," I say to Ethan.

"You may be better at ordering food. But I made some beverage decisions for the evening," he says.

"This is crazy. This bottle must have been so expensive. Why are we drinking champagne?" I ask.

"We're celebrating your promotion," Ethan says nonchalantly.

"What? How did you even know about that? It just happened today!" I say. My head is spinning as I try to figure out how he could have possibly heard the news. My presentation on the skincare rebrand was a huge success – even Janet was impressed. Frederic assured me that my promotion was guaranteed in the coming weeks, but I was still so nervous that I didn't want to jinx anything by talking about it, even to Ethan. I was ecstatic when Janet called me into her office today to give me the news. Then Ethan called me this afternoon and said he wasn't having a great day, so I decided to wait and tell him later tonight or maybe even another day.

"Would you believe me if I said that I just figured it out?" Ethan asks. He looks adorable when he says this, and yet again, I can't believe that he's sitting here with me, and it's finally my turn to be in a good relationship.

"My sense of curiosity won't let it go that easily," I laugh.

"It's a small world New York City kind of story," Ethan says.

"Those are the best kind."

"You know how I said I wasn't having a great day earlier?" Ethan asks. I nod to show that I remember, and he keeps going. "I was upset because it was one of my friend's last days at work today. He's leaving the company to go work at a consulting firm. They are expanding their offerings into environmental consulting and will be paying more than we do at Tishman. The building is practically next door, but he's going to be traveling a lot, and it's not the same as working together," Ethan says sadly.

"Sorry about that," I say. I have no clue how this relates to him hearing about my promotion, although it seems rude to try and get him back on track now when he's clearly upset about his friend leaving, and that's what he wants to talk about.

"I helped him bring a couple of boxes of stuff to his new office after the little going-away party we had today, and as I was walking back to the elevator, guess who I saw?" he says. Now he sounds excited; all traces of sadness from a moment ago are gone.

"I have no idea," I say.

"Jessica!" he says excitedly. "That's where she works. Isn't that crazy? I recognized her right away, even though I met her for the first time the other night - when I was getting a glass of water," Ethan pauses and then blushes. He clearly remembers running into Jessica in the hallway, wearing only his boxer briefs. "She was so excited for you and told me about your promotion," he says.

"I was *going* to tell you. You sounded sad on the phone, so I thought I should wait." I'm not sure why I'm defending myself, but I hate the idea of Ethan being upset with me. I'm still trying to figure out how to navigate a relationship and what to do and not to do.

"You don't owe me any explanations," he says quickly. "I'm so happy for you and wanted to be able to celebrate together – I hope that's okay." He leans over and tenderly kisses me on the lips, and now I'm glad we're in a booth in the back of the restaurant so there isn't a crowd to watch when I grab the back of his head to pull him in closer. Ethan moans appreciatively and then mumbles in my ear, "Do you think it would be rude if we asked them to wrap up our food to go?"

"I know you're smart, but that may be your best idea yet," I whisper back. I scoot closer to him to feel his leg against mine. Ethan raises his arm to signal for the waiter, and I take that moment to gratefully acknowledge the one-eighty my life has taken.

Chapter 48

Jessica

It's weird to be in the same building, on the same floor, but in a different apartment. I was so relieved when I learned that I would be able to simply move down the hall into Robin's apartment. It meant that I didn't need to face Craigslist again, consider an inferior location, or imagine unaffordable rent. It also meant that I could easily escape the awkwardness of living in the same apartment with Zach, with a shared living room and kitchen.

What I didn't consider was that I would be back at my same boring job, albeit with a wonderful roommate, but one who is never home because she is consumed by her blossoming relationship. And now I'm four doors away from the place I'm supposedly avoiding, and all I can think about is Zach!

The first few days back, I busied myself with setting up my bedroom and trying to spend time with Robin during the few moments when she wasn't with Ethan. It's gotten progressively harder since then. I've tried to throw myself into work, although I can only muster so much excitement about pitch decks and change management slideshows. The other night I decided I was going to look online for freelance photography opportunities, and I found a few that looked promising until I remembered that I no longer have my own camera. I don't know what part of my brain was missing when I forgot that vital piece of information. It's just further proof that I'm completely out of sorts.

I've tried to time my elevator use, so I won't run into Zach, and then I'm secretly disappointed every time I don't see him. I heard Robin talking to him in the hall the other evening, and I got as close to the door as possible to listen to their conversation. I was one step away from turning into a sitcom character with a glass pressed up against the door. I didn't catch much. I think Zach was paying the delivery guy, and Robin was merely saying hello. I desperately wanted to ask Robin what kind of food he got delivered and if it looked like there was enough for two people, but it seemed too desperate.

Robin is out with Ethan again tonight, and I'm on the couch trying to find something to watch on TV. As I'm flipping through the channels, I remember that my mom called me this afternoon, and I told her I'd call her back. I try the house line, and it rings four times, and then I get the answering machine. It's still early out in California, and she may be in the office, so I try her there. She picks up on the first ring. "Hey, sweetie, how are you?" she says.

"I'm fine; how are you?" I ask.

"I'm good. I'm just looking through the recent orders on

my fancy new system," she laughs. "Your friend really is a lifesaver."

"Yeah, that was nice of him," I offer. "How's your leg? How are you feeling?"

"Oh, I'm fine. It's barely anything now," she says, dismissing me. I know from my dad that she's still wearing a boot and using a cane, although she's moving around quite well and should be back to normal soon. "How's everything in New York?"

"It's fine. Nothing really to report," I sigh.

"In the *city that never sleeps*? How's that possible?" she jokes. "How's Zach doing?" she asks.

"I don't know. I haven't seen him," I say.

"Why is that?"

"I haven't run into him," I offer lamely.

"He lives down the hall from you. I don't think seeing him should be that hard," she says.

"It just hasn't happened," I tell her.

"You're going to do what you want. I know that's how you do things, and I love that about you. But you're the one that's getting in the way of your own happiness," she says firmly.

"What are you talking about?" There's a whiny quality to my voice that makes me sound about twelve, and I wonder if she's going to call me on it.

"It's obvious you have feelings for Zach. And it's painfully obvious that he has feelings for you. I understand that you were upset that he wasn't honest with you, but as far as I can tell, he's cleared that up and then some. He may not be your soul mate, but maybe he is – who knows? You'll never know what it could be if you don't give it a chance. And the way you're acting, you're not even giving him a chance to be your friend. Zach sure seems like someone I'd like to have as my friend."

"I've got to go," I say abruptly.

"Alright, talk to you later," she sighs. I can tell that she's annoyed with me, but I can't handle the lecture.

I pick up the remote and mindlessly flip through the channels. I don't know what I'm in the mood for, but I'm sure I'll know it when I see it. Unfortunately, with this many channels and poor programming, I could be here for a long time and still not find anything I want to watch. I'm all the way up to the movie channels when I land on *Ocean's Eleven*. Without thinking, I turn toward the other end of the couch to remind Zach of the first time we watched the movie together, but of course, he's not there. I settle into the corner of the couch and try to get comfortable to watch Brad Pitt in his barely-buttoned button-down.

No matter what I do, I can't get comfortable, and I can't focus on the movie. All I can think about is watching this with Zach. We had such a good time laughing about the absurdity of the plot, and he didn't make me feel dumb when I needed a minute to figure out the twist. I find myself wishing I was sitting on Zach's couch right now, cuddled up and watching a movie, or maybe going out together for a late-night walk for ice cream or grabbing a drink at the bar on the corner. To deter this line of thinking, I try to summon up the anger I had toward him when I fled to California, and I find that it's just not there. I wish that he'd been upfront with me about Cassie and what prompted the roommate offer. Sadly, now that I know everything that happened with Cassie in college, I can understand why he might not have been able to do that.

I don't give my brain another chance to mess things up. The next thing I know, I'm out the front door and walking down the hall. I knock twice and wait to see if he's home – *and* if he's home alone. I'm unsure I'll have the courage to do this again. When Zach opens the door, it's clear from the look on his face that he's surprised to see me, and I also detect signs of joy and relief.

"Hi, I'm Jess. I live down the hall. I was wondering if you'd like to go out sometime?"

Epilogue

Tory

Six Months Later

"I can't believe it's so cold outside!" is the first thing Jessica says when she walks through the door to my apartment. She's wrapped up in a giant down coat that makes it look like she's three times her actual size.

"You've lived on the East Coast for long enough; you should be used to this," I joke.

"I know. Still, I'm never ready for that first really cold day in December. And I only got back from California a few days ago; I haven't properly adjusted," Jess says.

"Let me take your coat," I offer. "You can have a drink to warm up." Jess shrugs off the giant coat, which barely weighs anything considering its bulk, and hands me her hat and gloves as well. Her cheeks are still pink from the cold, but there's a glow on her face that's hard to hide. She rubs her arms to warm up, even though they are already encased in a buttery soft cashmere sweater.

"The place looks great, Tory. Every time I come over, you've added something else," she exclaims. "I can't believe you turned the dining room into a music studio."

"It's *hardly* a music studio," I reply shyly, though I am quite proud of my work. "I didn't need a formal dining room, so I used half the space for my office and the other half as a practice area for my violin."

"Whatever you call it, it looks amazing. And Robin mentioned that you are going to be performing soon; is that right?" Jess asks.

"It's only a little quartet for a holiday thing. It's not a big deal, but it *will* be my first time playing in front of an audience in almost fifteen years, so that's kind of exciting and terrifying," I admit.

"That's so exciting. Congratulations," Jess says and then changes gears. "And the Christmas decorations in here are beautiful. I can't believe you found time to decorate with everything you have going on."

"I can't take any credit for the Christmas decorations," I confess. "My mom came over last week, and when I told her I didn't think I'd have time to do any decorating, she was appalled. I was out all day on Tuesday at meetings, and when I came home, the place looked like this," I say, gesturing to the stunning nine-foot tall perfectly trimmed Christmas tree behind me and the elegant decorations that adorn the living and dining rooms.

"That seems like something your mom would do," Jess laughs. "She's too funny."

I absolutely love that Jess can casually make these comments. Anyone who knew my mom when I was growing up only knew her as the meek socialite who lived in my father's shadow – except for the few friends who were unfortunate enough to be around when they'd both been drinking. Then they knew her as the angry woman who fought with her husband. And then, I didn't bring anyone around my parents for a long time because I was too embarrassed. Now, my friends all know my mom and know her as the slightly eccentric, well-meaning, over-the-top, and loving mother that she has become.

"What can I get you to drink?" I ask.

"Let me take a look at your enormous bar and see what looks good," Jess says as she walks over to the black and chrome built-in bar and floor-to-ceiling wine fridge in the corner of the living room. "I can't get over how different this place is from our apartments on West 78th Street. We're like eighteen blocks away, and we might as well be in a different world," she gushes.

"This place may be a little over the top," I admit. "I was desperate to have something new and different, and The Time Warner Center felt like it was calling to me. I signed a two-year lease, which gives me another year and a half here. Maybe I'll be ready to move into something a little less ridiculous then," I laugh.

"Knock, knock, we're here," Robin says. She pushes open the front door, and I realize I must not have properly closed it after Jess came in. "Are your neighbors so rich that you don't even lock your doors? That's a whole different kind of

Manhattan," Robin laughs, and Ethan laughs alongside her as he helps her off with her coat.

"Come in! I'm so excited you could make it! And close the door behind you. Apparently, I'm not very good at doing that," I say.

"Wait, don't close it quite yet," a voice says as Zach appears in the entryway.

"I thought the security was better at a luxury building like this. It looks like they'll let anyone up," Ethan jokes, and Zach playfully punches him on the arm while Ethan fakes like he's going to hit him back. Neither of them is the type of guy that is believable as someone who even knows how to throw a punch, but it's funny watching them try. It's even funnier watching them rib each other since Ethan and Zach have become such close friends over the past few months.

We were all thrilled for Robin when she met Ethan, and it was clear that he was the kind of wonderful guy she deserved. We didn't know that he would also turn out to be the best friend Zach had been looking for. I occasionally feel a twinge of jealousy when the four of them hang out in their neighboring apartments or go out on double dates. However, I'm too focused on work and not remotely interested in dating right now, so that wouldn't suit me anyway.

"Are you bartending tonight?" Zach asks Jessica. He hangs his coat in the front closet, walks over, and kisses Jess. "What are you going to make us?"

"You know my specialty is pouring wine," she says. "If you want anything much more complicated than that, you're going to have to ask someone else."

"Is everyone good with Manhattans?" Ethan asks. "It's a good drink for a cold night and feels appropriate."

There's a chorus of "yeses" and "fine by me," and Ethan proceeds to take ownership of the bar and gets to work mixing drinks. He finds a tray from somewhere (I'm guessing my mother bought it) and brings five beautiful Manhattans in crystal old-fashioned glasses to the table where we are all gathered. I've dimmed the lights so we have a better view out of the floor-to-ceiling windows that overlook Central Park and much of Midtown Manhattan.

"I have an announcement to make if that's okay," Robin says. We all turn to look at her, and I see Ethan mouth something, but it's too dark to make out the words.

"Ethan and I are moving in together," she says joyfully. Glasses are immediately clinked together, although my only thought is, "What about Jessica?" When everyone turns to stare at me, I realize that I must have said it out loud.

"I'm moving back in with Zach," she smiles. "You probably think we're crazy, but we're going to try it for real this time."

"That's great. I'm really happy for you," I say to the four of them. Ordinarily, I might feel left out since it's clear that I'm the only one who wasn't in on the plan. However, I have my own news to share tonight, so it doesn't even phase me.

"Jess has something else she wants to share," Zach claims.

"It's not a big thing," Jess insists, though the grin on her face says otherwise. "You all know how I've been helping my parents with the vineyard. With Zach's assistance, we've made it more of a travel 'destination,' and people are now booking it for day trips, weddings, and corporate events. I did all the photography for the website, and then I did the website design. When I was out there this past week to help and take pictures at their big holiday event, I ran into the owner of a neighboring vineyard and hotel, and he asked if I could do a photoshoot of his property."

"That's amazing!" Robin says. "Congratulations," Ethan adds. "I'm so excited for you," I say to Jess.

"Although it isn't exactly the type of photography I've always dreamed about, it's a good start, and I'm finally moving in the right direction," she says proudly.

"In a few years, all of your work is going to be in a gallery in SoHo, and none of us will be able to afford it," Zach beams.

"I'm not so sure about that," Jess laughs.

"Yeah, I'll still be able to afford it," I say, and everyone laughs along with me. "Actually, I also have something exciting to share."

"Really? What is it?" Robin questions. "It seems like we're all full of happy news."

"We sold the book to Penguin Random House," I say nonchalantly, although I know it's huge.

"Oh, my God!" Jessica squeals and jumps out of her chair to hug me.

"And they gave us a two-book deal," I add.

"Tory, that's absolutely amazing!" Robin gushes and runs over to join the group hug. "Why didn't you tell us right away? I can't believe you've been letting us talk about our living arrangements while you've been sitting on this earth-shattering news."

"I only found out yesterday," I say sheepishly, although it feels wonderful to be able to share it with my friends and have them be this excited for me. Throughout all the edits and rewrites, our agent was optimistic that we would be able to sell the book, but that didn't mean it would actually happen. And even if it did sell, there was no guarantee it would sell for a big advance or to a great publishing house. She's tried to prepare me and my co-author for the inevitable next round of rewrites, but I know we are both too excited to contemplate that yet. Right now, I want to sit back with my friends and rejoice in the amazing transformation my life and all our lives have taken this year.

"This calls for a toast," Zach says.

"What should we toast to?" Jess asks.

"To friendship?" Robin offers.

"That's lame," Jess replies, and we all laugh.

"To new careers?" Zach suggests.

"That's even worse," Robin chides.

"To the Upper West Side," I say. "If it hadn't been for our chance encounters and random roommate matches, who knows where we would be today."

"To the Upper West Side," we all say together and ceremoniously polish off our Manhattans in one final swallow.

THE END

Acknowledgments

As always, I am eternally grateful to you – my readers. I don't know how many of you are reading the acknowledgments page, but if you are, I want you to know how much I appreciate you. Thank you for reading the words that I write. I hope that this book entertained you and provided a temporary escape into the world of The Upper West Side in the early 2000s.

When writing this book, I constantly returned to my life in Manhattan almost twenty years ago. Of course, this book is purely fictional, but I loved reminiscing about that time in the city when I was in my mid-twenties and revisiting bars, restaurants, and landmarks from two decades ago.

In a way, this book is my love letter to New York City. I've lived close to Manhattan for most of my life, but I only actually lived there for five years. And what a wonderful five years it was. I look back on that time in my life with rose-colored glasses, but even the bad things from those years have good parts now in my memory. So, my second acknowledgment will go to Manhattan and its fabulous neighborhoods, although I'll always have a particular affinity for the Upper West Side.

Thank you to my sister, Sarah Nelson, for continuing to

be an early reader and one of my biggest fans; your unwavering support means so much to me.

Thank you to my parents and my entire family for believing in me and supporting me. And a special thank you to my mom, Vicki Nelson, for doing a final read-through of the book to check for problems – your meticulous nature is much appreciated!

Thank you to my early readers and amazing friends, Kathy Soderberg and Aimee Kaplan - I am so lucky that you continue to find time to provide such meaningful feedback with your busy lives.

A big thank you to my friends near and far - whether grabbing a cup of coffee, walking our dogs together, or exchanging rapid-fire texts, you are there for me, offering support and words of encouragement and generally helping me keep it all together. And a particular note of appreciation for my paddle tennis friends – I wrote a lot of this book during the winter, and it would have been a lot harder if I didn't have that as a delightful diversion.

And last but certainly not least – I must thank my three exceptional children and my husband. Morgan, Sam, and Lexi – you encourage and inspire me daily. Although these may not be "your kind of books," I love that you are still proud of them. Finally, to my amazing husband, Doug – my rock. Thank you for having faith in me and supporting me on this journey. Sorry, I didn't work Baker Street into this one :)

About the Author

Rachel Cullen is a graduate of Northwestern University and NYU Stern School of Business. She worked in consulting and marketing in San Francisco, London, and New York and currently lives in Westchester, New York, with her husband, three children, and her two large dogs. *an Upper west side story* is her seventh novel.

www.rachelcullenauthor.com

Also by Rachel Cullen

www.ingramcontent.com/pod-product-compliance
Lightning Source LLC
Chambersburg PA
CBHW030136310726

48970CB00005B/1458